"I, PRINCESS CLAUDIA, BRING YOU A SPECIAL TREAT—THE LEGAL ASSASSINATION OF THE INFAMOUS BOUNTY HUNTER, SAM McCADE!"

The aerial team arrived first. They opened fire at long range, liberally spraying the terrace with lead and coherent energy. He killed the first by carefully punching an energy beam through his reflective visor. The pulse of coherent energy burned a perfect hole through the man's head, while his belt continued to keep his body aloft and propel it forward . . .

Praise for WAR WORLD

"Adventure and mystery in a future space empire."
—F.M. Busby

"Slam-bang action."
—David Drake

"Good, solid space-opera, well told."
—*Science Fiction Chronicle*

"All-out space action!"
—*Starlog*

Ace books by William C. Dietz

WAR WORLD
IMPERIAL BOUNTY

IMPERIAL BOUNTY

WILLIAM C. DIETZ

ACE BOOKS, NEW YORK

This one is for my father,
William Holt Dietz.

Prologue

MCCADE WAS HUNTING an icecat. Or maybe the icecat was hunting him. It wasn't clear which, but it didn't matter much, since he was in deep trouble either way. First, because he didn't know much about hunting icecats, and second, because icecats knew a lot about hunting people. Which wasn't too surprising since they'd been at it for fifty years. That's how long humans had been on the iceworld called Alice. The process of natural evolution had molded icecats into killers, and to them, humans were targets just like everything else.

Naturally the colonists had fought back, but it wasn't easy. Icecats can move with amazing speed, and never give up. Their name comes from a vague resemblance to Terran cats. Unlike Terran felines however, icecats have heat-sensitive membranes located in the center of their foreheads. Operating like infrared scanners, these membranes allow them to lock onto radiated heat, and follow it even through a raging blizzard if necessary. They also have excellent vision, good hearing, and lots of teeth. All of which explains why icecats are normally hunted by well-armed groups instead of individuals. "Not that I planned it this way," McCade said to himself.

It had all begun when a roaming icecat attacked a small herd of variant caribou about twenty miles to the south. In a matter of minutes the rampaging beast had almost wiped them out. By the time Lane Conners arrived, there were bodies everywhere. And when Conners attempted to defend a wounded animal, the icecat jumped him too. He had used his pocket com to call for help. Moments later his wife, Liz, hit the big red panic button just inside the door of their pre-fab dome and raced to his side. A general distress call went out, and as luck would have it, McCade was closest.

McCade was returning home from a series of routine law and order visits to the small mining settlements which dotted Alice when the alarm came in. It had been a long trip. But on Alice you don't ignore a distress call. Not if you want anyone to show up when it's *your* ass on the line. Amazingly enough the rancher was still conscious when the medics arrived. As they loaded him into the chopper he grabbed McCade's arm. "Get the sonovabitch for me, Sam. Otherwise he'll be back . . . and next time it might be Liz or one of the boys."

McCade saw such agony in the rancher's eyes that like a fool he agreed, ready to say anything to get Lane into the helicopter and on his way. So as the med evac chopper disappeared into the southern sky, McCade got into his air-car and took off toward the north. What looked stupid now had seemed reasonable back then. Rather than wait for help, or take the time to put together a pack, he'd decided to follow the icecat's tracks north hoping for a quick, easy kill. He should've known better. When it comes to icecats . . . there's no such thing as a quick, easy kill.

So he'd dropped his aircar into a clearing, and set out on

foot, trying to get ahead of the beast and ambush it. But so far all he'd seen was ice, snow, and the low, twisted evergreens which passed for trees on Alice. "Where the hell are you anyway?" he asked in frustration, but there was no answer except the crunching sound of his own footsteps as he walked through the ice and snow. Around him the shadows grew longer and darker, creating a thousand hiding places, any of which might conceal an icecat.

As evening approached it brought with it a frigid breeze, supercooled by glaciers a hundred miles to the north, and sharp as a knife against the small area of unprotected skin at his throat. Walking cautiously he reached down to turn up the internal temperature of his heatsuit. Eventually he'd run out of power for it. Maybe he'd freeze to death while waiting for an icecat to kill him. The thought struck him as funny somehow, so why wasn't he laughing? "You're losing it, Sam old boy," he said to himself. "Pull yourself together. You've been in worse spots."

And it was true. In his days as a professional bounty hunter he'd come close to death many times. But somehow those encounters were different. He'd been in control, always the hunter, never the hunted. Here that was reversed; the icecat was in control. It could fight or disappear, and whichever it chose, there wasn't a damn thing he could do about it.

Suddenly he stopped, his eyes riveted to the snow in front of him. The icecat was close. There was no mistaking the huge plate-sized paw prints which overlaid the crosshatched pattern of his own boots. The sonovabitch was following him! And had been for some time. Together they'd made a large figure eight. With a sinking feeling McCade realized how far he'd come. The aircar was miles away.

He glanced over his shoulder one more time, and started up a nearby slope, instinctively seeking higher ground. Perhaps he could find a better vantage point toward the top. Eventually his path was blocked by the sheer face of a cliff. Locating a small crevice which would protect his back, he forced his way in, and did his best to make himself comfortable.

During his climb, the already dim sun had sunk farther in the overcast sky, making it even colder. McCade reached down to turn up the gain on his heatsuit, and then thought better of it. Even on its present setting the power pak wouldn't get him through the night. He did his best to settle down and concentrate on the task at hand. "All right you flea-bitten sonovabitch . . . I'm ready when you are . . . come and get it."

Another hour passed. He scanned the area below for the umpteenth time. Even under his visor's high mag setting, there wasn't much to see. He was about to give up when he saw something move out of the corner of his eye. Or had he? Maybe it was just a trick of evening's half light. No, there it was again, a shadow among shadows, a momentary blur only half seen.

Then he had it, a long low body, winter white giving way to summer gray, almost invisible against the volcanic rock. A strong neck supported a large triangular head, with two fan-shaped ears that twitched slightly as they sampled the evening breeze. Huge eyes moved this way and that, each independently scanning the area for any signs of danger. If they looked his way would they see him? And what about the animal's ability to sense radiated heat? Could it detect him?

McCade felt a lead weight drop into his gut as the beast's hideous head swiveled toward him and stopped. How good was his heat shielding? Maybe there was some leakage that the icecat could detect. The icecat snarled, the thin lips of its false mouth pulled back to reveal razor-sharp teeth. The sound echoed back and forth off the cliffs.

The last echo of the icecat's snarl was still dying away

when the animal vanished into the shadows. McCade thought about all those teeth and shuddered. The ones he'd seen were bad enough, but he knew there were still others located in its abdomen. Icecats have two mouths. A false mouth used for breathing and killing, and a real mouth, exclusively devoted to eating. Having made a kill, icecats immediately drape themselves over the body to keep it from freezing, thus bringing their real mouths into contact with the carcass. By sliding this way and that, icecats can efficiently strip a man-sized carcass in minutes, all the while keeping their false mouths and sensory organs available for defense. It is, the biologists like to point out, a very efficient adaptation to conditions on Alice. McCade didn't doubt it, but had no desire to take part in the process himself.

Nonetheless he stood up. To hell with waiting. If he didn't move soon he'd freeze to death. So if the icecat wouldn't come to him . . . he'd go to it. He felt the muscle in his left cheek twitch as he shifted the comforting weight of the slug thrower from one arm to the other. The weapon had a rotary magazine filled with alternating hollow point slugs and shot shells. As the planet's only police officer, it was just one of the many weapons McCade carried in his aircar. Properly handled it could take out a squad of Imperial Marines. Unfortunately, he thought, icecats are tougher than marines, and probably smarter.

Carefully he eased his way out of the rocky crevice. There wasn't much cover as he moved downslope, but he used what there was, pausing every now and then behind outcroppings of rock to check his surroundings. He was almost at the bottom when he spotted the icecat making its way across the opposite slope, pausing every now and then to scan ahead for radiated heat, or sniffing the breeze for a foreign scent.

Apparently satisfied with its surroundings, the beast moved off toward a patch of bare rock, attracted perhaps by the glow of radiated heat surrounding it. A few more yards and McCade would be close enough. He flicked the weapon's safety to the off position and moved forward.

Later he wasn't sure what warned him, whether it was an almost imperceptible sound, a tiny disturbance in the air, or some sixth sense, but whatever it was caused him to step right, and saved his life.

The second icecat hit him a glancing blow as it went past, knocking him down, and jarring the weapon out of his hands. Fighting its own inertia, the big animal scrambled to turn around, while McCade clawed desperately for his sidearm. He felt the slug gun come free just as the icecat leaped. The gun roared four times before the huge body landed on him, driving all breath from his body and plunging him into suffocating darkness.

Pushing up with all his might, he fought desperately to get his breath, almost gagging on the animal's stench. In spite of his efforts the icecat's muscular body didn't give an inch. Instead it squirmed, and slid this way and that, trying to bring its real mouth into contact with his flesh. The intervening heatsuit was the only thing between him and all those teeth. In a few seconds those teeth would make contact with the wire mesh of the suit's heating elements, eat through those, and go to work on him. Wire mesh! It gave him an idea.

He pushed up as hard as he could with his left hand, and managed to slide his right down until he found the heatsuit's controls. Fingers fumbling, he accidently turned the knob to the right, before realizing his mistake and turning it to the left. He prayed there was enough juice left in the power pak to do some good. A second later the icecat's teeth came through the suit's tough outer fabric and made contact with the inner wire mesh. As the power pak's full output hit the icecat's nervous system, the cat convulsed and jerked away.

Momentarily freed, McCade quickly rolled left, and

landed on the auto-slug thrower he'd lost earlier. As he picked it up he saw the icecat was already back on its feet, shaking its head like a dazed prizefighter, and preparing to attack again. The weapon in his hands seemed to weigh a ton. With a strange sense of detachment he watched the icecat shift its weight, gather itself, and leap into the air. Meanwhile the barrel of his weapon continued its slow journey upward. Some distant part of his mind noticed the animal was bleeding profusely from six or seven bullet wounds, and wondered if anything could kill it. Finally the slug thrower completed its upward arc and he touched the trigger. The icecat seemed to run into an invisible wall. It crumpled in midair, and for a moment it was enveloped in a pink mist, as blood and flesh sprayed out behind it. Then it landed with an audible thud, and slid the last couple of feet, until its head almost touched the barrel of his gun.

For a moment he just sat there, too shocked to move. Finally he struggled to his feet, unable to take his eyes off the icecat's huge body, shaking like a leaf. Then he heard the other icecat roar and, whirling, heard the sound of his weapon merge with his own screams. The animal was already in the air, his slugs stitching a bloody line across its chest, when his weapon clicked empty. Closing his eyes McCade waited for the inevitable impact. Instead there was just a dull thump followed by silence.

Opening his eyes, he saw the second icecat was also dead, lying only a few feet from the first. Suddenly his legs gave way and dumped him on the ground. He did his best to throw up, but failed. When the dry heaves finally stopped, he leaned back, and took a look around. It was almost completely dark. He shivered. A quick check confirmed that his suit's power pak was completely exhausted. Well, he couldn't complain about that since it had saved his life. Of course, what good was that if he froze to death?

"You're losing it again," he told himself, "cut the crap and do something useful." Shivering, he tried to think. The aircar was miles away, and he wasn't sure he could find it in the dark. So he should stay put and build a fire. With what? He knew from previous experience the low scrubby vegetation didn't burn worth a damn. Still, he had to do something. Trying to stand, he reached out to steady himself, and his hand encountered something warm. The body of the first icecat.

Of course! Given their bulk the dead icecats would take a while to freeze. Maybe even all night. That gave him an idea. It wasn't pleasant, but it might save his life.

Taking a deep breath, he drew his power knife, flicked on the blade, and went to work. Twenty back-breaking minutes later, he'd finished, and was curled up inside the icecat's warm abdominal cavity. Outside, large piles of entrails lay where he'd thrown them, steaming as they released their warmth into the cold night air, twitching as smaller nocturnal animals gathered to share the unexpected feast. Eventually larger animals would arrive, and start in on the main carcass, but by then it would be morning, and they'd be welcome to it. That was the theory anyway. By now he was so tired he didn't care if it worked or not. Sleep was all that mattered. Doing his best to ignore where he was, and the stench that went with it, McCade curled up even tighter and drifted off to sleep.

One

THE OUTER LAYERS of the icecat's body had frozen during the night. Now he was trapped. Panic began to crowd in around his thoughts but he pushed it back, swallowing the bile which rose to fill his mouth, forcing himself to think rather than feel. Gritting his teeth, McCade slid one hand down to the cargo pocket on his right thigh, fumbled for a moment, and then retrieved the power knife. Moving carefully so he wouldn't drop it, he brought the knife up in front of him, flicked it on, and heard the reassuring hum as its sealed energy beam came to life. It sliced effortlessly through frozen flesh and bone. Moments later he was crawling out of the animal's carcass onto the snow and ice.

He stood slowly, stretching cramped muscles as he looked around. Nothing. The ship he'd heard must have landed some distance away.

Taking his helmet off, McCade strolled over to the other carcass and sat down. It was hard as rock, and somewhat

9

ragged, since small animals had been nibbling on it during the night.

Grinning, he fumbled around inside his heatsuit for a moment, found a broken cigar, and lit the longer half with his lighter. He took a long satisfying drag. As he blew a thin streamer of smoke toward the sky, the sun suddenly broke through the clouds, and he felt its warmth touch his cheek. He smiled. It felt good to be alive.

A few moments later a familiar figure rounded an outcropping of rock and headed his way. McCade waved and the other man waved back. Rico moved easily for a big man. And he *was* big. His extra-large heatsuit bulged over his muscles and his enormous strides quickly ate up the distance between them.

He looked at McCade and shook his head in pretended amazement. "Well, sport, I guess I've seen it all now." Rico's tiny eyes twinkled merrily as he spoke. "First ya catch an icecat and rip him apart with your bare hands. Then, just for the fun of it, ya ambush a second one and kill him too. No offense, Sam, but at this rate we're gonna run outta icecats in a week or so, and then what'll we do for fun?" Rico shook his head again in mock concern.

McCade grinned as he stood up and extinguished the cigar butt under the heel of his boot. "Very funny, Rico. Now cut the comedy and give me a hand. I lost a couple of slug throwers around here somewhere . . . and certain members of the Council are notoriously tight with a credit."

Rico laughed. "Tight ain't the word for it," he agreed. "Downright stingy's more like it. But as long as your wife's headin' the Council we'll be runnin' a tight ship. Hell, you're lucky Sara ain't countin' your ammo."

"Don't give her any ideas, Rico, or I'll be throwing rocks at icecats from now on."

"Speakin' o' which, Sam, how the hell'd ya manage ta get into this mess anyhow?"

While they searched for the weapons, McCade told him the whole story. "All things considered, I was incredibly stupid," he finished.

"True," Rico said with a big grin.

McCade laughed. "Up yours, Rico."

Rico poked an icecat carcass with the toe of one boot. "All jokin' aside, you're damn lucky to be alive, ol' sport," he said soberly. "Looks like a mated pair. Well, come on . . . we've got places ta go an people ta see."

"Bullshit," McCade replied as they crunched through the ice and snow. "I'm going home. First Sara's gonna chew me out for being so stupid, and then I'm going to bed."

"Well, you're right about Sara chewing ya out, but ya ain't going ta bed, not yet anyway," Rico answered with a grin.

"Why not?"

"You'll see," Rico said mysteriously, and steadfastly refused to say more until they reached the clearing where McCade had left his aircar. As they broke into the open space, McCade saw one whole end of the clearing had been scorched all the way down to the permafrost, and sitting in the middle of the burned area was a small ship. Not just any ship, but a captain's gig, the kind that belongs to an Imperial Cruiser. It had fast lines and a flawless paint job.

"What the hell is that doing here?" McCade demanded.

"Your old friend what's-his-name sent it. The one with two last names."

"Swanson-Pierce? You mean he's here?"

Rico nodded and pointed one index finger upward. "He's got a cruiser, a tin can, and two DEs up there, and wants ta see ya."

McCade scowled and turned toward his aircar. "Whatever he wants can wait. By now Sara's worried and I need some sleep."

Rico shrugged. "Suit yourself, ol' sport, but Sara's up there too."

McCade sighed. Swanson-Pierce could mean only one thing, trouble. And as usual he'd managed to set up things his way. By getting Sara aboard he'd made sure McCade would come to him, plus they'd meet on his turf, and he'd set the agenda. It was all vintage Swanson-Pierce.

They were met just inside the lock by a solicitous young officer who introduced himself as Ensign Peel. He had a soft, friendly face and a firm handshake. Peel showed them into a small cabin just aft of the control room and disappeared forward to assume his duties as copilot.

As they strapped themselves into acceleration couches, McCade took a look around. Someone had lavished a great deal of attention on the ship's interior. The bulkheads and acceleration couches were covered in carefully muted fabrics and, here and there, the polished glow of ornamental brass and exotic wood caught and held his eye. The whole merged to convey a sense of restrained elegance. It all screamed—no, murmured—Swanson-Pierce.

McCade felt himself pushed down into his seat as the ship roared upward. The pilot knew her business and cleared atmosphere only a quarter rotation away from the large Imperial cruiser orbiting Alice. McCade watched the overhead screens as they approached and the vessel grew even larger.

She was one of the new Jupiter Class ships. Miles long, she was a tracery of gun platforms, missile tubes, laser mounts, and other less identifiable installations. She had none of the streamlined beauty common to ships designed for atmospheric use, but what she lacked in grace, she made up for in raw power. In minutes she could lay waste to all but the most heavily fortified cities. Beyond her McCade saw a glint of reflected sunlight marking the location of an escort.

Ahead a small rectangle of light appeared as a hatch slid

open to admit them. As their pilot skillfully matched velocity with the larger craft and slipped into the launching bay, McCade felt like a minnow being swallowed by a whale. Inside were rows of neatly parked Interceptors, their sleek deadly shapes reminiscent of bullets waiting to be fired.

As always, four were on condition red: tubes hot, weapons armed, ready for launch. McCade knew how it felt. You were proud to slide into the cramped cockpit because Interceptor pilots were the elite. The cream of the Academy. And you were scared, not of the enemy, but of yourself. You'd rather die than screw up.

Then one day the waiting was over. Wing after wing of Interceptors blasted out to give and receive death over the planet Hell. Entire fleets maneuvered through complex computer-generated patterns probing for strength and weakness. But for you the battle was much more personal. It was you against them. Your skill, your reflexes, your ship against them.

Finally the moment came, and with it a strangely silent explosion as a pirate ship blossomed into a miniature sun. You scanned your screens searching for the next target. There it was. A large ship just ahead. You felt the groove, the almost magical connection between you and it, and knew you couldn't miss. Relying on muscle memory, and years of training, you lined it up and prepared to fire. Suddenly a voice breaks your concentration.

"Please, in the name of whatever gods you worship, I implore you, please don't fire. My ship is unarmed. I have only women, children, and old men aboard . . . please listen to me."

And listen you did. You believed her. But a second voice comes over your headset. The voice of your commanding officer, Captain Ian Bridgar, hoarse from hours of shouting orders, tense with hatred for the pirates who took his wife and daughter. "Fire, Lieutenant! That's an order! She's lying. Fire, damn you!"

But you didn't fire. Instead you watched the pirate ship slide out of sight, taking with it your career, identity, and honor. For you have disobeyed a direct order from your commanding officer and his word is law.

McCade's thoughts were interrupted as the pilot's voice came over the intercom. "Welcome aboard *Victory*, gentlemen, Ensign Peel will act as your guide."

There was lots of traffic in the corridor as the third watch went off duty and the first came on. The two colonists attracted a good deal of attention as they walked along. Especially McCade. His blood-smeared heatsuit, two-day stubble, and hard eyes were difficult to miss.

Ignoring the stares, they followed Ensign Peel through a maze of corridors and passageways. Eventually, they moved into officer territory, passing a spacious wardroom, and arriving in front of a large open hatch. A pair of marine guards snapped to attention and presented arms. Peel saluted in reply and announced his party. "I have the honor to present Council Member Fredrico Jose Romero, and Citizen Sam McCade."

Suddenly a shapely female figure in a blue one-piece ship-suit burst through the hatch and threw herself into McCade's arms. She proceeded to kiss him, hug him, and scold him all at once. "Going after an icecat all by yourself...you are the most hopeless man I've ever met ...are you all right...is this your blood...how could you..."

McCade covered her lips with his, and marveled for the millionth time that this wonderful armful could be the daughter of the same man who'd court-martialed him. There was silence for a moment as she melted against him, before suddenly pulling away. "Oh, no, you don't, Sam McCade. You're not getting off that easy, not until you admit you were stupid."

He looked down into large hazel eyes set above a straight, determined mouth. A terrible white scar slashed

down across the soft roundness of her face. She'd been
aboard the liner *Mars* when it was attacked and boarded by
pirates. As they burst through the main lock Sara had been
there, fighting shoulder to shoulder with the ship's crew.
Coolly she had aimed and fired, killing at least two, before
a boarding pike had knocked her unconscious, and left her
scarred for life.

In a way the disfigurement had saved her. Instead of
selling her as a slave, the pirates had held her for ransom.
Ironically she and her mother ended up aboard the very
ship which McCade had refused to destroy during the Battle of Hell. In a desperate attempt to save her damaged
vessel, the pirate captain had made a random hyperspace
jump but it was too late. Knowing the drives were going to
blow, the captain ordered those who could to abandon ship.
Sara and her mother were among those shoved into a
crowded life raft and launched into the darkness of space.

Minutes later the larger vessel exploded, leaving them
alone and far from any civilized world. Being a step below
a lifeboat, the raft had no drive of its own, so for weeks
they drifted aimlessly in space. One by one they began to
die. Her heart broken by her husband's insane ravings,
Sara's mother was among the first to go. More time
passed, until only Sara and two others survived. Finally
rescued by a tramp freighter, Sara had made her way to
Alice, and never looked back.

Then McCade had shown up, searching for her father,
determined to kill him if necessary rather than allow the
secret of the War World to fall into Il Ronnian hands. Mutual dislike slowly gave way to wary cooperation, friendship, and then love. So McCade saw past the scar, seeing
only the love and concern in her eyes. She was still waiting. "I was stupid," he said, grinning.

Suddenly she was back in his arms, planting kisses all
over his face, and fussing over his appearance. Then she

leaned back and wrinkled her nose. "Great Sol, what's that odor?"

Meanwhile, the two marine guards did their best to ignore the whole thing and failed. Both were losing the battle to keep a straight face. Flushing slightly, McCade gently disentangled himself and followed her into the large cabin. It reflected the same elegant taste he'd seen inside the gig, which wasn't too surprising, since both belonged to the same man, Walter Swanson-Pierce.

As Walt moved out from behind his rosewood desk to shake hands with Rico, McCade saw the naval officer was at his perfectionistic best. Body trim and fit, uniform just so, graying hair carefully combed, calculated smile firmly in place.

Then it was McCade's turn, and as they shook, McCade noticed the thick gold stripe on the naval officer's space-black sleeve. He grinned. "So it's Rear Admiral now. Congratulations, Walt. Rear Admiral—a rank that describes you perfectly. A reward for cleaning out all the War World's little secrets, I assume."

Swanson-Pierce chose to ignore the dig. Instead, he looked McCade carefully up and down, eyes lingering here and there, as though counting each bloodstain. "Why thanks, Sam, I suppose you're right. I'm sure the successful disposition of that problem did play a part in my promotion. Nice of you to help. Meanwhile, I see you've managed to maintain your usual standard of sartorial elegance—no, that's not quite true—actually, you look even worse than usual."

Rico and Sara looked at each other and shrugged. They'd seen it all before. They'd have to wait it out. They dropped into chairs, Rico grinning in anticipation, Sara frowning in disapproval.

"So," McCade said, also dropping into a chair, and swinging his filthy boots up onto the polished surface of the officer's desk. "What brings the mighty Imperial Navy to this corner of the frontier? Slumming?"

As he moved around behind his desk Swanson-Pierce did his best to avoid seeing McCade's boots. "No," he answered evenly, "actually we're on our way somewhere else." He gestured vaguely. "I thought it would be nice to visit old friends."

McCade snorted in disbelief. "Get serious, Walt. You haven't got any friends. Nobody's got that strong a stomach." Ignoring Sara's look of disapproval, he took out a bent cigar, and talked around it as he puffed it alight. "Besides, you wouldn't go ten feet out of your way to visit your own mother."

Swanson-Pierce shook his head in mock concern. "Well, I see life on Alice has done nothing to improve your temperament, Sam. Sad, very sad. I don't know how you stand it, Sara. You deserve better. But," he said airily, "I will admit there's a matter of business I'd like to discuss."

McCade swung his feet down and stood up. "Come on, Sara. We don't need whatever this is. Nice seeing you, Walt. Don't trip on any pirates as you leave."

But to his surprise Sara remained seated. And a stubborn look had come over her face. He knew that look and groaned inwardly. "I think you should hear what he has to say, Sam," she said. "Then, if you still feel the same way, we'll leave together."

McCade knew when he was beat. He fell back into his chair, knocking a large lump of ash off his cigar. Swanson-Pierce watched in horrified fascination as it fell and then exploded against the rich carpeting. He winced as McCade automatically placed a boot over the ashes and rubbed them in.

"OK," McCade said. "So what's this all about?"

Swanson-Pierce looked up from the stained carpet and forced a smile. "Admiral Keaton and I want you to find someone for us."

McCade shook his head. "Forget it. I gave up bounty hunting."

"Even if you could prevent a war?"

"War, hell." Ten to one that was just more of Walt's bullshit. The old patriotic approach. Well, it wouldn't work this time. McCade was tired of chasing fugitives from planet to planet, tired of living the way they lived, alone and afraid. Besides, Sara didn't want him to. She detested bounty hunters. But why hadn't she objected? Because she believed whatever Walt was selling. He looked over and found her face a purposeful blank. She was trying her best not to sway him any more than she had already. Meanwhile Swanson-Pierce was grinning, aware of McCade's inner conflict, and enjoying it.

"All right," McCade said reluctantly, "I'll consider it. Who's the mark?"

Swanson-Pierce took his time, leaning back in his chair, obviously savoring the moment. "We want you to find the Emperor."

McCade's eyebrows shot up in surprise, but before he could ask the obvious questions, an emergency klaxon went off. The ship was under attack.

Two

Six torpedoes were launched at *Victory*. Two hit, and obliterated the Destroyer Escort which happened to be coming alongside at that particular moment. One malfunctioned, and raced off toward the warmth of the sun. Another was intercepted, and destroyed by an unusually alert Interceptor pilot. The last two hit *Victory* and blew up.

McCade and the others were thrown to the deck by the force of the explosions. A host of alarms and klaxons went off. All over the ship hatches automatically slammed shut, turning the vessel into a honeycomb of airtight compartments. The lights flickered, went off, and then came back on again. They were dimmer now since all available power had been automatically shunted to the defensive screens.

The com screen lit up before the naval officer could touch it. "Lt. Commander Muncy reporting, sir. Battle status negative. We have no targets on our screens . . . with cross-confirmation from our surviving Escorts. Initial evidence suggests a single vessel, a destroyer, or perhaps a light cruiser. It entered normal space approximately a quarter light out, fired six torpedoes, and immediately reentered hyperspace. Two hit us, two hit and destroyed the *Amazon*, one was intercepted, and one malfunctioned. Our remaining Escorts and Interceptors have assumed a defensive formation in case of further attack."

Standing now, McCade looked at the screen and saw there was pandemonium behind Muncy. Medics were running by with stretchers, officers were shouting orders, and a damage-control party was busy fighting a small electrical fire. But Muncy's face showed no trace of concern. Only a subtle tightness around her eyes betrayed the pressure she was under. A real pro, McCade thought to himself.

"Thank you," Swanson-Pierce replied evenly. "You may proceed with your report."

Muncy nodded. "I'm sorry to report that the bridge took a direct hit. Captain Blaine and his executive officer were killed instantly. The second officer is missing, and the third is severely wounded. I have assumed command."

"Noted and approved, Captain," Swanson-Pierce said briskly. "Extent of damage?"

"The bridge, main computer, and all primary controls were completely destroyed, sir. Ten killed, three wounded." She glanced over her shoulder and saw the damage-control party extinguishing the last of the flames. "All fires are out and the worst sections have been sealed off. Initial analysis indicates secondary computer and main peripherals are undamaged. Estimated time to sixty percent effectiveness, one hour forty minutes. We also took a torp in the galley and hydroponics section. Four killed, two wounded. We'll be on emergency rations until further notice."

By now both Sara and Rico were standing next to McCade. Neither was injured. "Speaking for Alice, our hospital and its staff are at your disposal, Captain," Sara said. "Plus any other assistance we can provide."

McCade saw gratitude in the officer's eyes. "Thank you. I'll notify medical."

"One last thing, Captain," Swanson-Pierce said, "and then I'll let you get back to your duties. Did we ID the enemy ship?"

"Negative, Admiral," Muncy answered evenly. "No positive identification. Since our hostile was in normal space for only five seconds, there wasn't much time. And what data we had on her was lost along with the main computer. However, our Escorts say her parameters provide a ninety percent match with Imperial design. As you know, both the pirates and Il Ronn have taken a few of our ships over the last few years."

"Yes, yes," Swanson-Pierce replied vaguely. "That would account for it." As he spoke, McCade noticed the other man had turned pale, and his knuckles were white where they gripped the edge of the com console.

"Well, thank you, Captain. You've done an excellent job under trying circumstances. Carry on, and let me know if there's anything I can do to help." Swanson-Pierce forced a smile. "At the moment, however, I imagine you can get along without an Admiral peeking over your shoulder."

Muncy grinned her agreement, but replied tactfully, "Over the next few hours I suspect I'll have lots of questions. With your permission, I'll call back then?"

"Of course," Swanson-Pierce said. Muncy nodded and the screen faded to black.

McCade lit a cigar and blew a stream of smoke toward the ceiling, where it was sucked toward the nearest vent. "Maybe you'd better take it from the top, Walt. Including that stuff about finding the Emperor. How did you manage to misplace him?"

Swanson-Pierce grinned crookedly at McCade. "Well, I'm afraid it's a bit complicated."

"Surprise, surprise," McCade said sourly.

"Actually it *was* a bit of a surprise," the other man said

agreeably. "A somewhat nasty one. You see the Emperor died about a month ago."

McCade lifted an eyebrow. "It's a bit out of my line, Walt. What you need is an angel, not a bounty hunter."

Swanson-Pierce smiled patiently. "It's his successor we want you to find. We're reasonably sure the rightful heir is alive; we just don't know where. That of course is where you come in."

Rico shook his head in amazement. "I know we're pretty far out on the rim, but if the Emp croaked, even we'd hear about that."

The naval officer shook his head. "Normally you'd be right Rico . . . but in this case only a handful of people know. Until we've found the Emperor's rightful successor, it seems best to keep his death a secret. Although, I'm afraid . . ."

"Oh no," McCade groaned. "Don't tell me, let me guess. The people who just took a shot at us know, and they don't favor the rightful heir."

"I'd say give that man a cigar," Swanson-Pierce grinned, "except he's already got one."

"I knew it," McCade said. "As usual your people have screwed up, and you want us to bail you out. Well, forget it. We're sorry, but we've got enough problems of our own. If you folks want to squabble over the throne, what's it to us? The Empire has damned little say out here . . . and we prefer it that way." Out of the corner of his eye, McCade saw Sara start to speak, and then restrain herself. Damn. For some reason she was still on Walt's side.

Swanson-Pierce paused for a moment as if gathering his thoughts, and then spoke through steepled fingers. "To understand why it's important to you, and every other planet along the rim, you've got to understand the circumstances of the Emperor's death. Unfortunately the Emperor loved to hunt. It drove his staff crazy of course, but he insisted. He'd been doing it for years and from all accounts was quite good at it. His quarters were full of trophies from hundreds of planets. An uglier assortment of dead carcasses you never saw. Anyway, each year he looked forward to his annual safari. There was the thrill of the hunt, the companionship of his favorite cronies, and an escape from the pressures of office."

"Yeah," McCade added sarcastically, "it must be tough having everything you want."

Swanson-Pierce ignored the interruption and continued his narrative. "This year he decided to visit Envo IV, a primitive planet located on the far side of the Empire from here, and well known for its vicious animal life. Apparently he had his heart set on bagging an Envo Beast. From all accounts they're herbivores, but weigh a couple of tons apiece, and are extremely territorial. I understand both his bodyguard and the locals were aghast. They apparently run the damned things down with armored vehicles, and then finish them off with shoulder-launched missiles. But the Emperor wasn't having any of that."

The naval officer shook his head regretfully. "Say what you will... the man had guts. He insisted on going it alone... even against Envo Beasts."

McCade reached out to deposit some ash in an ashtray, and missed. It cascaded toward the rug. Sara gave him a dirty look which he somehow managed to avoid meeting.

"Anyway," Swanson-Pierce continued, "something went wrong. The Emperor missed his shot and was badly gored. He lived for about two days. They tried everything but it was hopeless. Medicine is still pretty primitive on Envo. All they could do was make him comfortable and wait for him to die. Knowing his death was imminent, the Emperor sent for a courier. When the courier arrived, the Emperor ordered everyone else out of his chambers. A short time later the courier disappeared, and the Emperor was found dead. Some said the courier had killed him, and a bounty was placed on his head, fifty thousand credits dead or alive."

Swanson-Pierce looked from one to another as if checking to make sure he had their attention. "Suffice it to say this courier is a very resourceful man, and eventually made it to Terra where he delivered the Emperor's message to Admiral Keaton."

The naval officer took a moment to study the cigar he was holding, intentionally allowing the suspense to build, watching McCade from the corner of one eye. Finally, much to the Admiral's satisfaction, McCade scowled his surrender. Victorious, Swanson-Pierce returned to his narrative. "Before he died the Emperor chose his successor, and sent word of his choice to Admiral Keaton, the one man he trusted to carry out his wishes."

McCade quickly reviewed what little knowledge he had about the Emperor's family. He knew the Emperor's wife had died quite young, and if he remembered correctly, there was a son named Alexander as well as a daughter named Claudia. It seemed the son was something of a playboy, always making headlines with his outrageous behavior, eventually disappearing some time ago en route to Mars. Needless to say there'd been an intensive search at the time but nothing was ever found. Most assumed Alexander was dead, but a few insisted he'd simply gone into hiding, and would eventually show up. Nobody, except possibly the Emperor, seemed very concerned.

Claudia, however, was another story. She'd taken her position very seriously indeed. While the sons and daughters of other high-ranking officials tried to discover new ways to have a good time, or pursued fashionable careers, she entered the Academy. At her own insistence she was shown absolutely no favoritism. So when Claudia graduated first in her class, it was due to her own ability, and not her father's influence. She was subsequently assigned to the cruiser *Defiance*. Not long thereafter, the *Defiance* had the misfortune to drop out of hyperspace almost on top of an Il Ronnian raider which was operating inside Imperial space. Even the navy couldn't ignore that.

"PRINCESS DEFEATS ALIEN HORDE" the headlines read. In truth the *Defiance* was twice the size of the Il Ronnian raider, and there were only thirty members of the "ALIEN HORDE." Nonetheless, the Il Ronn put up a tussle, Claudia was wounded, and the press had a field day. The net effect was even greater celebrity status for the princess. She continued to serve with distinction, and eventually left the navy with a reserve commission as a Commander, seemingly determined to follow in her father's footsteps. The navy first . . . then politics. If it was good enough for Daddy, it was good enough for her.

At first she headed a variety of commissions, represented her father at ceremonial occasions, and performed other largely symbolic functions. Gradually, however, Claudia worked her way into positions of genuine responsibility, heading up a succession of small governmental departments, until finally her father agreed to place her on the Board of Military Governors. It was a position of some power, since it was the Board's responsibility to oversee the military on the Emperor's behalf, and that included approving all promotions above the rank of commander. The Board also oversaw the navy's budget and general state of readiness. As a result, some very important people began to take Claudia seriously, and many wondered if the Emperor had already chosen her to succeed him.

McCade shrugged. "So I suppose he chose Princess Claudia."

Swanson-Pierce nodded understandingly. "A logical conclusion . . . but as it happens . . . he didn't."

"Ya mean he picked the boy instead?" Rico asked.

"Exactly," Swanson-Pierce said.

"But why?" McCade asked. "I'd always heard Prince

Alexander was about as worthless as they come. Surely the Emperor knew that."

"I honestly don't know why he picked Alexander," Swanson-Pierce said with a frown. "All I can tell you is that Admiral Keaton believes the Emperor had good reasons for his choice. According to Keaton, there was a special bond of some sort between father and son, even when Alexander was at his worst. The Admiral also believes the Emperor feared what Princess Claudia might do if she assumed the throne. Unlike her father, she's a hawk, and believes war with the Il Ronn is inevitable. In her opinion we're better off fighting them now, rather than waiting and being forced to do so later, when they're even stronger."

Now McCade was beginning to see why Sara had sided with Swanson-Pierce. If Princess Claudia took over, she might destroy the delicate balance of power preventing war between the human and Il Ronn empires. For a number of reasons humans and Il Ronn were natural enemies. Strangely enough, their mutual hostility stemmed more from similarities, than differences. Both races were ardently expansionist, and as their respective empires grew in size, the once-thick band of frontier worlds separating them grew constantly thinner. As this occurred, squabbles over real estate became increasingly common. Fortunately, the Il Ronn had evolved on a hot, dry world and, in spite of a reverence for water, detested the wet worlds so loved by humans. Nonetheless both sought certain rare ores and isotopes, and would fight for any planet which contained them.

However some of the mutual dislike stemmed from other, less obvious, causes. For one thing, the two races had very different histories and cultures. The Il Ronn had been around a long time. In fact, most authorities agreed they had preceded man into space by thousands of years. Had their culture allowed the giant leaps made possible by individualism, instead of the slow but steady growth of group consensus, chances are the Il Ronn would have rolled over the human race while it was still living in caves. But they didn't. They preferred instead a deliberate expansion, in which each potential acquisition was painstakingly studied, and then carefully annexed.

Not so the humans. Once in space, their sphere of influence expanded in rapid fits and starts, sometimes accomplishing in days what the Il Ronn might have taken centuries to do. Unfortunately, the opposite was also true. Internal dissension, bickering, and laziness often destroyed human gains more quickly than they were made. The result was two large empires of roughly equal size and power, both of which were inexorably expanding toward each other.

For years, the first emperor, and then his son, had worked to forstall the almost inevitable collision. While both had worked to prepare the Empire for the possibility of war, both had also done everything they could to avoid it. Even to the point of tolerating the pirates because they helped keep the Il Ronn in check.

Nonetheless, some had always felt conflict was certain, and couldn't be avoided. Claudia was one of these. So, if she took the throne, there was a good possibility that war would follow.

And, since only the frontier worlds separated the two empires, they would be the most likely battlefield. And that accounted for Sara's interest in helping Swanson-Pierce. She was trying to protect Alice.

McCade imagined hell bombs falling, entire cities turned to black slag, millions or even billions of lives lost, and all to please a few power-mad idiots on both sides. Viewed that way, he really didn't have much choice. For better or worse, he'd have to find the idiot prince, and put him on the throne. "OK," he said, looking from Swanson-Pierce to Sara. "I get the picture. It sounds like we don't have a helluva lot of choice."

Sara smiled, a look of relief in her eyes. "I'm sorry, Sam, but it's in our self-interest."

McCade blew a long streamer of smoke toward the floor. "As usual you're right, honey . . . but I'm still waiting to hear how Walt managed to lose a prince. I take it from what you said earlier that Alexander's still missing?"

The naval officer looked embarrassed and tugged at his cuffs. "I'm afraid so." He looked up resentfully. "And say what you will, it's not easy to keep track of somebody who's not only wealthy, but a bit looney to boot."

"Even so," Rico observed thoughtfully, "it seems ta me if ya turn the whole navy loose on it ya can't lose."

At that Swanson-Pierce looked even more embarrassed. "You're quite right, Rico. I wish we could. Unfortunately that's not possible."

"Why not?" McCade and Sara asked the question almost in unison. Sara was just as curious as McCade, since her earlier conversation with Swanson-Pierce hadn't proceeded this far.

The naval officer paused as he slumped farther down in his chair. "Because," he said, "at least half the navy doesn't want Prince Alexander found."

McCade slowly shook his head back and forth, marveling at his own stupidity. "Of course. I should have known. The ship which just popped out of hyperspace and slipped us those torps wasn't captured by the pirates or Il Ronn. It was navy, wasn't it? Somebody who doesn't want Alexander on the throne."

"Claudia," Sara said to herself. "It's got to be Claudia."

Swanson-Pierce nodded reluctantly. "Evidently the Emperor believed Alexander to be alive. Nonetheless, in his message to Admiral Keaton he indicated that if Alexander can't be found within three standard months, Claudia must ascend the throne for the good of the Empire. Claudia believes Alexander is dead . . . but she's not taking any chances."

McCade gave a long, low whistle. "Claudia doesn't want her brother on the throne . . . and knows you're trying to find him and put him there. My, my, Walt. She must want you in the worst way. Can't say as I blame her, of course. God knows you're irritating! Nonetheless, sending a light cruiser after you strikes me as a bit excessive."

The other man allowed himself a bleak smile. "I admit the princess is annoyed with me, and Admiral Keaton too for that matter. However, you'll be interested to learn she's not too thrilled with you either. In fact she's already hired the Assassin's Guild to kill you." For a long time only the hiss of the air conditioning filled the room.

Three

NO MATTER HOW many planets McCade saw, there would always be something special about Terra. Even though he'd spent far more time away from Earth than on her, she still seemed like home. And many others felt the same way. In fact, for most humans, Terra would always be the emotional center of the Empire. After all, it was from her ancient surface that thousands of ships had lifted and disappeared into the blackness of space. In those days there was no hyperdrive. The colonists had crawled toward the distant stars, often taking years to make the one-way journey. Many died along the way. Sometimes entire ships, and even groups of ships, disappeared without a trace. Of course, some made it too. Their weary worn-out vessels dropping out of alien skies never to rise again. But even then the struggle was far from over. Hostile environments, poor equipment, and a lack of experience finished most colonies off within a few years. But a precious few some-how managed to beat the odds. Through good planning, or just good luck, they managed to hang on. Over time, they grew more numerous, eventually prospered, and even formed an interstellar government. A virgin planet was chosen as a capital and populated with millions of people sent to represent thousands of worlds.

But it wasn't easy. Advantage for some always meant sacrifice for others. Special interest groups battled constantly, alliances were forged and then broken, laws passed and then ignored. Finally a coalition of systems seceded from the Confederation. A terrible civil war followed.

From the ensuing chaos there emerged a single man strong enough, and smart enough, to build something from the ashes. His followers proclaimed him Emperor.

Though many things to many people, the Emperor was above all else a master psychologist, a PR man par excellence. During the early days of his rule he sensed Terra's symbolic and emotional value, and decided to leave the bombed-out Confederation capital as it was. Rather than rebuild, he declared it a monument to peace, thereby creating a permanent reminder of his greatest victory, and restoring Earth to her former glory. It was a popular decision.

Of course, some refused his rule. Especially those who'd fought valiantly against him during the civil war. Many of them headed for the Empire's frontiers. They eventually became pirates, raiding the Empire's commerce, and plundering the frontier worlds along the rim. At first the Emperor tried to destroy them. He sent Admiral Keaton to find and wipe out the pirate fleet. Keaton found them near the planet Hell and, while soundly defeating them, didn't manage to destroy them.

Elements of the pirate fleet escaped, later attacking an Imperial prison world in an attempt to free their imprisoned comrades and, much to their own surprise, winning. Having no other place to go, they were eventually forced to make the prison their home. If you can call an impregnable fortress, surrounded by orbiting weapons platforms, "home."

Having no desire to waste ships or lives attacking the pirate headquarters, the Emperor decided to tolerate the pirates as long as they didn't get out of hand. A pragmatist to the end, the Emperor decided the pirates might feed off the Empire, but by god they would defend it as well. Their eternal skirmishes with the Il Ronn made for less pressure on the navy, which in turn lowered taxes, which made his wealthy supporters happy. Not long after making that decision, he died and his son took the throne. Now the son was also dead, and *his* son must follow, or the entire Empire might be lost.

McCade looked at Terra on his main viewscreen and sighed. She floated against the black backdrop of space like a blue-green jewel wrapped in cotton. He was approaching her slowly, almost reluctantly, delaying the moment when *Pegasus* entered Earth's gravitational field and was pulled down toward the surface. Once there he'd be committed, forced to begin the search for Alexander, and unable to quit once he got started. And it wouldn't be easy. Arrayed against him were Claudia, her personal retainers, and a vast number of governmental and military personnel willing to do her bidding.

According to Walt, a large number of people were betting their careers that the prince wouldn't be found. Or, he thought grimly, that if found, the prince wouldn't live long enough to take the throne.

And, if Claudia's plans for McCade were any example, they were probably right. She must have a spy on Admiral Keaton's staff, because within hours of his decision to solicit McCade's help, she'd filed with the Assassin's Guild for a level-three license on the bounty hunter. A level three would allow the assassins to kill not only McCade, but anyone else who happened to be in the way as well. It was legal, but damned expensive, and indicated how much she wanted him out of the way. And to make things even worse, he'd run up against the Guild in the past, and they were no doubt looking forward to evening the score. It was a depressing thought.

He shook his head ruefully, and Terra disappeared behind a cloud of smoke as he puffed a new cigar into life. He tapped a few keys on the control console. *Pegasus* picked up speed, and started down toward the planet below. Somewhere down there he'd find Alexander's trail. It was more than two years cold, but he'd find it. Just as he'd found so many others over the years.

Bounty hunters were a strange breed. Hated by fugitives, disliked by planetary police, and romanticized by the public, they lived a strange twilight existence between two worlds. Heroes one moment, villains the next, bounty hunters soon learned to trust no one but themselves. They lived to run up their score, both for the financial rewards involved, and for their own egos. In so doing they performed an important function.

Like every other human society the Empire generated its share of criminals, sociopaths, and perverts. While most planets had some form of police force, there was no interplanetary agency for law enforcement. Oh, it has been suggested often enough, but ultimately no one wanted to pay for it. The last thing people wanted was more taxes. Besides, the planets valued what independence they had, and weren't eager to create still another Imperial agency to start mucking around in their affairs. So, bounty hunters were just another expression of the Emperor's pragmatism. If it works, leave it alone. And it certainly worked.

Bounty hunters could access a current list of interplanetary fugitives on any public terminal. Listed were their names, aliases, histories, habitual weapons, and, most important of all, the size of the reward offered for their capture or death. Sometimes the reward was conditional, specifying a particular fugitive must be brought in alive, but that was rare. Normally dead was just fine. Having picked a particular fugitive, the bounty hunter would punch the person's name and ID number into the terminal, and request a hunting license for that particular individual. This was an important step, since capturing or killing a fugitive without a license was considered a public service, and produced nothing more than a thank you letter.

McCade grinned to himself. It had happened to *him* once. And he'd sworn it would never happen again. Which is why he'd spent a lot of time and energy convincing Swanson-Pierce to offer a little extra motivation in the form of a reward. A sort of Imperial bounty.

Public service was well and good, but there was retirement to think about and besides, there was always the chance somebody might blow his ass off. Deep down, however, he knew the idea of giving Walt something for free just plain grated on his nerves. So, one million credits seemed like a nice round number. Sara resisted at first, until McCade suggested that perhaps Swanson-Pierce should throw in a class "A" fusion reactor for Alice as well, and then she'd jumped on the bandwagon with a vengeance. A class "A" reactor would provide enough power for the planet's needs well into the future. Walt never knew what hit him. Sara quickly had him wrapped around her little finger. In fact, Walt was damned lucky to get off that easy. McCade smiled at the thought.

"You're grinnin' like a roid miner on his way out of a pleasure dome," Rico observed, dropping into the copilot's chair.

"Well, there she is, Rico," McCade replied, waving his cigar butt at the main viewscreen. Terra more than filled the screen now as McCade slipped them into a descending orbit. "Trouble."

Rico shrugged philosophically. "I dunno, ol' sport. Seems ta me we've got 'em outnumbered. Wait till they get load o' Phil."

Suddenly a rigidly calm female voice flooded the intercom. "Alert. Alert. My scanners indicate a dangerous carnivore is aboard and about to enter the control area. I recommend immediate use of class 'A' hand weapons."

"I thought you said you'd have that damned computer fixed," Phil growled as he stepped into the control room. The voice was a deep basso and emanated from a shaggy, bearlike form which had just appeared from the ship's lounge. Phil was a human variant, biosculpted for life on iceworlds like Alice. He was a highly trained biologist . . . although he didn't look it . . . since very few scientists are seven feet tall and weigh three hundred pounds. Clad only in a plaid kilt of his own design, Phil made an imposing figure. He had large rounded ears, a short snout, and a shiny black nose. But Phil also had other less obvious attributes. Among them were infrared vision, amplified muscle response, and razor-sharp durasteel claws. For short periods of time he could go into full augmentation making him the biological equivalent of a killing machine. Which accounted for his presence. The search for Alexander was likely to get rough, and since the other two had rescued him from the slave pens of Lakor, and paid off his indenture, he figured he owed them one.

"Sorry about the computer, Phil. I just haven't had time yet to get it fixed, but I will."

Phil sat down and lit a dope stick. "I hope so. A rude computer can turn into a dead computer real easy." He looked up at the main screen. "Well, there she is, the planet named dirt."

"Yup," McCade said, glancing over his shoulder. "Fortunately it's winter where we're going, but it's still going to be a bit warm for you."

Phil growled deep in his throat. "Maybe I'll luck out and run into a blizzard."

Pegasus bucked a little as she hit a layer of colder air, and McCade gently forced her nose back down. "Damned little chance of that, Phil. This isn't Alice, you know. Weather programmers don't go in for blizzards. It generates too many hysterical com calls. Hell, you'll be lucky if it rains."

"Yeah, I know," Phil agreed regretfully, "but a guy can hope."

No one answered, and all were silent for a moment as Terra rose to meet them. The vast blueness of the Atlantic Ocean rolled by, quickly followed by the neat symmetry of the coastal cities, and then the dark green of the interior. Eventually the huge forests gave way to the endless interlocking circles of irrigated roboculture. Wherever he looked, McCade saw a carefully maintained balance between man and nature. He knew that when they left the ship, they'd find only clean air, and pure water. Pollution and crowding were things of the past. The damage had been repaired, and where nature seemed flawed, man had put it right. So what if the forests tended to have square corners, and the mountains seemed unusually symmetrical, a clean, safe environment was well worth it. Or that was the theory anyway. In McCade's opinion the whole thing seemed too structured, too tidy. It reminded him of something Walt would put together. Besides, he knew the problems of crowding and pollution hadn't really been solved. They'd simply been exported. Heavy industry and excess population had been shipped to other less fortunate planets, in order to make way for the neat parks and beautiful cities which now graced Terra.

His thoughts were interrupted as they neared Main Port, better known to spacers as "The Glory Hole," the biggest civilian spaceport on the North American continent. It now covered the area which had once been designated as "Chicago." For hours now the ship's computer had been in communication with Imperial Ground Control. Initial identification, clearance, and navigational data had all been handled by the two computers. Now as they neared the spaceport, a series of approach parameters flashed on his com screen, and McCade's hands danced over the controls. Responsive as always, *Pegasus* wound her way through the thickening air traffic, and then lowered herself into her assigned berth.

Once the ship's engines were shut down and secured, McCade took a moment to sweep his scanners across the surrounding area. A wide assortment of ground vehicles hurried to and fro on various errands, ships lifted and landed, but no one seemed particularly interested in *Pegasus*. Good. He liked it that way, even though he knew it didn't mean much. By now, Claudia, and anyone else who cared, knew they had landed. He'd considered arriving incognito, but rejected it. In spite of Terra's defenses, McCade felt sure it could be done. But there just wasn't enough time. A really effective cover would take weeks, maybe months, to establish and use. Besides, according to Walt, there was only one person who might know where to start the search. And she was apparently one of Claudia's best friends. So why bother to arrive in secret, and then be forced to come out into the open?

Therefore, McCade had decided on the direct approach. Land, find Lady Linnea as quickly as possible, and depend on Rico and Phil to cover his back. That's why they planned to check into a hotel. Although they might be safer aboard the ship, it would be very easy to watch, and that would make it hard to slip away undetected. Hopefully the crowds and activity of a large hotel would help to cover his movements. If they were fast enough maybe they could pull it off without any trouble. "And maybe we'll run into some flying cows too," McCade muttered to himself as he strapped on his handgun, and settled its familiar weight low on his left thigh. He'd put on a new set of black leathers in honor of the occasion, and they creaked as he moved.

Rico and Phil were already in the main lock when he

arrived. Both were heavily armed. Phil wore a shoulder
holster with a small submachine gun nestled in it and carried an energy rifle over his shoulder. Rico wore a sidearm
and cradled a grenade launcher in his arms as well. Not
that anyone would notice. The societal price for legalized
assassination and interstellar bounty hunters is an armed
population.

They left the ship together, hopping aboard one of the
articulated shuttles which wound its way from ship to ship,
finally stopping at the main terminal. There they joined the
throng of fellow spacers, mostly human, but well sprinkled
with aliens as well. It was quite a mob. Among them were
the crisply uniformed officers of a deep-space liner, a bird-
like Finthian merchant-prince, complete with entourage, a
hard-looking freighter captain with two of her crew, and a
somewhat shabby Zordian diplomat, his oral tentacles
weaving a complicated thought into universal sign lan-
guage. McCade couldn't tell if the tall woman striding
along beside him understood or not. Also present, but less
conspicuous, were other bounty hunters. He even recognized some of them. But whether he knew them or not, a
practiced eye easily picked them out of the crowd. For one
thing, they were alone. Most bounty hunters made damned
poor team players. And for another, their eyes were constantly on the move, sweeping the crowd for memprinted
faces, like a beachcomber checking to see what the tides
brought in.

Gradually the crowd was funneled through a series of
robo booths. As McCade stepped inside, hidden scanners
searched his body for signs of contagious disease, his retinal and dental patterns were cross-checked with his stated
identity, his weapons were analyzed for illegal technology,
and an officious-sounding computer simulation demanded
to know what cargo he'd brought to Imperial Earth.
McCade indicated he had no cargo to declare, agreed to
obey all the laws, customs, and edicts of Imperial author-

ity. And promised he'd have a good day—something he wasn't sure of, but hoped would come true.

Because his variant status had slowed his identity check, Phil was the last one out of the booths. First his retinal patterns and dentition were considerably different than those he'd been born with. His biosculpting had been done right there on Terra, and after a little digging, the computer had found his records. Then the computer noticed he'd been indentured to United Biomed as a biologist. He was supposed to be on Frio IV working off his debt. So, what was he doing on Terra? After some hurried consultation with United Biomed's mainframe, the computer learned his indenture had been purchased six standard months before by the government of a planet called Alice. Not long thereafter Phil's certificate of indenture had been used to light one of McCade's cigars, and there'd been one hell of a party. Phil was growling as he emerged, swearing as those who had programmed the customs booth, and threatening them with immediate dismemberment.

Once outside the terminal there was a swirl of activity as a variety of vehicles fought for a position at the curb. There were shiny new hover limos, stately sedans, and more than a few beat-up old taxis. As McCade stepped up to the curb a particularly decrepit-looking ground car of ancient lineage slipped between a limo and another taxi with only an inch to spare, and then screeched to a halt right in front of them. The driver leapt out, and ignored the outraged horns and invective of his fellow drivers, to race around and open a rear door for them.

"Taxi, sirs?" The young man's insouciant grin and obvious eagerness were hard to resist. He had light brown hair, an average sort of face, and wore a disposable gray coverall. The words "Maxi Taxi" were imprinted over a pocket crammed with pens, pencils, a comb, and a cheap pair of sunglasses. McCade normally used the less expensive autocabs, but it was Walt's money, so what the hell. He nodded and preceded the other two into the back of the car. It smelled of the disinfectant robo cleaners sprayed on everything. Given Rico's and Phil's bulk, it was a bit crowded, but not uncomfortable. Moments later the car jerked into motion and they were off.

"Where to?" the driver inquired as he smoothly inserted the ungainly vehicle into the flow of traffic, and accelerated away from the terminal.

"The Main Port Hilton," McCade replied.

"Yes, sir!" their driver said enthusiastically, and the car picked up even more speed.

Suddenly McCade felt vaguely uneasy. He couldn't put his finger on it, but there was something familiar about the taxi driver. Like most bounty hunters, McCade had trained himself to remember faces, and he was increasingly sure he'd seen the one reflected in the rearview mirror before. Surreptitiously he reached down to try the door handle. It was locked. And even if it wasn't . . . by now the car was moving too fast to jump. Glancing up at the mirror, McCade's eyes met the driver's, and the young man grinned. Only there was no humor in the man's smile. Or was it his imagination? Maybe he was just jumpy knowing the Guild was after him. The Guild! Then he had it, but a moment too late. Just as he remembered where he'd seen the driver's face before, the car swerved into an alley and came to a screeching halt. The driver whirled and McCade found himself looking down the business end of a needle gun.

"Welcome to the Glory Hole, stupid," the driver said, all traces of boyish charm suddenly gone.

"I assume he's addressing you, Sam," Phil said calmly, measuring the distance between himself and the gun.

"Shut up, fur face," the driver grated, shifting the gun an inch toward Phil. "Go ahead and try it. I could use a fur rug for my living room."

"Relax, Phil," McCade cautioned. "I don't think our

friend here plans to kill us. At least not at the moment. For one thing he's trapped us, and for another he hasn't delivered a warning. So if he takes us out . . . the Guild will be forced to hunt him down themselves." McCade was referring to the fact that while assassination was legal, certain ground rules had been established to give the intended victim a fighting chance. After all, those who made the rules knew that unless specifically exempted by the Emperor, they could become targets themselves. According to the rules, intended victims couldn't be tricked into an enclosed area, or other physical trap. Assassins were supposed to reveal identifying clothing just prior to an attempt, deliver an audible warning, and allow their intended target five seconds to react. And the Guild was committed to hunting down and killing any assassin who broke the rules. Not because they were concerned with fair play, but because if they didn't, assassination might become illegal.

The driver nodded his agreement: "That's right, shitheads. Mr. big-deal bounty hunter knows the rules. But don't push me or I might break 'em and take my chances."

Right then Rico belched, causing the needle gun to jerk his way. Rico covered his mouth in mock embarrassment. "Excuse me, ol' sport. I didn't mean ta scare ya like that."

McCade noticed the flush that started around the young man's neck and worked its way up across his face. There was hatred in the eyes which met McCade's, and he was holding the needle gun so tightly his fingers had turned white. He spoke through gritted teeth. "Real cute, asshole. But just remember you're all dead meat. Especially you, McCade. I want you to know that, think about it, sweat it through your pores, and piss it into your pants. Just remember, when they make your breakfast, I'll be in the kitchen; when you walk on the street, I'll be in the crowd; and when you go to sleep, I'll be in your dreams. And then, when I'm good and ready, I'm gonna kill you, just like you killed my brother Deke."

It all came rushing back. There were three assassins. Spread out to place McCade and his two escorts in a cross fire. He remembered how the middle one's amplified voice had echoed off the walls of the corridor. "Attention! A level-three licensed assassination will be carried out on Citizen Sam McCade five seconds from now." He remembered diving and rolling, snatching up a fallen weapon and swinging it left until the sight was filled by an assassin. A slightly older version of the driver. He remembered the incandescent holes his weapon punched through the wall before it came to bear and tore the man into pieces of bloody flesh. "Your brother did his best to kill me," McCade said flatly.

But they were wasted words. The driver was so centered on his own hate and need for revenge that he didn't even hear. "Just remember my face, shithead—cause it's the last thing you're ever gonna see." And with that the assassin opened the door and was gone.

Four

McCADE OPENED THE door of the speeding hover car and jumped. The ground came up fast, and slammed into his left shoulder. He rolled, crashing through the low bushes and down into the bottom of a drainage ditch. He gritted his teeth against the pain and forced himself to remain motionless. It was pitch-black and damned cold. A few seconds later a second hover car roared past showering him with blown gravel and dirt. "Talk about adding insult to injury," McCade mumbled to himself. But at least they'd fallen for it. Painfully he rolled over, made it to his knees, and then his feet. Now the second car's taillights were tiny red eyes way down the road. One, then the other, winked out as the car took a curve.

Somebody was going to spend a boring evening following Phil and Rico all over Main Port. It had been a long day, and winding up in a ditch didn't make it any better. After their taxi driver-cum-assassin deserted them, McCade had managed to crawl into the front seat, and start the car. Later they'd left it a few blocks from the hotel and walked the rest of the way.

As they checked in, McCade insisted on the hotel's best, paying in advance from the generous wad of expense money he'd wangled out of Walt. For a moment it seemed as though the hotel manager might say something about Phil, but right then the biologist smiled, revealing rows of durasteel teeth. The manager had turned pale, and assigned Phil the ambassador's suite.

While McCade's suite was smaller than Phil's, it was still big enough, including a small swimming pool, exercise room, and office. The latter boasted a com set which would have looked right at home on the bridge of a battleship. He flopped into a chair and gave the com set Lady Linnea Forbes-Smith's unlisted number. Using a soft female voice, the com set thanked him, and promised to put the call through quickly and efficiently. Lady Linnea wasn't expecting his call, but Walt felt that if the prince was alive, she might be able to provide some sort of lead. McCade had his doubts. After all, Walt also said she was Claudia's best friend. So, if she knew something, why tell him? As usual Walt probably knew more than he was saying: part of the old "only tell 'em what they need to know" routine.

After an auto receptionist, a secretary, and a personal assistant, Lady Linnea finally came on the line. Hoping for the best, McCade tackled the subject head-on and, much to his surprise, found she was eager to see him. She was also quite concerned that no one find out that he had. They agreed to meet that evening.

McCade, Rico, and Phil had used the rest of the day for rest and relaxation, leaving the hotel just about dusk. Jumping into their rented hover car, they pulled out into light traffic and headed toward the fashionable suburbs. McCade had kept an eye on the vehicles behind them, and sure enough, there was a tail. It was a sloppy job, which suggested either incompetence or arrogance. Either way, he'd have to dump them. They might be assassins, Claudia's people, or even Naval Intelligence, acting on Admiral Keaton's behalf. But Lady Linnea's instructions were quite specific. No one must know that McCade had seen her.

So they'd checked for other ground vehicles, air surveillance, and everything else they could think of. Nothing. Someone thought the single ground car was enough. They were wrong.

Ignoring his aching shoulder, McCade climbed up the low bank and slipped through the shrubbery which fronted the road. A few feet farther on, he found the eight-foot-high stone wall which encircled Lady Linnea's suburban estate. Feeling his way along, he found the narrow gate exactly where she'd said it would be. And true to her word it was unlocked.

Was it all too easy? Was there an ambush waiting on the other side of the gate? He paused in the shadows and gave his eyes a few more seconds to adjust to the half light. It was dark, but the ambient light from distant streetlights, plus the light from the mansion itself, made it possible to see. He carefully eased his handgun out of its holster, and brought it up next to his left shoulder. You never ever go through a door handgun first. Not if you want to live anyway. Conscious that the split second in the gate would be the most dangerous, McCade went through fast and low, quickly ducking around the trunk of a large tree. Nothing. He heaved a sigh of relief. Now he heard faint sounds of music and laughter coming from the direction of the mansion. Lady Linnea was holding a party.

Moving quietly, he drifted from one pool of shadow to the next, sensitive to the smallest movement or noise. He passed through concentric rings of security scanners, an empty dog run, and then a fifty-foot stretch of lighted duracrete, all without detection. The lady was as good as her word. So far anyway.

McCade made his way to a small side entry. He passed his hand over the scanner three times in quick succession. He heard quick footsteps on the other side of the door. It slid open to reveal one of the most beautiful women he'd ever seen. And except for some expertly applied makeup, she was completely naked.

Working on the assumption that women who appear at the door naked want to be looked at, McCade looked. In fact he took his time, starting with her neatly manicured feet, and moving slowly upward. She had long shapely legs, softly flaring hips, a tiny waist, full pink-nippled breasts, and a beautiful face. Her dark swept-back hair had been dusted with something that sparkled, and reflected the light as the warm air blew through it. She had big brown eyes, a small straight nose, and a full sensuous mouth.

"Would you like to make love to me?" she asked with an amused smile.

"I'd love to . . . but unfortunately I'm married," McCade replied regretfully.

"How old-fashioned of you," she replied, somehow demure in spite of her nudity.

"I'm not," McCade countered with a grin. "It's my wife who's old-fashioned."

Her laughter was warm and open. "So what *can* I do for you?" she asked with a twinkle in her eye.

"I'm here to see Lady Linnea."

She smiled as her hands came up to cup her breasts and then run down along the smooth contours of her body. "But you have seen her, Sam McCade." A mischievous glint came into her eyes. "And rejected her. Not something I'm used to." She enjoyed his discomfort for a moment longer, before taking his hand and pulling him gently inside.

The door closed noiselessly behind them as she led him down a narrow corridor. Since she had a delightful walk, McCade found himself enjoying the journey, quite oblivious to the possibility of a trap. Fortunately there was none.

Instead, she led him up some stairs and down another corridor. A side door slid open at her touch and he followed
her inside.

As they entered, soft lighting brightened to illuminate a
comfortably furnished study. Real books lined one wall,
the latest in com equipment took up another, while a third
was hidden by a heavy curtain of red fabric. Lady Linnea
touched a button and the fourth wall became transparent.
Beyond it, thirty or forty naked men and women frolicked
in an indoor swimming pool. Though many were quite elderly in chronological terms, their biosculpted bodies
glowed with youthful vigor. "Don't worry," she said, "they
can't see us. Nude pool parties are all the rage right now."

Reaching into a closet, she withdrew a robe made of a
silky material. As she slipped it on, and cinched it around
her waist, she grinned in McCade's direction. "I wouldn't
want your wife to get mad at me."

"Neither would I," McCade replied, taking a seat in a
richly upholstered chair. Lady Linnea sat down opposite
him and regarded him seriously.

"I must warn you, Citizen McCade, that you're in great
danger."

"Sam," McCade replied. "My friends call me Sam."

"All right," she agreed. "Sam. But I'm not really your
friend, Sam . . . though I might like to be if things were
different. But with the possible exception of Admiral Keaton, I doubt you have any friends on Terra at the moment.
None that count anyway. And while I've done my best, I
can't guarantee your safety, or mine for that matter. The
simple fact is that Claudia doesn't want Alexander found
. . . and no one wants to offend Claudia. After all, in a few
months she may be an empress. So naturally everyone
wants to please her."

"And you?" McCade inquired. "What do you want?" He
wished he could light a cigar, but there wasn't an ashtray in
sight, and for some reason the thought of lighting up here,

in spite of that, never even crossed his mind.

In answer she reached out to touch a button. Powered by some hidden motor, the heavy curtain slid slowly aside to reveal a huge holo tank. It swirled into life revealing the likeness of a young man and woman standing in a garden. It took McCade only a moment to recognize the woman as a younger Linnea, and the man as Prince Alexander. It was a candid shot, taken at a moment when both people were aware only of each other. The look passing between them spoke louder than words. They were obviously in love. And, McCade realized, still were. At least Lady Linnea was. Otherwise why the curtain-covered holo tank?

As if reading his thoughts she said, "You ask what I want. The answer is simple; Alex is all I ever wanted."

"Then help me find him," McCade said, glancing from the holo to her.

There was pain in the eyes which met his. "I want to, Sam . . . but I can't do so openly. If Claudia found out, she could ruin me, and my father as well. His company depends on navy business, and as a member of the Board of Military Governors, she could make sure all the contracts go to someone else. Besides . . . she thinks of me as one of her best friends . . . and, in every way but this, I am. We grew up together, and were very close before she went off to the Academy. So, if it wasn't for Alex, I wouldn't be doing this."

"Then why ask me here? If you can't or won't help, what's the point of this?"

She sighed. "I can't help you directly, but as Walt told you, I may be able to steer you in the right direction. Did you know Walt and I are distant cousins by the way?"

"No," McCade replied thoughtfully as he looked around, "but somehow I'm not surprised. He'd be comfortable here."

"And you're not?"

"No offense," McCade said as he watched her wealthy

guests throw a large ball back and forth across the pool. "But you mentioned something about steering me in the right direction."

She nodded, a half smile touching her lips. "I know where he was when he disappeared."

McCade regarded her skeptically. "According to all the papers he boarded his yacht, took off for Mars, and never arrived."

"True as far as it goes," she agreed. "But I have something to show you." She stood and stepped over to her desk where she tapped a combination into the keypad inset into its surface. There was a tiny click, and the lap drawer popped slightly open. Taking out a small box covered with gold filigree, she opened it, removed a small object, and handed it to McCade.

It was a small cube made of cheap plastic. Turning it this way and that, he saw that five sides were inscribed with an apparently random series of numbers, seven, eighteen, fifty-six, two, and eighty. The sixth side bore the letter "J" with a circle around it. He held it up to her and said, "Mean anything to you?"

She nodded. "It's the Joyo logo." Then McCade understood. Everyone had heard of Joyo's Roid, though few had been there. Originally it was just one of the many asteroids orbiting between Mars and Jupiter. Then a miner named Jerome Joyo came along searching for rare ores, hot isotopes, or anything else he could dig out and sell. But when his robo driller broke through the asteroid's crust, he found a series of large empty caverns, and not much else. Most miners would have packed up and moved on, but not Jerome Joyo. He'd paid a hefty fee for the rights to that asteroid... and by god it better pay for itself. So he plugged up the holes he'd made, pressurized the interior, and rented caverns out to fellow miners for use as warehouse space. A nice safe place to store extra gear, the odd shipload of ore, or a few crates of stolen merchandise. It was a unique service, and much in demand. Soon there was a constant flow of miners coming and going. This inspired Joyo to open a saloon. After all, why not take advantage of all that traffic, and turn another credit or two? And turn a credit he did. He did so well, in fact, that the saloon grew into a gambling casino, which also prospered, eventually giving birth to other entertainments, until Joyo's Roid finally evolved into a playground for the extremely rich. Although some said there was still a darker side to Joyo's business activities as well.

"That came by regular mail about three months *after* Alex dropped out of sight," she said.

"Was there a note or some other kind of message with it?" McCade inquired as he handed her the six-sided piece.

"No," she answered simply, accepting the plastic cube as though it were a religious relic. "But I knew it was from him. It was his way of letting me know he was all right. He was always sending me symbolic gifts. That's the sort of thing that makes it hard to forget him."

McCade lifted one eyebrow in a silent question.

Lady Linnea dropped back into her chair and curled her feet under her. When she spoke it was with the calm deliberation of someone who's given the subject a lot of thought. "Sam, it's important that you understand that Alex wasn't just another rich playboy. Oh, he was for a while, but that was just another in a long list of experiments. He also studied psychology for a while, then null G ballet, which somehow got him interested in unarmed combat, and that led him into a fascination with human history, and so forth. I guess you could say Alex is something of a romantic. It used to drive his father crazy. The Emperor wanted him to settle down, and prepare himself to rule. But Alex wanted to examine all the possibilities. All the things he could potentially be . . . instead of the next emperor."

"And you think he disappeared on purpose," McCade

finished for her, "as part of another experiment."

She nodded eagerly. "Exactly. Before he left on that trip, he was talking about how hard it is to know yourself when everything you do ends up on the holo. I think he wanted to find out what he could do without either the advantages or disadvantages of his position."

"I see," McCade said thoughtfully. Though he didn't really. The whole thing didn't make much sense to him. While everyone else is out working their butts off trying to make money, this bozo has tons of it, and doesn't want it. Instead he wants to find out what life's like without it. Hell, it's miserable. Everyone knows that. But she obviously believed and understood Alex. They were both silent for a while.

After a moment McCade asked, "Feeling as you do, why didn't you go with him?"

Much to his surprise, she looked down at her lap, apparently ashamed. "He didn't ask me. I'm afraid he didn't trust me." She looked up, and he saw a tear trickling gently down her cheek. "And he was right. At first I didn't understand. If I'd known I would have betrayed him, thinking it was for his own good." She wiped the tear away with the sleeve of her robe. "But not anymore. I've done a lot of thinking since then. Anyway, I'm sure he'd want to know about his father's death."

McCade rose to go, impatient now that he had a lead. "Thank you, Lady Linnea. I appreciate your help."

"You'll go to Joyo's Roid?"

McCade nodded. "It's the only lead I have."

Silently she led him back to the small side entry, and out into the chill night air. The warm-air blowers came on, but she unconsciously cinched the robe more tightly anyway. She turned toward him and paused. For a moment her eyes searched his face, as though looking for some sign of what would come, and then, as if finding it, nodded to herself.

"You'll find him, Sam McCade. And when you do . . . tell him I love him . . . tell him we need him."

McCade found himself nodding in agreement. She smiled, stood on her tiptoes, and kissed him on the cheek. "And tell your wife I think she's a very lucky lady." With that she was gone. The door hissed closed and he was alone.

This time he didn't bother to dash from shadow to shadow. Instead he just strolled through the trees as though he owned the place. A few minutes later he stepped out of the bushes and onto the road. A light flashed twice from down the road, and he heard the sound of a hover car starting up. Phil and Rico had dumped the tail and come back for him. Good, it would have been a long hike to the nearest transcar terminal. The car pulled up next to him, and the blast of warm air felt good as the door opened, and he climbed inside.

"Good ta see ya, sport. Where to?" Rico asked cheerfully.

"The hotel, Rico. And in the morning we'll get our butts off this planet while they're still intact."

"A wise decision indeed," Phil agreed soberly as he fed more power to the big turbine, and they accelerated smoothly away from Lady Linnea's estate.

Five

THE SUN WAS barely in the sky when they left the hotel for the spaceport. No one said anything, but all three were nervous. Why hadn't the assassins struck? Surely they wouldn't allow their prey to leave Terra unmolested? Yet nothing happened. Hands hovered near gun butts as they entered their rented hover car, eyes scanned the sparse early morning traffic as they drove toward the spaceport, and minds grew edgy waiting.

As they neared the spaceport, they heard the rolling thunder as ships lifted off, and saw distant sparks of light shoot upward toward the blackness of space. Then the green belt surrounding the spaceport came and went, followed by the outer perimeter security fence, and the outlying buildings. Still no assassins.

So as they pulled up in front of the main terminal, the muscle in McCade's left cheek had begun to twitch, and his gut felt like it was full of liquid lead. Where the hell were they? He felt like screaming, "Come on out, you bastards, and let's get it over with!" Nonetheless he did his best to hide it. Never let 'em see you sweat.

They took turns going through the customs booths. While one was processed the other two stood guard. When all three had been cleared, they left the terminal and jumped on a shuttle bus. As it neared *Pegasus*, McCade's spirits began to soar. "We made it, by God!" For some reason the assassins had left them alone, and soon they'd be safely off-planet.

Then as quickly as they'd gone up, his spirits came tumbling down. "Looks like trouble up ahead, Sam," Phil said tensely. "There's about twenty marines waiting by the ship." McCade wished he had Phil's enhanced vision. Without it the marines looked like little dots.

"Marines?" McCade wondered aloud. What the hell were marines doing here? Could they be assassins disguised as marines? No, that was expressly forbidden by law. But it didn't bode well. Marines meant the government, which in turn meant Claudia, and all things considered, he'd rather deal with the assassins. At least you could shoot at them.

As the bus began to slow, they looked at each other and shrugged. "We'll have to play it by ear, gentlemen," McCade said.

"Somebody already played with *his* ear," Rico commented, inclining his head toward the marines. Rico was referring to the marine major who stood facing the shuttle, his back ramrod straight, a leather-covered swagger stick tapping one leg. Where his left ear should have been, there was only scar tissue. His bullet-shaped head was shaved in the style of the elite Star Guard, and his features seemed made of stone. A real hard ass. McCade knew the type and didn't like them.

"Citizen Sam McCade?" The authority in the Major's voice evoked the many years McCade had spent in uniform, and he almost replied with a conditioned "Yes, sir!"

Instead he took his time, looking the Major over, as though examining a strange species of alien insect under the microscope. A scarlet flush started at the Major's stiff collar and worked its way up across his face. Finally, just when it appeared the Major might explode, McCade said, "I'm Sam McCade. Nice of you to drop in. Are you here to help with the luggage?"

By now a vein throbbed in the Major's forehead, and only his iron will, wedded to thirty-two years of disciplined service, was keeping McCade alive. The Major's eyes narrowed as Phil and Rico drifted off to each side. Three targets instead of one. They'd take on twenty marines by God! If only his orders allowed, but there was no point in wishing, best to just swallow his pride and get it over with. "Citizen McCade," he said formally, "I am Major Tellor. It is my honor to convey a message from the Imperial household. You and your companions are hereby invited to attend the finals of the 3-D games as guests of her royal highness, Princess Claudia. We are your escort."

McCade eyed the front rank of marines. They had a choice. Take on the marines, or accept the so-called "invitation." And McCade didn't like orders. But taking on the marines looked like a major project. Each held his energy weapon at port arms. Within a second they could bring them up and fire. And these were not recruits. They were hand-picked veterans. The choice was really no choice at all. "Well, Major," McCade replied lightly, "this is an honor. We'd love to come. Right, men?"

"Wouldn't miss it for the world," Rico replied with mock gravity.

"Charmed, I'm sure," Phil added in a bass growl.

McCade thought he saw a flash of disappointment in the Major's eyes as he murmured an order into his wrist com. Moments later, three helicopter gunships clattered in out of the sun and blew dust in every direction as they touched down. Climbing aboard the nearest chopper, McCade knew he'd made the right decision. Even if they'd managed to take out the marines, the gunships would have arrived a few seconds later and cut them to shreds. At least they still had their weapons and therefore a chance, however small.

It took about an hour to reach the Imperial Coliseum. McCade tried to use the time constructively by imagining what Claudia might say and how he'd respond. He quickly bogged down in all the possibilities and decided to watch the scenery instead. As they approached the coliseum McCade remembered that the ancient city of Detroit had been completely leveled to make room for it. First came the miles of green fields and forest which served as a buffer between the coliseum and the surrounding suburbs. Then came the vast parking lots filled with ground cars, aircars, hover cars, and more. They sparkled and glittered in the morning sun.

Then came the coliseum itself. It had been excavated rather than built. Layer after layer of earth had been carved away to create broad terraces, each cascading downward to the next, until finally reaching the flat playing field hundreds of feet below. Each terrace had been carpeted with variant green grass so tough it could compete with the strongest synthetic carpeting. Then the terraces had been divided into sections. Patrons could choose the type of seating they preferred. There were large sections of comfortable seats, complete with built-in holo tanks, on which they could watch the action below. Or, they could lounge about in the open grassy areas, appropriate for picnics or sunbathing. Tastefully placed clumps of trees offered shade and pleased the eye. Gone was the duracrete ugliness of most arenas. The whole thing was more like a park than a coliseum. Each terrace also offered a variety of restaurants and snack bars to serve the multitude of people who packed the place. People were everywhere. Their clothing created a multicolored moving mosaic that shifted endlessly over the green grass. McCade estimated there were at least a million people in the coliseum, and room for more.

At the very center of the coliseum stood a tower as tall as the arena itself. In spite of its location, the tower's slim profile blocked very little of the playing field. It too was terraced, offered a variety of seating choices, and a number of open-air restaurants. But there was more. This was the province of the rich and powerful. Streams and waterfalls cascaded down the sides of the tower, to feed countless swimming pools, and eventually fill the moat below. Miniature villas dotted its sides, each a small mansion in itself, each the private preserve of a wealthy individual or family.

Above, the climate-controlled blue sky promised only the best of weather, and below, the miles and miles of now-empty playing surface promised moments of excitement in otherwise dull and pampered lives. As their chopper lost altitude, McCade wondered what sort of games were popular these days.

McCade put those thoughts aside. Claudia was waiting somewhere below, and he wasn't looking forward to meeting her.

The chopper landed with a gentle thump, and they were quickly herded into some sort of a lift tube. The platform dropped quickly before coming to an abrupt stop. From the tube's banged-up interior, McCade got the impression it was normally used for freight. A subtle insult by Major Tellor? Probably.

They were led off the platform, and through a bewildering maze of halls and corridors. When they finally emerged into sunlight once more, they were standing on a narrow terrace, with an incredible view of the surrounding coliseum. However, the quality of the view suddenly deteriorated as Major Tellor stepped into it. His expression was anything but pleasant. Glancing around to make sure no one was listening, he spoke in tones pitched so low, they couldn't be heard even a few feet away.

"Now, you three clowns listen, and listen good. You're

about to have an audience with Princess Claudia. For some reason she insists you be allowed to keep your weapons. I recommended against it, and was overruled. I don't like to be overruled, so I'm pissed. And when I'm pissed, I like to hurt people. I'd like to hurt you. So I'm going to watch everything you do . . . and if one of you even brushes a weapon with his hand . . . he's dead meat. Maybe one of you will give me an excuse—and please, God—let it be you." The Major drove the last word home by stabbing a stiffened index finger into McCade's chest. Because McCade was wearing body armor under his clothes he didn't feel it. He looked down at the Major's finger and then up into his eyes. Slowly he smiled his most insulting smile.

"Yes, mommy, we promise to be good. Now get lost."

For a moment Phil thought McCade had pushed the Major too far. Murder blazed in his eyes. With a major effort, Tellor managed to bring his anger under control, and take a step backward. "You've been warned, scum." With that he executed a perfect about-face, and disappeared to their left. No sooner was the marine gone than a beautiful woman appeared. At first McCade couldn't quite place her. Then she smiled, and he realized it was Lady Linnea Forbes-Smith. She looked different with her clothes on.

In fact she was like another person, cold, distant, and imperial. As she introduced herself, she allowed no flicker of recognition to touch her features, and when she asked them to follow, it was more an order than a request. She led them toward the far end of the terrace, where McCade saw a single glass-topped table, and two chairs. One was already occupied by a young woman, who could be none other than Princess Claudia. He wasn't sure, because her face was shaded by a large disk of brightly colored fabric which hovered above her. He assumed it was kept there by some sort of anti-grav device.

They were still fifteen feet away from Claudia's table

when Lady Linnea paused, and skillfully guided Rico and
Phil into waiting chairs. Apparently the princess wanted to
speak privately with McCade. Rico and Phil were more
than a little relieved. Neither wanted to sit down and make
polite conversation with Claudia. "Try not to do anything
crude, Sam," Phil cautioned airily. "Rico and I have our
reputations to consider."

"I'll keep your reputations in mind throughout,"
McCade promised dryly.

"The princess will see you now, Citizen McCade," Lady
Linnea said tactfully.

"I think she means you should get your butt in gear,"
Rico suggested as he lit a cigar.

Linnea smiled in spite of herself, and said, "We
shouldn't keep the princess waiting."

McCade nodded, and as he turned to go, he would've
sworn he heard her whisper, "Good luck, Sam!" but
couldn't be sure. As he approached Claudia's table, he was
surprised to see how young she was. Thirty at the most.
Somehow he'd thought of her as older than that. She had
hard blue eyes, a long straight nose, thin lips, and
shoulder-length blond hair. Her clothes were fashionable,
but cut with almost military severity, and seemed too big
for her thin body. She was playing with a silver stylus. He
noticed that her nails were clipped short and blunt and her
fingers were heavily stained by some sort of chemicals.
Later he learned her hobby was experimental hydroponics.
A little something she'd picked up in the navy.

She looked up at his approach, her eyes quickly taking
him apart, and putting him back together. Having found no
surprises, she smiled slowly and said, "Have a seat, Citizen McCade. You may address me as Princess, or Your
Highness, whichever you choose. Based on your computer
profile, I suspect you'll find 'Princess' to be more comfortable. It allows one the semblance of equality...and I
sense that's important to you. After all, you've always had

trouble dealing with authority, haven't you?"

McCade couldn't help but admire her style. In seconds she'd managed to take complete control of the situation, remind him of her powerful position, and put him on the defensive. He forced a smile as he sat down. "You're quite right, Princess. But perhaps my distaste for authority is something we have in common. For example . . . it's my understanding that your father chose your brother to rule the Empire . . . yet you're trying to take the throne. Aren't you acting against your father's wishes?"

Claudia's eyes narrowed momentarily. She wasn't accustomed to open criticism, and didn't like it. Nonetheless there was an opportunity here, and like her father she was a pragmatist, so she suppressed her anger. "You have a quick tongue," Claudia said dryly, pointing the stylus at him like a spear. "However I admire directness. It's one of the many military virtues." She paused, leaning forward slightly. "So, by all means . . . let's be direct."

As she locked her eyes with his, and focused the raw power of her iron will on him, McCade felt an almost physical impact. "You're right. I do intend to take the throne." As she spoke she jabbed the stylus into the air in front of her to emphasize her words. "First, because I'm best qualified; second, because I'm convinced my brother is dead; and third, because I want to, and there's nobody strong enough to stop me."

She leaned back as though giving McCade time to absorb what she'd said. When she continued her voice was calm, almost reflective. "Even though I believe my brother is dead, there's always the chance I'm wrong. And it's a chance I don't plan to take. That's the bad news for idiots like yourself who want my brother on the throne." She smiled humorlessly and said, "However, here's the good news. You don't have to die. In fact, I'm the reason you aren't dead already. Haven't you wondered why the assassins didn't attack? Because I ordered them not to, that's why. And I can cancel that level-three license altogether. Then you could even earn that bounty you're after. In fact," she added, leaning forward eagerly, "I'll add fifty thousand credits to whatever they've offered you."

"That's a lot to pay for *not* finding someone," McCade said evenly.

Claudia laughed. "You misunderstand me. If my brother's alive I *do* want him found. Better now than later." She paused for a moment, tapping the stylus against the palm of her left hand. "Yes, if he's alive, I want you to find him, and then I want you to kill him."

A chill ran down McCade's spine, and he sat speechless. He'd expected her to be hard, but not cold-blooded. Maybe the Emperor had known what he was doing after all. Whatever Alexander was like, he couldn't be as bad as his sister. She was waiting, so he tried to come up with a reply, but was saved by the resonant male voice which suddenly filled the coliseum. "Ladies and gentlemen, citizens of the Empire, fellow sentients of all races, welcome to the finals of Three-Dimensional Combat. Today's games are brought to you by Princess Claudia."

Right on cue, a boxy-looking robocam floated silently up and over the edge of the terrace, zoomed in on the princess, and flashed her picture to the thousands of holo tanks located throughout the arena. She smiled and waved. A roar of approval filled the coliseum. McCade was suddenly reminded of what he'd heard about the ancient Roman emperors. They too had traded games for public approval.

Then the camera was gone, and the announcer's voice flooded in over the applause. His voice had taken on a decidedly somber tone. "After months of bloody combat . . . only two of the original thirty-two teams remain. Many have died, or suffered permanent disfigurement for the sake of our entertainment. Others have fought valiantly but lost . . . and now dwell on some distant prison planet. I ask you, one and all, for a moment of silence, during which we can pay our respects to those who have fallen, or lost everything but their lives." His voice echoed away into stillness as the moment of silence began. McCade noticed Claudia was using the stylus to beat out an impatient rhythm on the edge of the table. The clicking sound seemed amplified by the surrounding silence.

Then the announcer was back, cheerful now, as he warmed up the audience for the coming events. "Now, ladies and gentlemen, fellow citizens and sentients, prepare yourselves for the unbelievable spectacle of the 3-D finals, as our skilled warrior teams take their respective positions. At the north end of the coliseum . . . it is my honor to introduce the Green Rippers!"

A tremendous cheer went up, as a forest of green lasers flashed, pulsed, and rippled across the north end of the playing field. Loud pulsating background music filled the air, its heavy bass beat throbbing and ominous, quickly building toward a climax of sound. As the climax came, so did a brilliant flash of green light, which slowly faded from McCade's retinas to reveal the Green Rippers. There were nine altogether. Each was dressed from head to toe in green. Three wore light armor and anti-grav belts which allowed them to hover in midair. Below them were three more, dressed in heavy-duty body armor suitable for fighting on the ground. They sat on three-wheeled vehicles. Rocket launchers had been mounted right in front of the drivers. The last three members of the team wore medium-weight armor and jump paks. McCade quickly realized they would make or break their teams. Their jump paks would allow them either short hops in the air, or sustained ground combat, whichever they chose. So being the most versatile players, they would be the most critical.

As the applause died down, the announcer came on once again. "And entering the south end of the coliseum— still undefeated after weeks of grueling combat—are the

Red Zombies!" There was a flash and the quick crack of an explosion. Red smoke filled the south end of the stadium. An eerie whine filled the coliseum, steady at first, and then pulsating. The smoke pulsed too, glowing now as though invested with a life of its own, so that when the Zombies emerged, it seemed as though they'd stepped out of hell itself.

Once again, the crowd went wild. Only this time the cheering was even louder. Apparently the Zombies were favored to win. McCade noted with interest that Princess Claudia applauded enthusiastically with the rest as the red-suited team took up their positions. Like the Rippers, they had an air squad, a ground squad, and three jumpers. McCade noted with professional interest that the Green Rippers' weapons were anything but uniform. Apparently each warrior was free to choose whatever weapons they thought best. A glance at the Zombies confirmed his theory. They too were armed with a bewildering array of weapons, including at least one ancient battle axe.

McCade glanced at Claudia, but she seemed intent on the upcoming contest, so he turned his attention in that direction as well. A member of the Rippers' ground squad stepped forward with raised hand. The crowd quieted and, in marked contrast to her warlike image, the woman's voice had a melodic quality, hinting at a less violent past. McCade wondered what she looked like. But whatever her face might reveal was hidden by the reflective visor covering her face. When she spoke, there was pride and determination in her voice. "Ladies and gentlemen, citizens of the Empire, fellow sentients, the Green Rippers salute you. Let victory be ours!" Then she stepped back between the other two members of the ground squad and mounted her vehicle as the crowd roared its approval. McCade found himself gripping the arm of his chair so tightly his knuckles were white. He wanted her to win.

Looking at Claudia, he saw her grin savagely as the

center member of the Zombies' ground squad dismounted, and took a step forward. "Ladies and gentlemen, citizens of the Empire, fellow sentients, the Zombies salute you. Let it be ours to live, and theirs to die!"

The crowd went berserk, almost drowning out the announcer as he said, "Let the games begin!"

The contest was short and brutal. These were professional killers, their skills honed to razor sharpness by months of relentless battle, interested in one thing, and one thing only, killing the members of the opposing team as quickly and efficiently as possible. And they were very good. Those who weren't had died long ago.

Both teams employed some common strategies. Because both teams had to traverse at least half the length of the field before the fight could begin, naturally the air teams came into contact first. Nonetheless, it was the ground teams which got off the first shots. As their heavy tricycles roared toward center field, both sides launched heat-seeking missiles. First blood went to the Rippers, as a Zombie bike blew up in an orange-red ball, and hurled hot shrapnel in every direction.

Meanwhile a Zombie missile homed in on some poorly shielded hot-water pipes and blew up. The initial explosion didn't kill anyone, but the resulting steam and scalding hot water badly burned those sitting nearby. Now, as robo repair units and medics hurried to help, there were two sources of excitement for the bloodthirsty crowd.

The air teams made contact slightly north of Claudia's villa, soaring and swooping as each tried to outmaneuver the other, their terse comments flooding the PA system. The jumpers arrived second, and the ground team showed up last. Now, with all members present, a pattern began to emerge.

Rockets expended, the ground teams dismounted to fight it out toe to toe, three Rippers against the two remaining Zombies. Meanwhile, both squads of jumpers concentrated on the opposing team's air squad, trying to take them out of action as quickly as possible. Energy weapons flared, chemical weapons boomed, blades flashed, and at least one mini-missile exploded, turning a Ripper into red mist.

Suddenly a battle axe flashed, slicing through green body armor to bury itself in a Ripper. As her scream filled the air, McCade knew it was the woman who'd spoken for the green team, and felt a lump rise to block his throat. As she fell, the fortunes of the Green Rippers seemed to fall with her. Two members of their aerial squad tumbled out of the air, one after the other. Then they lost a jumper. The two remaining green jumpers did their best to assist the remaining airborne Ripper, but it was too late. Moments later, he too died, the jumpers followed, and then the remaining members of the green ground squad. The battle was over. The Zombies had won.

The crowd cheered, and the medics arrived to sort out the wounded from the dead. McCade felt empty inside, watching with sick fascination as a medic put a foot on the woman's body, and pried the bloody battle axe loose.

"So," Claudia said casually, picking up where they'd left off, "what's it gong to be . . . death for you . . . or for my brother?" He noticed the excitement of the battle still colored Claudia's cheeks, and her breathing was quick and shallow.

McCade pulled out a cigar and lit it without asking permission. Once he had it going, he inhaled deeply. The smoke came out with his next words. "I'm not a hired killer."

Claudia sneered. "A fine point, I would think. Frankly, the difference between a bounty hunter and a hired killer escapes me. Nonetheless I suppose that's your final word?"

"I'm afraid so," McCade agreed calmly.

"Then good-bye, McCade." With that she stood and brought the stylus-shaped microphone up to her mouth. A robocam had appeared to hover in front of her. Thousands of Claudias filled thousands of holo tanks as the audience turned their attention to her. "Ladies and gentlemen, citizens of the Empire, and my fellow sentients, I, Princess Claudia, bring you a special treat." She paused, turning to point a quivering finger at McCade. "The legal assassination of the infamous bounty hunter, Sam McCade!"

Six

"HOLY SOL!" THE announcer swore to himself as he swung his feet down off the console. This was going to be something special! He grinned in anticipation as his fingers flew over the keyboard. A hundred feet under the surface of the playing field, he was all alone in the control room, except for a variety of robotechs which kept things running. While he tended to be messy, the robotechs were relentlessly tidy, and more than made up for his sloppiness. The control area gleamed, polished surfaces reflecting the muted glow of a thousand indicator lights, cool air whispering through the ducts overhead. He sat on a raised dais, in front of a huge console, watching the thirty monitors mounted above it. Each had a different shot, and represented a different robocam. And the robocams were the least of his minions. There were also the computers and a small army of specialized robots to do his bidding. With their help he ran the enormous facility all by himself. And a boring job it was. After you've seen a few thousand combats they all start to look the same. Nonetheless, he prided himself on his ability to manipulate the crowd's emotions. He could have delegated the task of announcing to a computer, but didn't because it felt good to make the crowd roar with approval, or groan with disgust. It was in fact the only redeeming aspect of his job.

He sighed, shifted position, and ignored the hiss of pneumatics as his large power chair tried to adjust to his small frame. In spite of his deep, resonant voice, the announcer was a little man, and as unlike the warriors who battled above as night is from day. He had beady brown eyes, shoulder-length hair, and skin the color of white chalk. As usual he was dressed in a robe and sandals. By personal choice he lived under the playing field, and rarely ventured out. Years before he and society had mutually rejected each other, and neither had come to regret the decision.

Quickly scanning the monitors, he saw the robocams had dutifully responded to his commands, and positioned themselves to give him good shots of the action. He cut from the shot of Princess Claudia, to a wide shot with the Red Zombies in the foreground and the audience beyond. He knew the princess wouldn't appreciate a televised exit. She really had it in for this McCade guy. Whatever the reason, it must be something big. He might be a bit isolated, but he knew major league politics when they slapped him in the face. After all, it's not every day the princess personally fingers somebody for the assassins. Yeah, he had a special feeling about this one, and knew the audience did too. The excitement was almost palpable. He activated the wireless mike at his throat. "Come on . . . let's show the princess some appreciation!"

The roar of the crowd filled the coliseum as a squad of marines led by Major Tellor rushed in to surround Princess Claudia and escort her off the terrace. As she left, Claudia didn't even glance at the men she'd condemned to death.

That was already part of the past, and her mind was on the future. Her future, the way she wanted it to be.

As the princess and her escort disappeared through durasteel doors, Major Tellor turned and shouted, "Good riddance, asshole!" Then he was gone.

No sooner had the Major spoken than a voice McCade recognized as that of the taxi-driving assassin filled the arena. "Get ready to die, McCade!"

"Doesn't anybody like you?" Phil asked calmly as he checked the action on his submachine gun, and then tucked it back into its shoulder holster.

"It's his breath," Rico interjected as he made sure the safety on his grenade launcher was in the off position. "Sam's breath would kill an Il Ronnian Sand Sept Trooper at thirty paces."

"I'm forced to disagree," Phil replied thoughtfully, sighting down the length of his energy rifle. "The truth is he's ugly. Uglier'n a swamp beast headed south. Sorry, Sam, but somebody had to tell you."

McCade's reply was forever lost, as the word "assassin" began to flash on and off across each Zombies' chest, and a cheer went up from the crowd. The formal warning had begun. Assassins must also reveal red clothing, but since the Zombies were already dressed in red, that rule had been fulfilled. It occurred to McCade that a 3-D team comprised of professional assassins was hardly fair to the other teams. But, he reflected as he checked the load on his handgun, what else is new. Now he understood why they'd been allowed to keep their weapons, so that the assassination would be completely legal.

It was the taxi driver who delivered the formal warning. "Attention! A level-three licensed assassination will be carried out on Citizen Sam McCade five seconds from now!"

The announcer cut from the tight shot of the assassin, to a tight shot of McCade. The bounty hunter exhaled a tight stream of cigar smoke, flicked the butt over the edge of the terrace, and said something to the shaggy variant on his right. Damn! If there was only some way to mic them. Oh, well, it would still be good. Of course with, let's see, eight Zombies left, the three of them probably wouldn't last long. But on the other hand, none of them looked scared, and from all appearances they knew how to handle their weapons, and that was a good sign. Maybe they had a chance after all. Holy Sol—what if they won—that would really give the crowd something to cheer about! The underdogs come from behind and all that. Attendance would soar, and bigger crowds were more fun to manipulate. The announcer began to hope.

"There's not much the ground team can do to us off the top . . . since we're up here . . . and they're down there," McCade observed. "Nonetheless, when they get into range, Rico can work them over with the grenade launcher. Phil, I'm afraid you're the only one who can deal with their aerial squad, and I'll try to keep the jumpers busy. Questions?"

"Yeah," Phil replied, "what's a nice variant like me doing in a place like this?"

"Talkin' too damn much," Rico said with a grin. "Here they come."

Naturally the aerial team arrived first. They opened fire at long range, liberally spraying the terrace with lead and coherent energy. Ducking down behind the low wall which ran the length of the terrace, McCade forced himself to wait. Rico did likewise. Neither had weapons appropriate to the situation. Phil however was another story. Resting his energy rifle on the top of the wall, he fired with scientific precision. Meanwhile, the Zombie air team twisted and turned trying to throw off his aim. And it would have worked on anyone but a variant. But Phil had gone into full augmentation, and his enhanced vision, combined with perfect coordination, cost two Zombies their lives.

He killed the first by carefully punching an energy beam through his reflective visor. The pulse of coherent energy burned a perfect hole through the man's head, while simultaneously pushing his brains ahead of it. So as the energy beam emerged from the back of his helmet a jet of blood and brains came with it. Meanwhile, his belt continued to keep his body aloft and propel it forward. Seconds later it crashed into the side of the tower and slowly cartwheeled to the ground below.

Phil's second kill was less elegant than the first, but equally effective. He aimed for the woman's chest, but as if sensing his intention, she suddenly tried for more altitude. As a result his shot hit her anti-grav belt and destroyed its power pak. She fell like a rock, and her scream followed her down to the hard surface of the playing field.

As the second member of the aerial squad died, the volume of incoming fire fell off, and McCade stuck his head up to take a look around. The jumpers were damned near on top of them. Scrambling to his feet, he realized they intended to jump over him and land on the inside of the terrace. Then with the jumpers behind, and the remaining member of the air team in front, they'd be caught in a cross fire. He jumped to the top of the wall and yelled, "Clear the terrace!"

Following his own advice, McCade leaped out and away from the terrace. As he fell toward the playing field far below, there was a sickening moment when he thought he'd misjudged the distance, but then the robocam was there, floating below him, and as he hit, he threw his arms around it and held on.

As luck would have it, the announcer had activated that particular camera just before McCade jumped from the terrace, so the whole crowd lived the moment with him. The announcer swore happily as he fought to keep the robocam from crashing. What a shot! The crowd watched as McCade struggled to obtain a one-armed grip, finally managed to do so, and then pulled his handgun. Suddenly the crowd began to cheer. Deep underground, the announcer grinned. Their sympathies had shifted.

McCade felt the robocam slowly sinking, and heard a grinding noise from inside it as the announcer pushed its drive to the edge of burnout. Then he saw that the jumpers had landed on the terrace, and one was now bouncing out toward him. But the Zombie had jumped too hard and was coming almost straight down. As he went past, McCade fired four times, and saw all four slugs hit their mark. The jumper continued on down to crash into the ground.

Meanwhile, the two remaining members of the Zombie ground team had taken up positions below McCade, and were firing upward. McCade almost lost his grip as two slugs hit him and were deflected by his body armor. Any closer and they'd have gone right through. Then he felt the robocam jerk as a slug hit it. It was sinking even faster now, and trailing gray smoke. In a few seconds he'd land right in their laps.

Suddenly there was a loud cracking sound, and a Zombie disappeared in a red-orange ball of flame. Rico had managed to scramble down to the next terrace, and bring the grenade launcher into play. But now McCade was so low the big man couldn't fire again. If he did, the flying shrapnel might kill both friend and foe.

McCade twisted around, trying to bring his gun to bear on the man below, but found he was unable to do so. He watched helplessly as the Zombie took off his helmet and threw it down. It was the taxi driver. Grinning a sadistic grin, the assassin raised a minilauncher, and took careful aim. He squeezed the trigger, and then watched with amazement as another robocam swooped in front of the tiny missile, and disappeared in a flash of light. The small explosion peppered McCade with tiny pieces of plastic and metal but none of it penetrated his body armor.

"That's one for me, you bastards!" the announcer

shouted gleefully as he banged his fist on the console. "This is my show . . . and it's gonna end my way!"

McCade let go of the robocam and jumped. His feet hit the assassin right in the chest, and threw him over backward. Falling backward himself, McCade hit the surface of the playing field hard, and had the wind knocked out of him. His mind ordered his body to get up, but nothing happened. All his effort seemed centered on sucking precious oxygen into his lungs. Not so the assassin. Shaken but not hurt, he staggered to his feet, and pulled a sidearm. McCade felt the oxygen hit his lungs and the energy flow through his body at the same time. He rolled right just as the Zombie pumped two large caliber slugs into the ground where he'd been. Coming up on one knee McCade fired three times, the first shot taking the assassin in his right knee, the second in his chest, and the last between his eyes. As he toppled and fell a tremendous cheer went up from the now-partisan crowd.

McCade looked up as he heard a string of shots from above. A jumper tumbled end over end to crash onto a distant terrace, and Rico uttered a defiant battle cry. Then McCade's heart fell as the big man's scream of victory ended in a grunt, and he crumpled to the ground. The last of the aerial assassins had nailed him from above.

With a growl of rage, Phil leaped thirty feet straight up, and wrapped the flying assassin in a bear hug. Locked together, they began to drop as Phil's additional weight overloaded the anti-grav belt. As they fell, Phil slowly closed the circle of his arms. The assassin listened helplessly as his armor started to creak and groan. Then with a sort of morbid fascination, he heard loud cracking noises as it began to break, followed by the snapping of his own bones. Mercifully he lost consciousness before he hit the playing field and Phil landed on top of him.

By the time McCade arrived, Phil was already starting to get up, the assassin's body having cushioned his fall.

"Thought I'd drop in and give you a hand," the big variant growled.

The last Zombie was a jumper and he moved as though his heart wasn't in it. He jumped from a high terrace, and McCade picked him off with a single shot. After his body hit the field there was total silence for a moment, followed by wild unrestrained applause as the entire audience came to its feet. Not only had the underdog won, he'd done it in spectacular fashion, and they loved it.

McCade wasted no time basking in their applause. Rico was down. He couldn't tell if the big man was dead or wounded, but either way, that was his first priority. And his second priority would be getting the hell out of there, before Claudia could arrange another attempt on their lives. To his surprise a robocam bumped into his arm and the unmistakable voice of the announcer issued forth. "Your friend is only wounded. He'll be okay. My robots have him in an automedic right now. Is there somewhere you'd like to go?"

"The spaceport," McCade replied gratefully. "We've got a ship there."

"Gotcha," the announcer replied. "Do exactly as I say and you'll reach the spaceport without further trouble. After that, you're on your own."

McCade agreed, and soon found himself in a robo-controlled aircar along with Phil, and an unconscious Rico, whose entire right leg had disappeared inside an automedic. A cloud of brightly colored aircars flitted all around them. They were all listening to the announcer on their radios and, urged on by his voice, they waved and cheered. Doing their best to smile cheerfully, McCade and Phil dutifully waved back. The unofficial escort was the announcer's idea, and a very effective one. Not only would the crowd make it difficult to execute an attack, they also made it stupid to launch one. With McCade and his companions riding a wave of public approval, to attack them within minutes of their victory would not only smack of poor sportsmanship, it would also amount to very stupid politics. McCade knew Claudia was a lot of things, but stupid wasn't one of them. To take and hold power she would need a good measure of public approval. She'd just lost some by taking a public position and losing. At this point a public attack could turn a minor loss into a major public relations disaster. So McCade felt fairly sure she'd control her temper and bide her time. Meanwhile, they'd get the hell off Terra and into the relative safety of space.

A few minutes later the aircar landed next to *Pegasus*. Under McCade's watchful eye, two robots transferred Rico from the aircar to the ship. Then he and Phil engaged in one last round of waving and smiling, before ducking into the main lock, and cycling the outer hatch closed. Once in the control room, McCade was amused to find that a second customs inspection had been waived, and *Pegasus* was already cleared for lift-off. Apparently Claudia was as eager to get rid of them as they were to go.

After considerable urging from Main Port ground control, the swarm of aircars backed off to a safe distance, and gave *Pegasus* enough room to lift. As she roared toward the sky, the announcer swung his feet up onto the console, and lifted a glass in salute. For the first time in many years he felt good about himself. "Good luck, McCade. We made one helluva team."

Seven

"MORE FOOD, SLAVES, and while you're at it, more cigars!" Rico's voice boomed over the intercom.

"Shall I kill him, or would you like the honor?" McCade asked Phil.

Phil shook his shaggy head in amazement. "I'm a trained biologist, and I can't believe that a single man can eat that much, and be that big a pain in the ass. It isn't normal."

McCade grinned. "If you're suggesting that Rico isn't normal . . . I'll go along with that."

"I heard that!" Rico said accusingly. "Here I am, layin' wounded . . . nearly starvin' ta death . . . and my friends sit around insultin' me . . . me—the one that saved their miserable lives . . ."

McCade reached up and flipped a switch, cutting Rico off in mid-complaint. "Well, much as I'd like to hang around and shoot the breeze with you guys, it's time to get to work."

"Sure," Phil grumbled, "you take off for Joyo's Roid while I stay here with the crazed convalescent. Why don't I go while you stay?"

McCade grinned as he got to his feet. "Because I'm the bounty hunter, remember? And besides, from what I hear, it's damn hard to get off Joyo's Roid unless they decide to let you. So somebody's got to be here to save my ass if I get in trouble."

Phil sniffed loudly, only partly mollified. "Maybe, but just make sure you don't have too much fun."

"I promise," McCade replied readily, and flipped the intercom back on.

". . . not to mention the many favors I done them. By the way, did I mention cigars? How many cigars have I given you, Sam McCade? A hundred? A thousand? And you won't bring Rico a cigar? Shame on you . . ."

Phil groaned out loud, and McCade gave him a jaunty wave as he slid out of the control room. Stopping by his cabin he grabbed a box of cigars, took a fistful for himself, and then threw the rest into Rico's cabin. Grabbing his carryall he headed for the lifeboat.

It was a tubby little affair, barely large enough to hold six very friendly adults. McCade secured the tiny lock, slid behind the rudimentary controls, and strapped in. He had a choice between Emergency Launch and Normal Launch. He chose normal. As the boat's computer ran an automated pre-flight check, atmosphere was pumped out of the launching bay, and the outer doors cycled open. He felt the gentle push of a repellor beam, and the boat floated free of the larger ship. As usual, zero gravity caused McCade a momentary queasiness, but he did his best to ignore it, and it soon passed. A quick scan of the boat's control board showed all systems were go. Looking up he saw *Pegasus* and felt a momentary pride. Her long graceful shape reflected the sunlight and he paused for a moment to admire her.

Originally a navy scout, she'd been decommissioned during a round of budget cutbacks, and purchased by a wealthy businessman. He'd converted her to a yacht. She was comfortable, fast, and very well armed. Unfortunately the businessman was accused and found guilty of drug smuggling. He went to a prison planet, and *Pegasus* was returned to the navy. Eventually she'd been given to McCade as partial payment for services rendered while searching for the War World. Yes, outside of a computer which occasionally said strange things, she was a good little ship. Confident that Phil and Rico would take care of her, he tapped a course and new identification code into the boat's computer, and settled back for the ride.

An hour later Joyo's Roid loomed large in his single viewscreen. He saw the occasional gleam of reflected light as another ship arrived or took off, but otherwise the asteroid appeared lifeless, a huge chunk of rock following its own lonely path through the solar system. Years before, Joyo had put some spin on the asteroid to create a little gravity, but not too much. That way his rich, but sometimes corpulent, guests could enjoy some of the more rigorous sexual entertainments normally off limits to them. And that, like everything else Jerome Joyo did, was calculated to put even more money in his pockets.

But regardless of whatever commercial benefits gravity might confer on Joyo's wallet, the asteroid's spin could make for a tricky landing, and McCade was just about to ask for landing instructions when his com set buzzed softly. He touched the accept key and was greeted by a face so androgynous he couldn't tell if it was male or female. He or she had long blue hair, big blue eyes, full red lips, perfect teeth, and a long straight nose. Regardless of sex, there was something exquisite about the face, something compelling, and quite exciting. His or her voice had a soft sexy quality. "Welcome to Joyo's Roid, gentle being. A thousand pleasures await you." He or she paused to run a pink tongue over red lips, and then smiled, as if aware of the thoughts running through McCade's mind.

"If this is your first visit to Joyo's Roid, please turn your ship's navigation over to our computer and answer the questions on the rest of the form."

The information requested was mostly financial in nature, addressing the crucial question of whether he could afford Joyo's pricey pleasures, or should be politely turned away.

His answers were all lies with one exception. When asked for a credit reference, he provided an account number for the Imperial Bank on Terra, registered to one Samuel Lane. Seconds later, confirmation was flashed back from Terra, and Joyo's computer practically kissed his rear end. Apparently Walt, or Naval Intelligence, had a sizable number of credits in that account. Too bad Walt hadn't provided an access code as well. He could've retired early.

Now the pitted brown surface of the asteroid was only a hundred feet away. Thanks to Joyo's computer, the boat had matched the roid's spin, but the surface was still coming up fast. McCade was starting to worry when two enormous doors slid aside to reveal a lighted tunnel. He watched as a large yacht moved majestically out of the tunnel, and slowly accelerated toward Earth.

Then his boat rocked a tiny bit, as a tractor beam locked on, and pulled it into the tunnel. It was perfectly symmetrical and lined with duracrete. Tractor-beam projectors studded the walls at regular intervals, and McCade wondered why, until dozens of colorized beams suddenly shot out to lock the ship in a matrix of energy. The tractor beams would be used to move the boat from one end of the tunnel to the other. Otherwise, vessels entering or leaving the asteroid would be forced to use their repellors. The roid's gravity might be weak, but it must still be dealt with. And dancing a ship down a long narrow tunnel on repellors takes a lot of skill, more skill than the average pilot's got, so McCade figured the expensive tractor-beam system had probably prevented lots of accidents. And accidents would cost Joyo money, not to mention bad press. The man thought of everything.

The colored tractor beams were a good example. They were normally invisible, but by colorizing them, something boring and mechanical had been transformed into a work of art. The beams were all colors of the rainbow, and as they crisscrossed each other, they created endless geometric shapes. McCade was impressed.

The com set buzzed again, and McCade was disappointed when a man in evening clothes appeared. He was thin to the point of emaciation, his voice was smooth and oily, and he wasn't half as interesting as the exotic creature who'd come on before. He had a receding hairline, bored eyes, and a professional smile. "Welcome to Joyo's Roid. I am your host Jerome Joyo. The tunnel will be pressurized in a few moments, but please don't attempt to leave your ship, it will be transported into our parking area where you can disembark in comfort. If there's anything that I or my staff can do to make your stay even more enjoyable, please don't hesitate to ask. Thank you." The screen faded to black. The head man himself. McCade wasn't impressed.

Moments later the large external doors closed, and McCade's small craft began to move forward, still carried along by the rippling tractor beams. Up ahead were another set of durasteel doors. They would open as soon as the tunnel was pressurized. Meanwhile McCade sat back to enjoy the light show.

As the boat approached, the gigantic doors slid aside to reveal a large chamber beyond. At least three or four hundred ships of all shapes and sizes were parked in neat rows. There were yachts, some large enough to carry hundreds of people, a couple of small excursion liners, and all sorts of smaller craft. McCade saw everything from tiny two-person speedsters to sturdy tugs and freighters. Apparently not all of Joyo's customers were wealthy.

As the boat moved through the doors and into the cavern, new tractor beams took over, carefully transporting the boat over the rows of neatly parked ships, and gently dropping it into a vacant slot. McCade noticed he'd been sorted by size, and dropped into a row of smaller vessels.

Once again the com set buzzed softly. This time text flooded the screen, accompanied by a computer-simulated voice. "Welcome to Joyo's Roid, Citizen Lane. There is a selection of free gifts waiting for you in the reception area compliments of Jerome Joyo himself. Please enjoy your stay, and let us know if there's anything which fails to please you."

As the text and voice faded away, McCade made a mental note to remember his new name. It wasn't much of a disguise, but it couldn't hurt. By now Claudia's people were probably burning vacuum looking for him. But it was a big empire, and assuming Lady Linnea hadn't spilled her guts, they had no reason to look for him on Joyo's Roid.

He shut down all the boat's systems, grabbed his carryall, and stepped through the tiny lock. An obliging robot had already placed a rolling set of stairs there for his convenience. As he stepped off the stairs onto the duracrete surface of the parking area, an autocar rolled up, and offered him a ride. McCade declined, preferring to walk the half mile to the reception area. It wouldn't hurt to know the layout just in case he wanted to leave in a hurry. The tunnel and lock arrangement would make a quick departure difficult; nonetheless, such precautions had paid off in the past. With that in mind he did his best to memorize the area as he walked along between the rows of parked ships. The lighter gravity put a spring in his step, and it felt good to stretch his legs.

* * *

Cy could barely see as he rolled the last few feet to the power outlet. For hours he'd been hiding among the parked ships, dodging both people and robots, waiting for his chance. But he couldn't wait any longer. He had to get some juice or it was all over. The tiny trickle of power remaining in his storage banks was being diverted to life support, and it wouldn't last much longer. Most of his peripherals were down, and his mains were malfunctioning, which explained why he could barely see. So he'd left his hiding place and made a run for the DC receptacle. Most of the asteroid's electrical systems ran off alternating current and there were only three direct current outlets on the whole damned rock. That miserable bastard Joyo had sealed two of them just for the fun of it. And that left only one, a maintenance outlet which should be right ahead. And there it was, the blessed three-prong receptacle, the very center of his collapsing universe. Summoning the last few ergs of energy left him, he extruded a power pickup, and tried to ram it home. He missed. Damn it! He could barely see through the fuzzy vid pickup. Was this the way he'd die? Unable to get it up and in? He laughed deep in the recesses of his metal body. It was a long time since he'd had to worry about getting it up. One more try. Just one more try. He'd just have to take more power from life support and hope for the best. Reaching way down to the very bottom of his being, he found a tiny bit of remaining strength, and shoved it up and out. The power pickup twitched, and then launched itself toward the receptacle. It made a perfect connection.

Cy's spirits soared as he felt the power and energy flow through his systems. Greedily he guzzled DC current, reveling in his new found strength. Suddenly his audio pickups came back on, and the first thing he heard was the sound of Rad's hoarse laughter, and that meant he was in deep trouble.

Rad was one of Joyo's drive techs. Most of the time he worked on Joyo's private fleet, but sometimes he filled in for the techs who worked on customers' ships, and today was such an occasion. "Well . . . what have we here . . . a power pirate that's what. Mr. Joyo isn't gonna like this. You know you're supposed to pay for what you get. Hey, Dag, look what I've got here!"

Cy's world was suddenly plunged into darkness as Rad pulled his power lead and picked him up. Desperately Cy dumped all systems except life support. They'd tortured him before, and there'd be pain enough without watching and hearing them do it. Hunkering down inside himself, he waited for it to begin.

"Here catch!" With that Rad launched Cy into air like a big beach ball. As the silver globe spun toward him, Dag danced back and forth, as if unsure where it might land. A stupid grin split his fat face as he dodged this way and that.

"I've got it . . . I've got it," Dag shouted confidently, and then just as the metal sphere was about to land in his arms, he pretended to trip, allowing it to fall and hit the deck. As Cy hit the duracrete millions of tiny feedback circuits fed pain directly into his brain. The pain came in waves, in hard jagged spears, in explosions so intense he wished he were dead.

Rad laughed uproariously. "Jeez, Dag, you've gotta be more careful, you might scramble what brains Cy's got left. Now com' on and pass him back to me."

Dag grinned, and walked around and around the metal ball as if picking his shot. Then with considerable drama, he lined the ball up with Rad, drew back a huge boot, and kicked it as hard as he could. Another tidal wave of pain hit Cy's brain as he rolled across the floor toward Rad. One or two more and it would be over. The small amount of power he'd received would be exhausted and the internal systems cushioning his plastic brain pan would stop functioning. Then one final concussion would put him out of his misery. He found he was looking forward to it.

Rad blocked the rolling sphere, paused to make sure of his aim, and then put everything he had into the kick. Cy screamed, unconsciously activating his speech synthesizer, so the sound echoed off the cavern walls. Even as he screamed Cy cursed himself for his weakness, and swore he wouldn't make another sound. Then he felt himself jerked to a halt. He waited for Dag to pick him up or kick him. Nothing. Not knowing was driving him crazy. He activated a single vid pickup. Someone had placed a large boot on top of him. A tall man with black hair and hard eyes. He had a cigar clenched in his teeth and smoke dribbled out the corner of his mouth. Friend or foe? Hoping for the best, but expecting the worst, he opened an audio pickup.

The man with the hard eyes spoke first. "Hello, gentlemen . . . what's up?"

"Just havin' a little fun's all," Rad replied resentfully. "Now if you'll jus' pass me that ball I'd sure appreciate it."

The tall man nodded thoughtfully as he dropped a carryall next to Cy, and allowed his left hand to fall on the butt of his handgun. Dag looked at the man and then at Rad. He didn't like this. This guy looked like trouble. He tried to catch Rad's attention, but the drive tech's glittering eyes were locked on the stranger.

"Maybe you didn't hear me," Rad said through gritted teeth. "I said pass me that ball."

"First time I ever heard a ball scream in pain," the man replied calmly. "Now that's a real curiosity. And I like curiosities. In fact I collect 'em. So I think I'll just keep this ball for myself. I hope that meets with your approval." The man grinned, and Dag knew he didn't care if they approved or not.

For a long moment Rad considered using the wrist gun

tucked up his right sleeve. Sure, Joyo'd be pissed, but this guy didn't look like any big deal, and Dag would back his story. But something held him back, a primitive sense of survival which had managed to keep him alive for thirty-two years. The way the other man waited, the way his fingers brushed that gun butt, he was different somehow. Deep down Rad knew, that in spite of the spring-loaded holster, he'd be dead before the wrist gun even slapped his palm. He shrugged his shoulders and spat onto the dura-crete. "So keep it . . . who gives a shit? Come, on Dag . . . we've got work to do."

As the two men departed, McCade bent over and picked up the metal sphere. Holding Cy with one arm, he picked up his carryall with the other, and headed for the reception area. It was clearly marked with a neon sign.

"DC power . . . I need DC power soon . . . dying." The weak voice came from the metal sphere.

It was weird, but if a metal ball could scream, then talking seemed reasonable too. "OK, my friend," McCade said, "DC power it is. My treat just as soon as I check in."

Cy wanted to express his gratitude but couldn't find the energy, so he allowed himself to sink back into darkness, carefully monitoring the trickle of energy which flowed to his life support systems.

The reception area was huge, and sparkled with a thousand lights. Tiers of balconies reached up to a ceiling hewed from brownish rock. Gentle music merged with the hum of subdued conversation to create a comfortable jumble of background sound. Thick carpeting, comfortable furniture, and tasteful decorations all added to a feeling of restrained elegance.

In fact, the check-in counter even boasted a live receptionist. She was young, quite pretty, and well aware of it. Flanking her on both sides were the latest in autotellers. They did the actual work of checking people in and out. She was supposed to provide the human touch. But right now her practiced smile couldn't quite conceal her disapproval. She'd recognized Cy immediately. "Is that, er, thing yours, sir? I hope it hasn't been bothering you."

"What this?" McCade asked in mock surprise. "Certainly not. This is my portable gatzfratz. Never leave home without it. Hope you have some DC power in my room. Damned thing won't work off AC."

"Certainly not," the receptionist sniffed, appalled by McCade's obvious lie. "None of our rooms supply DC power."

"Well, mine had better supply some, and damned fast," McCade said, eyes narrowing. "I'll be happy to pay whatever costs are involved."

The receptionist gulped. "Just a moment, sir, I'll check." She didn't like this man's expression. She punched some keys on her com set and explained the situation to her supervisor.

He laughed, and said, "Sounds like Cy found himself a sucker . . . well, what the hell . . . give the man what he wants. Like Mr. Joyo says, 'The customer's always right.'"

Half an hour later McCade was thanking the maintenance tech, and showing him out. The tech had managed to run a cable from a junction box thirty feet down the hall, under McCade's door, and into his room. He closed the door and turned to see Cy extrude a power pickup and plug in. He yawned. "Enjoy, my little friend. Meanwhile I need a nap." With that he stretched out on the bed and was asleep ten seconds later.

Eight

McCADE AWOKE TO find the metal ball floating ominously over his head. In one fluid motion his gun came up and centered on Cy. "You'd better have one helluva good reason for being up there," he said levelly.

"Ooops, sorry," Cy replied, and used a squirt of compressed air to propel himself toward the far wall. "It's been a while since I could afford to run my anti-grav unit. I'm afraid I drifted off to sleep . . . and was blown over you by the air conditioning."

"No problem," McCade said, holstering his gun. He swung his feet over the side of the bed, stood, and headed for the bathroom. He stripped to the waist and smeared his face with shaving cream. It was sort of old-fashioned, but he liked the ritual. The metal sphere had followed him, and now hung suspended in the doorway. "So," he said, shaving the left side of his face, "did you get enough power?"

"Oh, yes," Cy answered eagerly. "I don't know how to thank you. It's been months since I've been able to bring storage up to max. They don't pay me much . . . so I can rarely afford more than a half charge."

"They charge you for power?"

The metal ball bobbed up and down as though nodding in agreement. "Oh, yes . . . nothing's free on Joyo's Roid."

McCade studied the hovering sphere in the mirror for a moment before starting in on the right side of his face. "No offense, but what are you anyway, some sort of advanced robot?"

A distinct sigh emanated from the silver ball. "That's what everyone thinks . . . but I'm not." Cy paused for a moment getting ready to say it. The words never came easily. Finally he steeled himself and said, "I'm a cyborg."

"Part man and part machine?" McCade asked. He'd heard of them but never met one.

"That's right," Cy replied, "although I'm mostly machine, and very little man. In fact my brain's all that's left of the man."

McCade regarded the cyborg thoughtfully as he wiped his face with a soft white towel. "So you must have a name . . . I'm Sam Lane." He'd almost said "McCade" but caught himself just in time.

"Glad to meet you, Sam. I'm Cy Borg."

"No, that's what you are . . . I asked *who* you are."

"No," Cy said stubbornly, "that's who I am too. The old me is dead."

"OK, have it your way," McCade replied, walking into the bedroom. "Mind if I ask how you wound up in your present, ah, condition?"

Cy spun back and forth as if shaking his head. "Why not? It's common knowledge. I gambled myself away."

McCade finished putting on a fresh set of leathers and zipped them up. "You what? How the hell d'you manage that?"

Cy bobbed up and down slightly as he passed through the cold air being blown out of a vent. "I'm afraid I was a very sick man. Believe it or not, I used to be wealthy. Made it all myself too. I was a whiz at electromechanical miniaturization, computers, stuff like that. In fact, I designed myself. What do you think?" Cy spun full circle like a model showing off a new gown.

"You're the best-looking metal ball I've ever seen," McCade answered dryly. "So how did you gamble yourself away?"

"Oh, that," Cy replied, as if coming back to an uncomfortable subject. "Well, I came here like most people do, just looking for a good time, you know, a little fun and relaxation. So I tried a little of his, and a little of that, and then I discovered gambling. I'd never gambled before . . . and, I loved it. I loved the risk, the excitement, the pure adventure of it. Well, to make a long story short, before I knew it I'd gambled away all my money. And when that was gone, I gambled away my business and my yacht. Then I tried to stop. But it was too late. I couldn't. So I gambled the only things I had left, my bodily organs. And I lost."

For a moment there was silence as McCade tried to imagine what it would be like. Being wheeled into surgery, knowing they were about to take your body apart, package it, and sell the pieces like so much meat. Then awaking to find they had left only your brain. It was horrible, but all too possible, since there was quite a market for organs and anything with value could be gambled away. He thought of the people cavorting around Lady Linnea's pool in their biosculpted bodies. Maybe some of them were using Cy's organs. He shuddered. "I'm sorry, Cy . . . that's a tough break. But it looks like you did a good job redesigning yourself."

"Yeah, it ain't too bad," Cy agreed, extruding a vid pickup to examine himself. "Although I should have gone for a better AC converter. But I only had a week to design and build my new body, so I had to work with what I could get. Most of me came from junked robots," Cy added proudly.

"Well, you did a damned fine job," McCade said thoughtfully as he pulled out a cigar and puffed it alight. "Now it happens that I need a guide. I don't suppose you'd have time to show me around? I'd be happy to pay you."

"Of course, Sam," Cy said eagerly. "I wish I could refuse the pay . . . but I'm afraid I need it."

"I'd insist anyway," McCade replied. "You mentioned a job earlier. Are you sure working for me won't interfere?"

Cy dropped a few inches as though hanging his head in shame. "It's not regular work, Sam. Sometimes they hire me to spy on people."

McCade raised one eyebrow. "Spy on people . . . whatever for?"

"You know," Cy said unhappily, "find out what they like, what they don't like. It helps the staff cheat them."

McCade considered the cyborg's small body and anti-grav capability. "I suppose you can go places the rest of us can't," McCade said, thinking out loud. A handy talent to have. The fact that Joyo cheated his customers didn't surprise McCade. He'd never seen an honest casino yet.

Cy bobbed in silent acknowledgment.

"Well, don't worry about it, partner," McCade said, patting Cy on his top surface. "We all survive as best we can. Let's see Joyo's Roid."

The two of them set off, and it didn't take long for McCade to discover that the asteroid was a maze of tunnels, corridors, and passageways. Some were natural and some artificial. Together they connected the countless bars, nightclubs, and casinos. Joyo knew that while all his customers wanted the same things, they didn't necessarily want them the same way. So while each area offered drugs, sex, and gambling, each made it seem like a different experience.

One area they visited was all brightly lit efficiency. Here

sex and drugs were offered by wholesome-looking types, and the whole thing looked like a health-food store. At the other end of the spectrum was an area called Hell's Basement. Here everything was sleazy and decadent, dark bars harbored leather-clad deviants, and customers felt they'd stumbled into hell itself. They loved it.

McCade thought it was funny. He'd spent a lot of time in bars that really were as decadent as this one pretended to be, and knew the richly clad customers who lined the bar, and filled the tables, wouldn't last ten minutes in the real thing. But they were having a good time living out their fantasies . . . so what the hell. He ordered another whiskey from the half-naked bartender, and turned to watch the threesome on stage. They were making love, if you could call their intricate gymnastics "love," and McCade was wondering how they did it. Double-jointed perhaps? Well, it didn't matter. He had work to do. And sitting around wasn't getting it done. Cy, it turned out, was a good guide, but also attracted a lot of attention.

For one thing, all of Joyo's staff knew Cy, the same way bartenders all know the local wino. And it was quickly apparent from the comments they made, that Cy still gambled whenever he got the chance. Plus the two of them were pretty visible. A hard-eyed man dressed in black leathers with a silver ball for a sidekick is hard to miss. So much for the low-key approach. So maybe he'd try something different.

"OK, Cy . . . I think I've got a feel for the basic layout. Now let's have some fun. A friend of mine told me about a game that uses oddly marked six-sided dice. I can't remember what he called it, but it sounded interesting."

Cy gave a metallic-sounding whistle. "Odd six-sided dice . . . your friend must have been a high roller . . . and a bit crazy to boot. Don't tell me, let me guess. When you talked to him he hadn't played Destiny, he was just planning to."

McCade nodded, playing along. "I thought so," Cy said knowingly. "Only crazies play Destiny. If they lose you never see them again. That's part of the game. Or used to be. I heard they shut it down. The payoffs were rare, but damned expensive when they came. Did your friend tell you how it worked? No? Well, it was supposed to be like getting born again. You know, sort of a second chance. An opportunity to overcome the cards dealt you at birth. That's why it was called Destiny. First they'd have you reach into an anti-grav cage where there were thousands of six-sided dice flying around. You'd grab one and check it out. You'd see it had numbers on five sides and Joyo's logo on the other. Each of the numbers would represent a possible life outcome, like with five you might end up a millionaire, and forty-two might mean you're a settler on some frontier planet, and so on. So each of those five numbers became your possible destinies. Then the game would begin. So you roll your dice. Let's say forty-two comes up, you're a settler on some Sol-forsaken frontier planet. But that's just the beginning. According to the rules you must roll sixty-six times. So you keep going. According to the next roll your first two crops fail, your net worth decreases, and your family starts to starve. But you roll again, good news, you discover rare metals on your land. However the next roll brings a pirate raid, and so forth. Once your sixty-six rolls are up, you receive your net worth, if any. From what I've heard most players were damned lucky to avoid slavery. That's right, Sam . . . slavery. If you ended up with a negative net worth you *belonged* to Joyo. Hey, you think I was stupid betting my organs? These people bet the rest of their lives. So, if they're still playing Destiny, I suggest you avoid it like the plague. Let's try mind-maze or roulette instead."

McCade groaned inwardly. Great. A game where a prince could wind up just as miserable as everyone else. Just Alexander's cup of tea. So if he wanted to find the prince, Destiny might be the path he'd have to follow. McCade assumed what he hoped was a nonchalant grin, and said, "Well, let's find out if they still play it, and then I'll decide."

Cy dipped in what might have been a shrug. "OK... it's your neck... but don't say I didn't warn you." With that Cy turned, and squirted himself toward the door.

McCade followed as Cy led him deeper and deeper into Hell's Basement. Finally, after what seemed like endless twistings and turnings, Cy rounded a corner and disappeared. McCade followed. But instead of another endless hallway, there was a door. Except it wasn't really a door— since only ribbons of multicolored cloth barred his way.

Brushing them aside, McCade stepped through it and into a tunnel of pink silk. A host of concealed lights made the fabric glow, and a steady breeze caused it to ripple gently, as though invested with a life of its own. Cool air touched his face with the slightest hint of perfume, and brought with it the half-heard strains of distant music. Then came the voices. There were dozens of them, all whispering, all saying the same thing. "Welcome to the Silk Road. Welcome to the Silk Road. Welcome to the Silk Road." They said it over and over, echoing each other endlessly, like ghosts speaking from beyond the grave. It sent a shiver down his spine.

As he walked down the tunnel, the whispers gradually died away, and the music grew gradually louder, its soft but insistent beat pounding with the same rhythm as his own pulse, ebbing and flowing around and through him. The Silk Road. The place the beautiful face on his com set had suggested he come. Perhaps he'd see her. He found himself walking a little faster, as the tunnel curved gently, and then emptied into a large circular room.

The walls were covered with the same pink silk which lined the tunnel. Tables circled the room, each protected by its own silk enclosure, granting those within a gauzy sort of privacy.

Dominating the center of the room was a sunken bar, also circular in shape. And there, bobbing gently in the air-conditioned breeze, was Cy. Autocarts scurried this way and that, serving their customers, and skillfully getting out of McCade's way as he headed for the bar.

The bar was practically empty, most customers evidently preferring the curtained pleasures of the surrounding tables, to the more standard liquid refreshments. Taking the empty seat next to Cy, McCade said, "Nice place, Cy . . . by far the fanciest whorehouse I've ever seen."

"Yes," Cy answered wistfully. "I can remember enjoying such things . . . but not very well." He sighed, and extruded an infrared pickup to supplement his vision. "When the bartender comes, tell him you wish to speak with Silk. She owns the place, and used to run the Destiny games. If they're still going she'll know. But I think you're crazy to even consider playing that game."

"You're probably right," McCade replied. "But I'd like to ask her a few questions." Moments later the bartender appeared from the other side of the bar, lumbered up, and ran his bar rag over the pink plastic countertop.

"Want?" His voice was a guttural rumble which sounded like distant thunder. Luminescent green eyes peered out from under craggy brows to regard McCade with generalized hostility. Like all his race, the Cellite was a humanoid mountain of muscle and bone, sculpted by the heavy gravity of his home world into a living Hercules. His oiled torso rippled when he moved.

"I'll take a whiskey and water," McCade answered. "Terran if you have it."

The bartender gave a grunt of assent, and tapped three keys on his automixer. The glass emerged with a whirring sound and disappeared into the bartender's huge hand. As he set it down, McCade said, "Thanks. And I'd like to have a word with Silk when she has a moment."

The bartender eyed him appraisingly, and then grunted, "Wait." With that he lumbered away and out of sight.

McCade eyed Cy as he lit a cigar, and took a sip of his drink. He had a feeling that direct questioning wasn't going to get him much. So he needed some help, but how far could the cyborg be trusted? He wasn't sure, but decided to take a chance. That way he could pursue the gambling angle, while Cy tried other less obvious possibilities. He cleared his throat. "Cy, I'm afraid I wasn't entirely honest with you earlier."

"I know that, Sam," the cyborg replied calmly, turning a vid pickup in McCade's direction. "Regular customers either ignore me, or just laugh at me. They'd never risk a fight with Rad. So," he added shrewdly, "since you aren't a customer, then you're after something, or somebody."

"Somebody," McCade answered evenly, blowing a thin stream of smoke toward the ceiling. "And I need your help."

"I owe you my life," Cy said simply. "If I can help you, I will."

McCade smiled. "Maybe you lost your body, Cy, but you've still got lots of guts. I'm trying to find someone who disappeared about two years ago. Here's what he looked like back then." McCade unzipped a pocket, and pulled out the vidfax of Alexander which Swanson-Pierce had supplied.

Cy extruded an articulated metal arm. He took the vidfax with his three-fingered hand, and held it up in front of a vid pickup. McCade searched for any sign of recognition. After all, Alexander's likeness had appeared on every vidcast in the Empire countless times before and after his disappearance. But either Cy didn't recognize him, or he did, and carefully concealed it. As he handed the vidfax back McCade wished Cy had a face. How the hell can you tell what a metal ball's thinking anyway? Talk about a poker face. . . .

"This is the friend you mentioned . . . the one who played Destiny?"

McCade nodded. "I'm trying to find him."

Cy bobbed his understanding. "As I explained earlier your friend could be anywhere, depending on how his game went. If he won, then perhaps he chooses to be elusive. If he lost . . . then who knows. But Joyo maintains an extensive data bank on all his customers. Since many come back again and again, the records help him keep track of what they like, what they don't, and how to maximize his take without driving them away. Anyway . . . if I'm very careful, I might be able to access his central computer."

"I was hoping for something like that," McCade admitted. "Have you got any storage compartments?"

There was a soft whirring noise as a small hatch slid aside to reveal a tiny recess in Cy's metal body. McCade reached into a pocket and pulled out the wad of expense money Walt had given him. Splitting it in two, he stuffed half into Cy's storage compartment. "There's no telling how things will go . . . so here's a little something to tide you over. If you're careful it should solve your DC problem for quite a while."

For a moment neither said anything. Finally Cy broke the silence. "This is very dangerous, Sam. Be careful what you say to Silk, she belongs to Royo mind and body. And he doesn't like people poking into his affairs."

"Thanks, Cy. I will. And the same to you. Don't take any unnecessary chances."

Cy bobbed in the affirmative. "I won't. Watch for me, Sam . . . I'll find you." And with that he was gone, sailing across the room toward the distant tunnel.

"Come."

McCade turned to find the bartender had returned.

Stubbing out his cigar in an ashtray, he stood and said, "After you, gabby."

The Cellite scowled, and did an abrupt about-face. McCade grinned, and followed the huge humanoid toward the far wall. As they approached, the bartender stopped and pointed to a curtained doorway. "In."

"Somehow I knew you were going to say that," McCade said, shaking his head in disappointment. The bartender scowled even harder as he stepped aside and motioned for McCade to enter. As he stepped through the curtained entranceway, McCade saw a luxuriously furnished office, and the woman called Silk. She was sitting on the corner of a large desk. The same beautiful face, blue hair, red lips, and long straight nose. And in spite of her somewhat androgynous look, there was no longer any question of her sex. Her red silk gown managed to both reveal and conceal a spectacular female body. Unfortunately she wasn't alone. A cadaverous-looking man, dressed entirely in black, sat behind the desk, smiling a thin smile. Jerome Joyo. And on either side of him there stood a Cellite bodyguard, their huge hands dwarfing the blasters which were pointed in McCade's direction. The thin man spoke first.

"Welcome, Citizen Lane, or whatever your real name is. You are in very deep trouble."

Nine

CY WAS SCARED. No, on second thought, he was terrified. For the last ten minutes he'd hovered in front of the open air vent, trying to work up enough courage to enter. He'd already unscrewed the grille and swung it out of the way. Now all he had to do was enter, find his way through the complex maze of ducts to Joyo's computer center, plug in, and run a high-speed data search. Not an easy task, but not all that hard either, except for the crawlies. They scared the hell out of him, and for a very good reason. If they found him in the ducts, they'd kill him. That was their job. Joyo was not a stupid man. He'd forseen that the air-conditioning ducts could be used against him. In fact, he used them himself. Cy knew, because on more than one occasion, he'd been sent into the ducts to spy on customers. For hours on end he'd waited by vents, forcing himself to listen to their boring talk, waiting for that one gem of information for which Joyo would pay. Joyo said it was cheaper than bugging all the rooms. But that was different. The crawlies had always been deactivated for his benefit. Now, however, they would be very much alive, just waiting for him.

Crawlies were rectangular in shape, and were designed so that they fit snugly inside the endless ducts supplying Joyo's Roid with warm and cool air. All four sides of their boxy bodies were equipped with traction drives, which enabled them to crawl through the ducts, and explained their name. Hollow in the middle, so they wouldn't obstruct the free flow of air through the system, crawlies were governed by a microcomputer so primitive, so simple, it was almost retarded by the normal standards of robotics. How much intelligence does it take to sense unusual amounts of heat, noise, or movement, and fire a battery of low-power lasers? Crawlies were equipped with low-power lasers so they wouldn't damage the ducts, but low power or not, they'd cook Cy in seconds.

Still, Cy thought to himself, trying to push the fear down and back, I'm smarter than they are, and that's an advantage. Plus I'm smaller, faster, and more maneuverable. He felt the fear retreat a ways, crouching like an animal in its lair, watching and waiting to see what he'd do. And there's one more thing, damnit! he thought defiantly. Sam said I've got guts. Machines don't have guts. Maybe I'm locked up in this tin can body, but by Sol I'm still a man! And with that he entered the duct, extruded an arm to pull the grille closed behind him, and squirted himself into the darkness. Let the crawlies come. . . . He'd show 'em a thing or two!

An hour later, he was still moving, but with a good deal less bravado. He sensed an intersection up ahead. As always he approached it with great care. He'd already dumped all but essential systems to minimize heat. His infrared and audio sensors were cranked up to max, and he was using his sonar to gently probe ahead. What was that? A noise. Inside the duct or out? Sometimes it was hard to tell. Nothing on sonar. Inside. Definitely inside. A slight grating of metal against metal, like a traction drive with a worn bearing, or a poorly adjusted servo. Oh, shit . . . it was just ahead . . . coming toward the intersection just like he was. Which duct? Well, it wasn't in his, so that left three possibilities. Should he just stop and hope for the best? Or should he attack? Attack? How the hell could he attack? The Sol-damned things had lasers and he didn't have shit. Oh, wait a minute . . . lasers . . . they literally cut both ways. If he could just work fast enough. . . .

Frantically he extruded three articulated arms, and went to work on his own metal housing, swearing when one screw refused to budge, then giving thanks as it finally came free. A distant part of his mind kept nagging him, pointing out he was making enough noise to raise the dead, reminding him the crawlie would reach the intersection in seconds. Then it would zap him, and a few days later the smell of his rotting brain would offend some guest, and they'd send in a maintenance bot to find him, and throw him in the recycler.

As half his housing came free, he spun it around, and sensed the flare of heat as the lasers hit. But there was no hot searing agony. No plunge into the darkness of death. Only an incandescent flash of light as the crawlie took the reflected laser blast, and died. It worked! The concave surface of his shiny metal housing had served to concentrate and reflect the lasers, turning them back against their source.

At first he couldn't believe it, and then suddenly he did, giving a whoop of joy, which scared the hell out of a couple making love in a nearby room. Pushing his way down the duct, Cy located the dead crawlie, and spent a moment gloating over his victory. Then, just as he was about to continue his journey, he remembered something. Quickly probing and touching, he found the crawlie's power pak, checked it for damage, and chuckled when he found none.

Ten minutes later he'd jury-rigged a connector, plugged in, and was happily draining delicious DC from the robot's storage cell. It took some time to suck up all the crawlie's power, but eventually the task was complete, and thus refreshed, Cy continued happily on his way. Now he moved with some speed, pushing his homemade laser reflector in front of him, almost daring crawlies to attack him. One did, and quickly suffered the same fate as its predecessor. This time Cy was forced to leave the corpse only partially drained, since his own storage capacity was up to max. Great Sol, it felt good!

He was close to the computer center now . . . so all he had to do . . . Then his thoughts were shattered, as someone slammed a grille against a wall up ahead, and he heard the sound of male voices. "Shit, I don't know, Vern . . . I mean how the hell would I know what trashed the crawlies? Meg told me one went off her board, and then another one croaked too. An like she says, two in one day's no accident. Somethun's in the vents. But whatever it is ain't gonna last long. Not after the snake finds 'em. Ain't that right, snaky?"

Snaky? Cy wondered. What the hell was a snaky? He'd never heard of such a thing. Up ahead there was a metallic slithering. Suddenly Cy had a feeling he'd get to meet snaky real soon.

The Cellite hit McCade with a massive open-handed blow. Pain rolled over the considerable pain he already felt. And when he hit the wall, the impact created a whole new wave of pain, which rolled over all those which had gone before. As he slid down the wall to the floor, he could detect distinct layers of pain, sort of like an archaeologist digging down through layers of artifact-laden soil, each telling its own special story.

"Why don't you just tell us what you're doing here?" Joyo asked reasonably. "It would save you so much pain."

From his vantage point on the floor McCade could see a certain logic to the suggestion. After all pain hurt, and hurting was bad, so anything that stopped the hurting was good. No wait a minute, telling was bad, so hurting was good. Oh, to hell with it, throwing up was good, so he'd do that. By expending a little extra effort, he managed to do it on Joyo's shiny boots. He watched dully as the boot went far away, and then came straight at him with incredible speed. The resulting darkness felt good.

The snake was about six feet long. Where a real snake's head would normally be, the robosnake had a bulbous housing containing sensors and weapons. Its brain, a microcomputer only marginally more intelligent than those issued to crawlies, was located in its tail, its designer having concluded this would be a safer place for it.

Cy, however, was in no mood to appreciate the subtlety of the robosnake's design. He just wanted to kill it, and do so as quickly and simply as possible. But how? Well, first he'd try the laser trick. It had worked on the crawlies, so maybe it would work on robosnakes too. He made a little noise, and waited for the lasers to hit. Nothing. Just more metallic slithering. Faster now that the snake had a target.

"Oh, shit," Cy said to himself as he struggled back into his housing and secured it. He hated to use up precious time, but he didn't want to fight the snake bare-assed naked either. The moment his housing was back in place, he activated his anti-grav unit, and whizzed back to the next intersection. He needed time to think.

Cy's mind was racing through the possibilities. Apparently the snake wasn't equipped with lasers or projectile weapons. The fact that he was still alive seemed proof of that. So the damned thing was designed to work in close, and since he had no defenses to speak of, it would be critical to keep the snake at a distance. But how? He could keep running, but eventually he'd make a mistake, or just run out of power, and the damn thing would have him. The snake had been designed to operate in the ducts and he hadn't. But wait a minute! *Outside* the ducts the electronic reptile couldn't touch him. Not while he had power for his anti-grav unit anyway, and thanks to the crawlies, he had power to burn. Cy zipped farther down the duct until he found a grille. The room beyond the grille was dark, and Cy couldn't hear any movement or conversation. With luck it would be vacant.

The scraping of metal on metal was closer now. Working quickly he reached through the grille with two articulated arms, undid the screws holding it in place, and pushed it aside. Turning to face the snake, Cy slid a section of his housing aside to reveal a high-intensity light. He flicked it on, and damned near scared himself to death. The snake was even closer than he'd thought, its bulbous head bristling with sensors, acid jets, and power drills, its brightly scaled metal body gathering itself for an attack.

McCade was dimly aware of being scooped up by one of the enormous Cellite bodyguards, and carried like a baby down a series of hallways and corridors, before being unceremoniously dumped into a small room. He heard the door slam, and the sound of retreating footsteps. He ordered his body to get up, and swore silently when it failed to respond. He understood the problem. It had to do with dispersal. Somehow he was everywhere, and in order to accomplish things, he had to be somewhere. He'd have to gather himself in and focus his energies. Easier said than done he concluded glumly. Nonetheless he had to try. Bit by bit he gathered himself together, and as he did, he became increasingly aware of his surroundings. The cold metal deck under his cheek, the reek of strong disinfectant, the glaring light of the room's single chem strip. Eventually, in what he considered a heroic expenditure of energy, McCade managed to roll over. From there it was a simple matter to crouch, and then stand. It only took an hour.

His whole body ached and throbbed from countless bruises. A careful inventory revealed a deep cut on his face where Joyo's boot had hit him, two black eyes, a broken tooth, two broken fingers on his left hand, and a sprained right ankle. His eyes were almost swollen shut, but from what he could see, the room was entirely bare. Naturally. Cells rarely come with a lot of furniture.

Hobbling toward a corner, McCade used his good hand to pat his pockets, searching for a surviving cigar butt. He found nothing but crumbs. The bastards had taken everything: his money, cigars, lighter, and, needless to say, his gun. Slowly he lowered himself to the floor and closed his eyes. He'd had better days.

As the snake struck, Cy propelled himself sideways, and through the open vent. The robosnake followed its target, launching itself into the darkened room, and then falling like a rock. There was a loud scream as the heavy metal snake fell across the large bed. Somewhat confused, but nonetheless determined, the snake sensed a spherical source of heat and attacked. The woman continued to scream as her husband managed to flick on the lights. To his utter amazement a six-foot-long metal snake was draped across his wife and seemed intent on destroying the globular com set located on their bedside stand. Being a retired general, the man had fairly good nerves, and the presence of mind to retrieve his handgun and blow the snake's head off. Much to his surprise this did nothing to stop the snake's determined attack. Denied its primary sensors, but still possessed of its limited intelligence, the robosnake reevaluated the situation, and mistakenly decided the rather large mass of warm tissue lying under it had been the source of the attack. Quickly wrapping itself around the lump of offending tissue, the snake began to squeeze. Unable to shoot at the snake's midsection for fear of hitting his wife, and no longer calm, the General blazed away at the only available target, the snake's tail. He got two solid hits and the snake went limp. His wife continued to scream as he tried to operate the destroyed com set, and neither of them noticed as two articulated arms finished screwing the air-conditioning grille back in place, and then disappeared.

Cy zipped through the ducts racing for the computer center. Once security found the robosnake, all hell was going to break loose. The fact that the grille was screwed shut might confuse things for a while, but not for long. Moments later he was peering out of a vent into a large, brightly lit room full of humming computers. There were two people in sight. From their tool belts Cy deduced they were repair techs rather than programmers. Good, he'd give them something to repair.

Seconds later he was at the far end of the computer center undoing a grille. Spying a likely printer, he squirted himself over, and started pulling a plastic print fax out of its box. Looping it around and around the printer he built quite a pile. Then, extruding a tiny arc welder, he lit the pile of plastic. Though not highly flammable, the stuff did manage to burn, giving off clouds of horrible-smelling smoke. Cy had no more than ducked back into the duct when the automatic alarms went off.

Both repair techs were up and running for the other end of the room seconds after the alarm went off. So, they failed to see the grille over their table swing open, and a metallic ball squirt out, heading for the control console. Cy extruded two articulated arms, both of which ended in three-fingered hands. As he hovered over the control board his fingers moved with blinding speed, first entering the access code which he'd seen and memorized while working for Joyo, and then setting up the program he wanted the computer to run. It was a large computer, but since it was early morning cycle on Joyo's Roid, largely unused at the moment. It ran Cy's program in forty-three seconds, and spit out three feet of print fax from the nearest printer when it was finished. Cy didn't take the time to look at it. He just rolled it up and clamped it to his side. Then working quickly, he dumped the program he'd set up, and cleared out. If they really checked, they'd find about a minute of unauthorized computer use, but since they had no reason to check, chances were they wouldn't.

As soon was the grille as screwed shut, he took off down the duct at high speed, before suddenly coming to an abrupt stop. What the hell was he doing? He didn't know where Sam was, and he could run into a crawlie anytime. Mentally gritting teeth he no longer had, he undid half his housing, and pushed it ahead of him as he moved through the maze of ducts at a more moderate pace.

A quick check of Sam's room found nothing. Literally nothing. Even his carryall was gone. Had he checked out? Not likely . . . no, this looked like Joyo's work.

Grimly Cy headed for the Silk Road. Along the way another crawlie attacked and fried itself. Cy didn't even pause. Finally he drifted silently along the duct which ran around the circumference of the silk-lined brothel. Each time he came to a grille he took a look. There were lots of people, doing some fairly amazing things, but none of them was Sam.

Damn! Sam could be anywhere. Cy racked his brain trying to think of some way to locate his friend. Nothing came. But chances were, if he waited by Joyo's office long enough, he'd hear something that would tell him what he needed to know. So he scooted over there and settled down to wait.

Cy awoke with a jerk. He heard voices. One he immediately recognized as Joyo's; the other, softer voice belonged to Silk. Extending a vid pickup, Cy peeked through the grille. Joyo was behind the desk, seated in his high-backed leather chair, speaking to Silk who was just out of sight.

". . . The man's nothing more than another two-bit chiseler. We'll turn his absurd lifeboat into scrap, and send him to Worm. As usual Torb's complaining about a shortage of slaves. I swear the ugly bastard uses them up like there's an endless supply."

"Maybe that's because you raise his production quota four times a year," Silk replied softly.

Cy couldn't see Joyo's face, but he sensed the scowl on it when he replied. "Don't lay that crap on me, lady. I don't see you turning down the flow of credits coming in from Worm."

"Granted," she said placatingly. "And I want that flow to continue. Which is why I wonder if we're doing the right thing. This Sam Lane smells like trouble. What about his lifeboat, for example? A lifeboat implies a larger ship. Where is it? Who's on it? There's too many unanswered questions." Her voice was so soft Cy had difficulty hearing it. He cranked up the gain on his audio pickups.

Joyo shrugged. "Maybe, but my people on Terra weren't able to come up with anything, except that there's no Sam Lane matching his description. Now we could take his retinals, cut a voiceprint, map his dentition, and send the whole mess to the Earth Central mainframe. Chances are it could tell us who he is, what he does, and the kind of cereal he likes for breakfast. But that could create as many problems as it solves. Asking Earth Central mainframe for information cuts both ways. You get it, but you also provide it. So, if he's wanted we could have bounty hunters all over the place, or if he's got powerful friends, they might give us trouble, or what, God forbid, if he's a pirate? That kind of trouble we don't need. No, a call to Rad and his lifeboat disappears, then a little trip to Worm, and the problem's solved."

Silk moved into sight and sat on Joyo's lap. She smiled. "Well, you're the boss . . . boss."

* * *

McCade heard the grille squeak open and looked up through bleary eyes. As Cy squirted himself into the room he tried to speak but only produced a croaking noise.

"Great Sol, Sam, are you all right? Ooops, stupid question, of course you aren't." Cy spun around helplessly, looking for some way to help.

McCade cleared his throat. "I'll be okay, Cy... just need some R & R, that's all. How'd it go? But before you answer... check to see if this cell's bugged. If it is... you better haul ass."

"Nah, it ain't bugged," Cy replied loftily. "I checked before I came in. As for how it went, I've got some good news and some bad news."

"Give me the good news first," McCade croaked, trying to find a more comfortable position against the hard wall.

"I got into Joyo's computer," Cy said proudly, "and here's what it coughed up." Cy unclipped the roll of print fax, and used an articulated arm to hand it to McCade.

As McCade accepted it he did his best to grin. It hurt. "You're quite a guy, Cy... nobody else could have done it."

Cy felt a pleasurable warmth inside at the praise, and a renewed determination to help Sam any way he could.

McCade unrolled the print-out, and scanned it through his blurred vision. His eyes were so swollen he could hardly get them open, plus his two broken fingers kept getting in the way. The computer had used the matrix of information supplied by Cy to search for men who'd played Destiny and matched Alexander's general description. McCade's heart sank as a quick scan failed to turn up a perfect match. Maybe Lady Linnea had tricked him, or maybe Alexander really was dead, or maybe a hundred different possibilities.

Nonetheless he turned his attention to those who most closely matched the prince's description. One caught his eye time after time. A man calling himself Idono H. Farigo. He'd arrived about the right time, played Destiny, and lost. The only trouble was that Joyo's computer placed him at only a ninety percent match for Alexander's physical description. Examining the detailed analysis which followed Farigo's summary, McCade noticed some interesting facts. First, Farigo's race and age matched Alexander's perfectly. Second, both men were exactly six feet one inch in height, and both weighed 178 pounds. And third, they both had blue eyes. However, where Alexander had light brown hair, Farigo's was black, and though both had even features, Farigo's were rougher and less refined.

As McCade leaned back to think, he ignored the pain of his various injuries, and wished he had a cigar. Forcing his mind to the task at hand, he considered the facts. On second thought, maybe a ninety percent match was pretty good. Especially when the two men were a one hundred percent perfect match in everything but facial appearance. And from years of bounty hunting, McCade knew how unimportant facial characteristics could be in tracking someone down. Given enough credits, a new face was as close as the nearest biosculptor, and the prince certainly had enough credits. What if he'd visited a biosculptor before coming to Joyo's Roid? And from what Lady Linnea had told him, it would be just like the prince to roughen, rather than refine his features. That way he'd have a face more in keeping with the common herd. Then, disguised as Farigo, he'd arrived on Joyo's Roid, played Destiny, lost as he'd no doubt hoped he would, and been sent to some miserable planet as a slave. It all made a crazy sort of sense . . . but what if he was wrong?

"Can I see that?" Cy asked, hovering in front of McCade.

McCade nodded and handed over the print-out. "As a matter of fact you can keep it. Otherwise I'd have a hell of a time explaining where I got it."

Cy bobbed in agreement. "Did you find anything?"

"I think so," McCade replied doubtfully. "Take a look at that Farigo guy. He seems like my best bet, but if I'm wrong I could waste a lot of time and energy on him."

Cy found Farigo's name on the print-out, and sounded it out, "I-do-no-H-Far-I-go . . . that's a weird name."

McCade sat up straight, and then wished he hadn't. Everything hurt. "Well, I'll be damned . . . at least the bastard has a sense of humor. How much you want to bet the 'H' stands for 'how.' 'I don't know how far I go.' That's got to be him. Thanks, Cy, now I'm sure Alexander and Farigo are the same man. You've been a big help. OK . . . you said there was some bad news . . . I guess I'm as ready for it as I'll ever be."

Cy felt happy and sad at the same time. He'd been able to help, but it wasn't going to do any good. "They're sending you to a slave planet called Worm," Cy replied sadly. "And they don't plan on you coming back."

To Cy's amazement, McCade broke into gales of laughter, grimacing at the pain it caused him, and pointing at the print-out clutched in Cy's metal fingers. Cy aimed a vid pickup at Farigo's entry, and there under "disposition," it said, "Manual labor, ten years, the planet Worm."

Ten

IN SOME WAYS, McCade actually enjoyed the trip to
Worm. While his quarters aboard Joyo's supply ship were
something less than luxurious, the chow wasn't bad, and
the ship's engineer was also a damned fine medic. She was
middle-aged, homely, and gruff. Though far from sweet,
even as a baby, hopeful parents had blessed her with the
somewhat unlikely name of Candy. But McCade liked her
nonetheless. And not just because she patched him up, and
brought his food each day. Behind Candy's rough facade
there was a quick mind, and a sharp wit. Plus she'd
knocked around the Empire even more than he had, and
when properly coaxed, knew how to spin a good yarn. So,
over time, he'd come to view her as more friend than
jailer, and suspected that, deep down, she felt the same
way about him. Of course both knew the trip would soon
end, and with it, their friendship. So McCade continued to
act out his role as miserable prisoner, while Candy did her
best to play the heartless jailer. Then they were in orbit

around Worm, and Candy was giving him one last examination.

"Flex your fingers," she said curtly. McCade obeyed, flexing all his fingers. They worked perfectly, including the two which Joyo's bodyguard had broken. The ship had been in transit for about three standard weeks, having come out of hyperspace just the cycle before, and the passage of time, plus the attentions of the ship's automedic, had healed his fractured bones. Now only the faintest shadow marked where his black eyes had once been, and Candy had closed the cut on his face so skillfully the scar was almost invisible. She grunted her approval.

"You're healthy as a horse. Might even last a month or so down there." McCade would've sworn he saw a trace of sadness in her eyes.

As the hatch clanged shut and locked behind her, McCade leaned back to stare at the overhead. He hoped her sadness was unnecessary. By now Cy should have delivered his message to Rico and Phil. If so, they'd soon drop out of hyperspace, and take up position a few lights out. Meanwhile he'd go dirtside. There he'd find the prince, signal his friends, and escape. Nice and simple. Sure, there were a few problems to iron out, like what if Cy hadn't delivered his message, or what if he couldn't figure out a way to signal Rico and Phil? But these were mere details, he told himself, in all other respects the plan was perfect. Then why was he so worried?

A few hours later McCade had been transferred to the freighter's shuttle, and was trying to cooperate as Candy ordered him to move this way and that. First she secured his nerve shackles. If he strained against them they'd deliver a powerful shock to his nervous system. Like most bounty hunters he'd used them on fugitives once or twice, so he knew what they could do, and had no desire to experience it himself. Especially since he wanted to go where they were taking him.

Once the nerve shackles were secure, Candy strapped him into the acceleration couch. As she double-checked his harness, she glanced forward to make sure the pilot and copilot weren't looking, and shoved a flat rectangle into the waistband of his pants. It felt cold against his back. "Cigars," she said gruffly. "Don't know why you insist on smoking the damned things. Go easy on 'em. You'll see why."

A few minutes later the pilot goosed the power, and nosed the shuttle down toward the surface of Worm. It was a smooth trip. After a flawless landing the copilot came back to release his harness, and lead him to the lock. She was young, badly in need of a bath, and amused by his condition. The inner and outer doors cycled open in turn, and McCade stepped out into hard yellow light. The heat hit him like a sledgehammer.

Seeing his reaction, the copilot grinned and said, "Welcome to Worm." Once the lock had closed behind them, she touched his nerve shackles with a small black wand, and they fell away. "Go ahead," she said. "You can run but you can't hide." Then she broke into peals of laughter as she strode off toward the distant complex. As he followed, McCade saw what she meant. Except for the shabby dome up ahead, the terrain was flat, only occasionally broken by spires of jagged rock. Heat waves shimmered in the distance, and he was already sweating like a pig. The copilot was right. You could run . . . but there was no place to hide.

A few more steps and he realized he was short of breath. Worm's atmosphere was low on oxygen. Plus, each step stirred up a small cloud of dust, and that made it even harder to get enough air. The copilot turned to hurry him up. Now he noticed the small canister she wore on the back of her belt, and the single tube leading up and over her left shoulder fed a nostril plug. No wonder she was so peppy. She was using supplemental oxygen. McCade offered her an ancient gesture which she returned with a smile.

By the time they reached the dome, McCade was out of breath, and very tired. The approach was littered with huge pieces of scrap metal, worn-out machinery, and other less identifiable junk. A well worn track wove its way between the larger obstacles and disappeared under a huge pair of sliding doors. Judging from the patterns they'd left behind, McCade guessed the vehicles were fairly large, and equipped with tracks. A smaller personnel entry whirred open at their approach, releasing a blast of cool air.

McCade followed the copilot inside, and heard the door close behind him. He saw sudden movement out of the corner of his eye, but moved way too late. A massive fist hit the side of his head and he fell like a rock. From his position on the ground, he decided someone was going to pay. And that meant getting up. Slowly, painfully, McCade made it to his knees and was about to stand when a huge boot kicked him in the side. The blow rolled him over so that he landed on his back.

He found himself looking up at one of the ugliest human beings he'd ever seen. Fire had twisted the man's features into a mass of ridged scar tissue. An intricate tattoo decorated his bald head, a gleaming ruby replaced his right eye, and his left ear sported an earring made of bone. At first McCade couldn't figure out why the bone looked so familiar, until he realized it was really three bones wired together, all of which had once been part of a human finger. A quick glance at the big man's hands confirmed an intuitive guess. The little finger on his left hand was missing. "Well, scum . . . what the hell are you staring at?"

Raising himself on one elbow, McCade shook his head tentatively to make sure it was still connected, and said, "Beats the hell out of me . . . but whatever it is . . . I like it."

The man threw back his head and roared out his laughter, then he reached down to offer McCade a hand. McCade took it, and was effortlessly jerked to his feet. The big man looked him up and down as though inspecting a side of beef. "Well, you've got balls—even if you won't be needin' 'em—and I like that. Name's Torb. Do what you're told and you'll live. Go against me and you're dead. It's as simple as that. Hey, Whitey, fresh meat . . . come'n get it." With that Torb put a massive arm around the copilot, and together they marched off toward a distant door.

Meanwhile a skinny man, with a shock of white hair, had appeared at McCade's side. In spite of his white hair he wasn't more than twenty-five. He had pale skin, pink eyes, and a very nasty smile. "Gotcha, Torb. Come on, meat, I haven't got all day." Whitey gave him a shove, and when McCade started to turn produced a nerve lash. "Come on, meat, you wanta taste of this?" For a long moment Whitey looked into hard gray eyes, and suddenly wished he was somewhere else. This was one of the crazy ones, the kind that didn't care, the kind that would take a nerve lash just to get their hands on you. "Move it." He did his best to sound hard, but even as the other man obeyed, Whitey knew he'd lost.

Now that he was inside the dome McCade found the air was cool and rich with oxygen. Overhead, the dome's armored plastic was so scratched from the abrasive action of wind and sand that it did little more than admit a hazy half light. Large crawlers were parked here and there in haphazard fashion, scarred flanks and worn tracks suggesting hard use, energy cannon hinting at hidden dangers. Except for the huge double doors somewhere behind him, the circumference of the dome was taken up by what he supposed were enclosed sleeping quarters, office space, and maintenance shops. As they walked along, McCade felt the box of cigars dig into his skin, and wondered why he hadn't been searched. They probably assumed there wouldn't be much point. He'd been a prisoner aboard the freighter, hadn't he? As he approached the far side of the dome, a door slid open to admit them, and then closed behind them, as they moved down a dimly lit hall. It ended in front of a lift tube. McCade looked at Whitey and lifted an eyebrow.

The guard threw him a metal disk on a plastic loop. "Put it around your neck if you wanta eat." McCade caught it and did as he was told. "Now, meat, into the tube." McCade obeyed, turning to see Whitey aim a remote control unit in his direction. The door whined shut on Whitey's nasty smile. "Sleep tight, meat. I'll see you in the morning."

There was a short drop before the doors hissed open. McCade stepped out into a huge underground cavern. Smoke filled the air, occasional lights cast deep shadows, and hundreds of men moved aimlessly this way and that, talking, gambling, or just killing time. The loud hum of their conversation suddenly stopped as the doors of the lift tube closed behind him.

"How many came with you?" The voice was strident, demanding. McCade scanned the faces nearby, searching for the one which went with the voice. With the exception of the occasional black or brown face, they were pale, like the grubs which inhabit the under surface of things, an army of zombies risen from the dead. Then he found two bright glowing eyes, which locked with his, and McCade knew he had the right man. His face was drawn and haggard, his clothes little more than rags.

"None," McCade replied. "I came alone."

"Shit." The other man turned away, and the hum of conversation returned to its previous level.

"We were hoping for more. The more men we've got, the easier it is to meet Torb's next quota." This voice came from slightly behind and to the right. McCade turned to find a wrinkled-up prune of a man, grinning a toothless smile. Bright little eyes regarded him with amusement. "They call me Spigot."

McCade accepted the little man's extended hand and found a grip as hard as durasteel. "Glad to meet you, Spigot, I'm Sam Lane." It seemed wise to stick with the name he'd arrived under. "How long have you been on this dirtball?"

Spigot's eyes seemed to go slightly out of focus as he thought back. "That's a tough one, Sam. It's hard to keep track . . . about twelve local years, I reckon . . . give or take one or two."

McCade nodded. "Then you're the man I'm looking for. I need someone who can give me the straight scoop, you know, who to look out for, how to avoid the worst work, that kind of stuff."

"You've been locked up before," Spigot observed slyly.

"A time or two," McCade agreed wryly. "But nothing like this." As he looked around he noticed a number of men eyeing him in a speculative fashion. They all wanted something. It might be his boots, his body, or just a new fund of dirty jokes, but each was a survivor, and saw McCade as something to be used.

"Let's find a place where we can sit and talk," McCade suggested.

Spigot grinned. "Make you nervous, do they? Sure, why not. But I'm no different. A man's gotta live, and what you want's worth something."

McCade felt the box of cigars pressing against his back. God bless Candy . . . properly used the cigars could make a big difference. "Damned right, Spigot, and pay I shall. How 'bout the next meal?" McCade saw no reason to let anyone know about his cigars until he'd found a good place to hide them. Otherwise they'd jump him the minute he fell asleep. Besides, he felt sure he could pass up one chance at whatever slop they were serving, without missing much.

Spigot pretended to consider McCade's proposal, finally nodding his agreement. "Normally I'd insist on two meals, but you seem a regular guy and there's no reason to take advantage."

McCade smiled. "Thanks, Spigot, I appreciate that."

He'd obviously overpaid. Nonetheless a little goodwill wouldn't hurt.

"Think nothing of it," Spigot said generously. "Follow me. I know a place where we can talk without those bone pickers staring at us." With that the little man moved off, his oversized rags swirling around his knobby knees, his feet moving among the litter of rocks with a sureness born of long experience.

As they wound their way between small clumps of men, McCade saw hard faces, and tough leathery bodies from which all but the essential juices had been evaporated out. These were the survivors. The ones who'd arrived with nothing, and still managed to live, not because they hoped to escape, but because they didn't know how to give up. Did one of those faces belong to Prince Alexander? Did he have the strength and the guts to survive in a place like this? McCade tried to find the face described on Joyo's print-out but failed. It was a big cavern. And life here could change the way a man looked. Finding the prince might take a while.

Now they'd left the open cavern far behind. Spigot led him around a rock pillar, and through a small opening in the rock, before climbing up and out of sight. McCade followed, and soon found himself sitting on a rock ledge overlooking the distant cavern, protected from observation by a low rock wall. "This is it," Spigot said proudly. "Home sweet home. I've never showed it to anyone else."

For some strange reason McCade believed him. A bundle of rags in one corner had the look of a crude bed, and a litter of empty meal paks and other junk testified to extended use. "Thanks, Spigot, I won't show it to anyone without asking you first."

Spigot nodded his approval. "OK, Sam, a deal's a deal. Shoot." As McCade asked questions, and the other man answered them, it quickly became apparent that Spigot liked to talk. Fortunately, he was pretty good at it, and had

something worthwhile to say. There was a good sharp brain
at work behind those bright eyes, and it had managed to
integrate twelve years of experience and observation into a
useful body of knowledge. So as Spigot talked, an overall
picture of life on Worm quickly emerged.

The planet itself had very little going for it. While it did
have some arable latitudes, these could not support Terran
crops due to the low levels of CO_2 in the atmosphere, and a
shortage of certain minerals. And while the planet did have
large deposits of iron ore, and certain other metals, these
were also available elsewhere closer in toward the heart of
the Empire. So all activity centered around the rockworms
which had given the planet its name. The rockworms were
huge, leathery gray tubes, averaging some thirty feet in
length, and six feet in diameter. As far as McCade could
gather they spent all their waking hours eating their way
through solid rock. Each had a circular mouth boasting
thousands of grinding teeth. The worms cut their way
through the rock by rotating their teeth back and forth in a
half circle. Then some sort of strong acidlike substance
secreted by glands in the worm's mouth went to work,
gradually turning the loosened rock into a thick jelly, which
they promptly ingested. From there the jelly went through
a series of five different stomachs, each serving to further
digest the rock, each responsible for leaching out certain
minerals.

The result was an incredible labyrinth of tunnels through
the solid bedrock which overlaid much of the planet. And
the way Spigot explained it, when the worms weren't eating, they were screwing, a life-style which he clearly en-
vied. The results of these amorous encounters were small
clutches of two or three eggs. These were deposited in
small rock alcoves created by the female worms. Then it
was the male's responsibility to fertilize the now-dormant
eggs, and seal them into the alcove with partially digested
rock. In due time the infant worms would hatch, eat their

way out, and the whole cycle would start over again. But every once in a while a clutch of eggs would escape fertilization. For years they would sit there, slowly crystallizing, their internal chemicals gradually recombining, changing consistency and color, until finally they became rock hard. Then careful cleaning in a series of chemical baths would reveal iridescent jewels, each different from every other, each invested with a brilliant fire deep in its center. Properly cleaned each would be worth a million credits or more. These were the fabulous Fire Eggs so sought after by the wealthy of many races. McCade had heard of them but never seen one.

But the worms didn't give up their unborn young easily. First you had to find them, and that meant venturing into their subterranean maze of endless tunnels, where your life expectancy was measured by your luck, and the amount of oxygen and power you had left. But even worse than the possibility of becoming lost, or dropping into the occasional vertical shafts created where tunnels crossed paths, were the worms themselves. It seemed the planet was calcium poor, and while the worms needed a certain amount of calcium to survive, it was very hard to come by. Which explained why the worms loved the rare, but calcium-rich limestone deposits that dotted the planet, and were equally fond of human bones. Where calcium was concerned, the worms had some very fine senses indeed, and the amount of calcium present in the human skeleton was sufficient to bring them galloping from miles away. "So," Spigot said succinctly, "the trick is to find their eggs without becoming a vitamin supplement."

McCade shifted position trying to find a more comfortable way to sit on the hard rock. Having a box of cigars shoved down his pants was damned uncomfortable. "Why not use robots?"

Spigot spat, the glob of spittle easily clearing the low

rock wall, to splatter somewhere below. "Cause we're cheaper. How much did they pay for you?"

McCade thought for a second, and said, "Outside of transportation . . . nothing."

"I rest my case," Spigot said with a grin.

"Still," McCade countered, "how do they make you work? Surely they can't send a guard along with each prisoner."

"Simple," Spigot replied. "There's a bonus for any man who finds an egg, extra food usually, and a penalty for the whole group if we don't make Torb's quota. And since we all want to stay alive, it works real well."

"OK," McCade said thoughtfully, "I've got the big picture. Now, how about people. Who's the top dog around here?"

Spigot eyed him sharply. "You don't miss much, Sam. I'll have to keep an eye on you. Well, topside Torb's the big cheese, but I suppose you already figured that out."

McCade rubbed the side of his jaw. It still hurt. "Yeah, he certainly has a way with words."

Spigot chuckled "That's Torb . . . he believes in making an impression on the new meat right away. Anyhow he's the boss, and under him there's a whole bunch of guards, nasty bastards most of them, though one or two are halfway human. Then there's our own pecking order to consider. Course it keeps changing as people buy the farm."

McCade nodded in sympathy. "Who's top man right now?"

"That'd be 'The Animal.' Of course that's just his nickname."

"Glad to hear it," McCade answered dryly. "I'd hate to think his parents named him that."

"Well, knowing him, it probably fit," Spigot replied with a shake of his head. "The Animal is not a nice man. But you'll find out soon enough. Just like Torb . . . he likes to make an impression on new meat."

"I can hardly wait," McCade answered dryly. "By the way, I haven't seen any women, what's the deal?"

Spigot looked wistful for a moment, and then shook his head sadly. "We had women up till about six years ago, but there wasn't enough, so Torb took 'em all away. Said there were too many fights."

Suddenly a klaxon went off, and Spigot stood up, all business. "Meal time," he said, and held out his hand. McCade removed the loop of plastic from around his neck and handed it over.

"Thanks," Spigot said. "I'll return it right after I eat. Be nice to feel full for once. Where shall we meet?"

"How about right here?" McCade asked. "If you don't mind."

"Nah, that's fine," Spigot answered as he started climbing down to the floor of the cavern. "Just don't let anyone see you coming or going. I like my privacy."

"You've got it," Sam promised, and followed the other man down. With a wave of a hand, Spigot disappeared into the maze of rock passageways which led back toward the open cavern. McCade waited a full five minutes, making sure the little man hadn't doubled back to spy on him, and climbed back up to the balcony. After a bit of exploration, he found a small dead-end tunnel, toward the rear of Spigot's living area, and a tiny niche high in its darkest corner. Removing the cigars from the waistband of his pants, he opened the box, withdrew a handful, closed the container, and slid it into the niche. As he retired to the balcony, he stuck one cigar in his mouth, and tucked the rest into an inner pocket. Selecting a comfortable seat, he puffed the self-igniting cigar into life, and took a long satisfying drag. There was plenty to think about.

Eleven

ONE LOOK AT the man in front of him, and McCade knew Animal's nickname fit like a glove. And not because of the way he looked. Animal was a lot better-looking than Torb. No, it was his eyes. They were hard black lumps of coal, dead things, empty of all feeling, set in a face of pallid white flesh. And he was tough. Not big, not muscular, just tough. It showed in the way he moved and held himself. McCade sighed. Animal held his position through physical force. That meant each new man had to be beaten into submission. And because he was a sadist, and enjoyed inflicting pain, no matter what McCade did or said, Animal would insist on a fight. So, it was a no-win situation. If McCade fought Animal and lost, he might be seriously injured, and if he won, he'd have a powerful enemy. Either way he was in trouble.

Six hours had passed since McCade's arrival. Spigot had returned from his double meal, belched a couple of times, and offered to take McCade on a tour of the cavern.

McCade had accepted, welcoming an opportunity to search for the prince among his fellow prisoners, and eager to learn the ropes. As they wandered through the cavern, McCade encouraged Spigot to introduce him to the men they ran into along the way, but none were Alexander.

So while McCade made no progress in his search for the prince, he found the cavern itself quite interesting. Thousands of years before, the huge subterranean vault had served as a sort of a natural terminal for the worms, providing them with a place to meet, and mate. At one time hundreds of their tunnels had branched off in all directions, but Torb and his guards had sealed the passageways with explosives, creating the perfect underground prison.

"Have the worms ever tried to tunnel in?" McCade asked.

Spigot looked surprised. The thought had never occurred to him. "Not that I ever heard of, Sam. Who knows, maybe they ate all the good rock way back then."

McCade nodded agreeably. "You're probably right, Spigot. Anyway, I'm glad they won't be interrupting our dinner." Thanks to Spigot's built-in timer, they had arrived in front of the lift tube just as the klaxon sounded and the next meal arrived. This, the little man explained, was breakfast. Not to be confused with the identical meal paks which were called dinner. Lunch didn't exist.

After breakfast they'd go to work. It would be dark outside in an hour or so, and it seemed the worms were less active at night, making it safer to enter the tunnels. It was a sensible policy, since it was always pitch-black in the worm tunnels anyway, and it did serve to reduce casualties. It didn't eliminate them entirely however, because there always seemed to be a few worms who liked to wander around at night. Anyway, no one wanted to eat in the tunnels, so "dinner" would be served when they returned from work. If they'd made the week's quota that is. Otherwise it was one meal a day. Eat, grab a few hours of sleep, and then do it all over again. It wasn't much of a career, although McCade imagined that it would beat hell out of working for Swanson-Pierce full-time.

So they got in line, displayed their disks to a bored guard, grabbed one of the identical meal paks, and headed for the open area where most of the men ate their meals. They were halfway there when Animal and two of his henchmen stepped into their path.

Although Animal directed his comments to Spigot, his dead eyes were on McCade. "So, Spigot, what's this piece of garbage you've been dragging around?" Spigot didn't answer. He just looked down and shuffled his feet.

McCade put down his meal pak and turned toward Animal. The facial tic which plagued him during moments of stress was twitching like crazy. He hoped Animal wouldn't notice it. "OK, you want to fight . . . so why don't we dispense with the preliminary bullshit and get on with it. Spigot, what's the penalty if I kill this sonovabitch?"

Spigot looked at him in openmouthed amazement, as did Animal's two toadies. Sensing entertainment, a crowd began to gather. Animal's eyes were unreadable, but a slight sheen of perspiration had appeared on his forehead. This wasn't the way things were supposed to work. He forced a grin. "That's big talk, meat, but talk's cheap. Try it."

McCade ignored him and turned to Spigot. "Well?" he demanded.

Spigot gulped, and said, "A day outside with no supplemental O_2."

McCade looked Animal up and down as though examining a new disease. He smiled. "It'll be worth it."

Over the years Animal had found that a sudden and unexpected attack often gave him the advantage. So, with a roar of self-induced rage, he charged straight at his opponent. Forcing himself to wait until the last second, McCade stood his ground. And then, when Animal was only inches away, McCade drove the six-inch piece of sharpened steel straight into Animal's heart. Animal jerked, gurgled, and then fell.

McCade wiped his slippery hands on his pants and picked up his meal pak. "Spigot, if you'd be so kind as to notify the guards of Animal's much deserved demise, I'd like to eat my dinner. I don't suppose there's much room service outside."

The crowd laughed, some stopping to slap him on the back, others shaking his hand, already ingratiating themselves with the new boss. Then they drifted away, talking excitedly among themselves. Who'd have thought someone could walk in and take Animal like that? What kind of taxes will he levy? Who is this guy anyway?

Meanwhile McCade pretended to eat his meal. But as soon as the crowd was gone, he stood and sauntered over toward the rocks surrounding the open latrine. Having made sure no one else was there, he promptly threw up. It was partly nervous reaction, and partly revulsion at what he'd done. He'd killed many times, but never so coldly, so calculatedly. The whole thing had gone exactly as planned.

First he'd pumped Spigot about Animal, then he'd verified the little man's observations with others, and finally he'd slipped away to buy the knife. Naturally Animal had lots of enemies, it showed in their eyes whenever his name was mentioned, and McCade had spotted one honing a handmade knife. He's spent half his cigars to get it. After that it was simply a matter of time. Animal wasn't all that bright and, being a creature of habit, used the same insults time after time to pick his fights, following up with his predictable charge. In a way the poor bastard had killed himself. McCade straightened up, wiped his mouth, and left the latrine. By the time he emerged he had a grin plastered on his face, and was pretending to zip his pants.

"I did like you told me, and they're waiting for you, Sam," Spigot said, nodding toward the lift tube.

"Thanks, Spigot," McCade replied. "You've been a big help. See you in . . . how many hours does it take this crud-ball to rotate anyway?"

"About twenty."

"OK, see you in twenty hours then." With that McCade walked over, and presented himself to Whitey. Taking no chances, the albino had armed himself with an ugly-look-ing riot gun, and his nasty smile made it clear he'd love an excuse to use it.

"So, meat, it didn't take you long to get your ass in trouble, did it? Well, get in, Torb wants to see you." McCade noticed that in spite of Whitey's tough talk, both he and the hulking neanderthal he'd brought with him kept their distance. Apparently anyone who could take out Ani-mal deserved a certain amount of respect. McCade grinned as he stepped into the tube.

"You know, Whitey, it doesn't seem possible, but I'd swear you're even uglier now than you were six hours ago. What is it . . . some sort of makeup?"

The neanderthal took a moment to process this, and then broke into deep grunting laughter. Whitey scowled at him and said, "Shut up, stupid. That goes for you too, meat. You're in enough trouble as it is."

McCade smiled, and they finished the ride in silence. When the door hissed open, Whitey motioned McCade out first. Together they marched across the center of the dome toward a door on the far side. Now it was dark outside and therefore cooler inside. When they reached the door Whi-tey gave a nod of approval, so McCade palmed it, and stepped through when it slid open.

He found himself in a surprisingly nice office. Though not fancy, it was clean and well furnished. Torb dominated the room. He was seated behind a large metal desk, his huge boots propped up on its bare surface. From what McCade could see he was surprisingly calm. Or at least that's the way it seemed, though with all that scar tissue it was hard to tell. Torb's ruby eye remained motionless, reflecting light, while his good eye looked McCade up and down. A full minute passed before he spoke.

"So, Animal's dead. Well, you certainly didn't waste any time." He paused reflectively, like a judge considering the merits of a difficult case. "On the one hand that really pisses me off, cause we're always short of meat, but on the other hand I kinda like it, cause that's the way I'd do it myself. My guess is you outsmarted him, which sure as hell didn't take much, and now you're king o' the heap." Suddenly Torb's single eye locked onto McCade like a tractor beam. "Well, that's just fine . . . but you'd better remember that it's my heap that you're king of . . . and when I say 'shit,' you'd better ask 'how high.' Do you hear me, meat?"

McCade nodded. "Loud and clear."

Torb nodded and seemed to relax a bit. "Good. You might be interested to know that the Animal and me had us a little understanding. He ran things down there, and I ran 'em up here. And between the two of us, we never let the meat get outta line. I ain't got time for riots and that kinda crap. So you run it the same way, and you can pick up where Animal left off. You know what this is?" Torb threw a rectangle of plastic on the top of his desk. McCade picked it up and looked at it.

"It's an account card drawn on Terra's Imperial Bank," McCade said, handing the card back.

Torb nodded approvingly. "That's right, meat. And there's about thirty thousand credits stashed in there that used to belong to Animal. You keep 'em in line and it's yours. Plus a tenth of one percent of what they find. That's how Animal made his. So whadaya say?"

"I'd say you can count on a very cooperative labor force," McCade answered with a grin.

Torb got up, came around to the other side of his desk, and brought his face within an inch of McCade's. Besides

being ugly he had very bad breath. McCade struggled not
to back away, and only barely succeeded. "Good," Torb
said. "Now I'm gonna have Whitey take you outside and
leave you for one rotation. And while you're out there . . .
suckin' what little air there is . . . sweatin' . . . and wishin'
to God you were dead, remember this: hit 'em, kick 'em,
but don't ever kill 'em. You got it?"

"I've got it," McCade answered, willing to agree to
anything that would put some distance between him and
Torb's breath.

"Take him away," Torb told Whitey, and minutes later
McCade was being marched out of the dome.

So when the big tracked carriers rumbled out into the
night, Spigot and all the rest crowded over to see where
McCade had been staked out. Whitey had an eye for the
dramatic, and had therefore chosen a slight rise, and even
rigged a battery-powered light to ensure a good view. Although his ankles and wrists were chained to deeply driven
stakes, McCade managed to wave one hand, and a cheer
went up from the carriers. For the moment he was their
hero.

As the crawlers disappeared over a rise, and the sound
of their engines slowly dwindled away to nothing, McCade
set to work testing his chains, and the stakes they were
connected to. They didn't budge an inch. But his efforts
used a lot of oxygen, and all of McCade's attention was
soon focused on the simple act of breathing, and the searing pain which went with it.

It took half an hour to get rid of the pain, and achieve
some sort of equilibrium. He found that by remaining absolutely motionless, and breathing slow deep breaths, he
could just barely take in enough oxygen. After that, it
wasn't too unpleasant. The night was cool, but not cold,
and he even managed a few short naps. Twice he was
awakened by a small animal that scurried over him, dash-
ing this way and that in search of food. And the crew woke

him a third time, as they returned from the tunnels, and yelled their encouragement.

Once again McCade waved a hand, and again they cheered, though less enthusiastically now that they were tired. And no matter how hard they tried to forget, many of them couldn't rid themselves of Samms' screams. Somehow a male worm had sensed him, and trapped him against a rockfall. The debris had completely blocked the tunnel, and Samms died trying to remove tons of fallen rock with his bare hands. Those working nearby tunnels had been forced to listen to his screams for a full five minutes. The worm had slowly ingested him, feet first, chewing carefully, savoring each milligram of calcium.

Not long after the crawlers had disappeared into the dome, Worm's sun poked its orange-yellow head over the far horizon, spearing McCade with its first rays. It was still cool at first, but as time passed he began to sweat, and before long trickles of precious moisture were vanishing into the dirt around him. One by one, the hours slowly dragged by, the sun doing its best to burn its way through the thin tissue of his eyelids, while he turned this way and that trying to escape. But there was no escape. Whichever way he turned the sun was there, anticipating his every move, trying to beat him into submission.

Eventually he began to slip in and out of consciousness. Pieces of his life seemed to come and go, an endless parade of old friends, enemies, and jumbled events. McCade allowed himself to drift with the flow, preferring it to reality, and hoping that when he came to, the torture would be over. Eventually he began to enjoy the visions, and became annoyed when a strange face appeared. It was a man's face, young and rather pleasant. But he'd never seen it before, and tried to get rid of it, preferring instead the jumbled flow of familiar people and places which had preceded it. But in spite of his efforts the face always came back. Cool green eyes regarded him with amusement, as though aware of his efforts, yet not offended by them.

Frustrated, McCade decided on direct confrontation. "OK, who the hell are you and what are you doing in my hallucinations? I don't remember meeting anyone like you."

The face smiled. "I'm the one they call Walker, and you're quite correct, we've never met."

"OK," McCade responded, doing his best to sound reasonable, "then why now? I'm kind of busy at the moment, and no offense, but you aren't as entertaining as some of my other hallucinations."

Walker laughed. "Sorry about that, but I thought that perhaps I could help, and besides, what makes you think I'm a hallucination?"

McCade considered that for a moment. It was hard to think without becoming conscious, and he wanted to avoid that at all costs. Perhaps if he humored this hallucination it would go away and be replaced by something more interesting, like naked women for example. McCade tried to grin. "Well, if you're not a hallucination, then you're damned stupid to be hanging around out here in the sun. Hey, if you want to help, how about some O_2 and water?"

Walker shook his head sadly. "Sorry, Sam, I wish I could, but that's not the kind of help I can offer."

"Terrific," McCade replied sarcastically. "So what kind of help *can* you offer?"

The other man grinned. "I thought you'd never ask. I can help you find the one you're looking for."

Suddenly McCade was completely conscious. The sun still seared his face, but now it was past its zenith, and already dipping toward the west. In a few hours it would set, and the torture would be over. McCade forced himself to look around. He saw nothing but hot emptiness. He felt strangely disappointed. Walker had seemed very real somehow, but apparently he was just another hallucination. Not that hallucinations were bad. In fact they beat the hell out of reality. He tried to slip into the half-conscious state he'd been in before, but found he couldn't.

So he just lay there, sweating out the minutes and hours until the sun finally set and twinkling stars filled the sky. As he watched them pop out one after another, he wondered if Rico and Phil were out there somewhere, drinking his booze, and breathing his nice clean oxygen. Silly question. Of course they were. The bastards.

By the time Whitey and the neanderthal came to release him, McCade was somehow floating above the pain and discomfort. It seemed as though he was a sponge which had absorbed all the pain and discomfort it could hold, and was therefore impervious to more. He even managed a grin and a croaked greeting. "Well, if it isn't Snow White and one of the seven dwarfs. It's amazing what crawls out at night."

Much to his amazement they didn't even hit him. They just looked at each other and shook their heads in amazement. First Whitey lifted his head and gave him a tiny sip of water. It was cold and tasted better than the finest wine. Then the neanderthal put a mask over his face, and his grateful lungs sucked in pure sweet oxygen. First it seemed to revive him, then it seemed to let him go, dropping him into a deep dreamless sleep.

"Wake up, Sam. Damnit, we gotta eat and go to work." Slowly McCade swam up out of comfortable darkness to feel a body which ached all over, and see a toothless grin which could only belong to Spigot. The little man waved a warm meal pak under his nose, and McCade felt an answering growl from his stomach.

Slowly he sat up, accepted the meal pak, and then leaned against a rock. He dimly remembered coming to, for short periods of time, someone holding water to his parched lips, and then more blissful sleep.

"Welcome back, boss," a voice said. "We missed ya." Now he saw there was a whole circle of faces beyond

Spigot's. There was general laughter and someone said,
"Let him eat. The poor bastard's about to meet the worms
... and they like 'em fat and sassy." There was more
laughter, and the crowd moved away.

McCade peeled the cover of the meal pak back, and dug
in. For once the bland stuff actually tasted good. Between
mouthfuls McCade said, "Thanks, Spigot, I owe you. How
long was I out?"

"A full rotation," the little man answered, "and that's all
Torb allows. That's why I had to wake you up."

McCade nodded. "And I certainly wouldn't want to dis-
appoint old Torb. Did you know that bastard and Animal
were working together to keep you guys in line?"

Spigot shrugged. "I didn't know, but it doesn't surprise
me. Did he offer you the same deal?"

McCade finished off the meal pak and threw it toward a
pile of empties. "Yup, one tenth of one percent of whatever
you guys find."

Spigot gave a low whistle. "You'd better keep that
under your hat, Sam, the guys wouldn't like it."

"I will for the moment," McCade agreed. "And then
we'll see what the future brings. Meanwhile, Spigot old
friend, an excellent meal like that calls for a good smoke.
Do you indulge?"

"I used to, Sam," Spigot said piously, "but my stay on
Worm has cured me of the nasty habit."

"Ah," McCade said understandingly. "Well, it happens
that I have a secret stash of cigars, and if you'd be so kind
as to go get one for me, I would be happy to help you
reinitiate the disgusting habit."

Spigot's eyes lit up. "Really? I swear I won't tell anyone where they are."

"And I believe you," McCade assured him. The little
man listened carefully as McCade explained where the
cigars were hidden, and then scurried away to get them. A
few minutes later he was back, cigars in hand. Together

they puffed the cigars into life, and then settled back to enjoy them. They were still smoking when the klaxon sounded again, and the men gathered in front of the lift tube.

There were quite a few envious looks as Spigot strutted importantly back and forth, emitting puffs of smoke like a runaway steam locomotive. But no one laughed when he got dizzy and almost fell down. Spigot was under McCade's protection, and therefore immune to the ribbing he'd once accepted as a matter of course. McCade didn't care for the dictatorial aspects of the situation, but he knew they were a natural outgrowth of the conditions the men lived under, and just might come in handy. So he did his best to play the part, waving his cigar expansively, and cracking jokes until the lift tube hissed open.

It took a number of trips for the lift to transport all of them to the surface. Once there, they stood in a sullen mob, each thinking about what lay ahead, each dealing with it in their own way. McCade did his best to scan their faces, and while there were a few possibles, none provided a perfect match with Alexander's latest looks.

Then the carriers coughed into life, and the guards herded them aboard. McCade crushed his cigar butt under a boot, and then followed the crowd as they moved up a ramp, and into one of the big tracked vehicles. Inside there were hard bench seats, one along each side, and one down the middle. McCade took a seat on the right side, and a moment later Spigot plopped down beside him. The little man had two five-gallon water containers with him. Each was equipped with a spigot and a cup on a string. "It's why they call me Spigot," the little man whispered cheerfully. "I bring the water. And that means I don't have to explore any tunnels by myself."

"Good thinking, Spigot," McCade said. And it was. Somehow he'd managed to stay alive for twelve years under appalling conditions.

McCade's thoughts were interrupted as two more prisoners appeared, each carrying a box. One passed out oxygen canisters with nostril plugs, while the other handed out headlamps. McCade watched the others as they hooked the oxygen canister to the back of their belts, and brought the small plastic hose up and over one shoulder. He did the same. "Don't turn on your O_2 till we're outside," Spigot advised. "You want all the margin you can get."

McCade nodded his agreement, and pulled the headlamp's elastic band down over his head. "Test it," Spigot suggested. "If the bastards forget to recharge one, you're shit out of luck."

McCade switched it on and off and found that it worked perfectly.

"Good," Spigot said approvingly. "Now whatever you do . . . don't lose it. There's a locater beacon built into the light. That way they can find you if you get lost or trapped by a rockfall."

"Now that's a cheerful thought," McCade said. "I notice the only way to get rid of the beacon is to throw away the light."

Spigot gave him a toothless grin. "You're catching on, Sam."

A few moments later, the vehicle jerked into motion, and headed outside. As the doors of the dome slid shut behind them, the men activated their oxygen canisters, and slipped in their nostril plugs. McCade did likewise. After a full rotation outside without it, the trickle of O_2 was quite comforting.

The crawler turned this way and that, following a twisted course between the huge spires of dark rock which punched their way up through the planet's skin. But they hadn't gone far when the vehicle suddenly slowed and came to a halt. The men all looked at the guard, but she pressed on her earplug for a second, and then shook her head. The ramp went down with a whine of hydraulics and then came right back up. A man came with it. McCade couldn't see what he looked like in the dim half light of the vehicle's interior, but whoever he was, he belonged somehow, because everyone greeted him as he moved down the aisle. Except the guards. They seemed to ignore him. So the man wasn't part of Torb's organization. Then why had they stopped for him?

McCade watched with interest as he felt the crawler jerk into motion, and the man continued to move up the aisle, stopping every now and then to talk with one of the men. Finally he dropped onto the center seat across from McCade, and a slash of light fell across his face. Their eyes made contact, and suddenly McCade found himself looking at a hallucination. The man smiled and stuck out his hand. "You remember me, I hope? The name's Walker. It's good to see you again, Sam."

Twelve

McCADE SHOOK WALKER'S extended hand. The other man had a firm grip, kind of surprising in a hallucination, but then McCade had very little experience in such matters. "And it's good to see you too," McCade said wryly, "or at least I assume it is. How do you do that?"

"What?" Walker asked innocently, his cool green eyes laughing merrily.

McCade looked around, wondering if his fellow prisoners were paying any attention to this somewhat bizarre conversation, but all the others were busy talking among themselves. "You know, appearing in someone's head like that. What is it, telepathy?"

Walker shook his head. "Nope. Physical bodies aren't everything, Sam. There's lots of other ways to get around." He gestured vaguely. "If you read Terran religious history you'll find all sorts of theories. Some of 'em are even true." He laughed.

"So you won't tell?"

Walker shrugged. "I can't. Not in the amount of time we've got anyway. But it's not magic, it's a skill, something you learn. Some people are better at that sort of stuff than others. I'm among the worst."

McCade lifted one eyebrow, and started to reply, but the crawler jerked to a halt and the guard said, "All right, worm meat, hit the ramp. This ain't no excursion bus." She ignored the prisoners' rude gestures, and motioned with her riot gun. The men obeyed.

As McCade stood, Walker said, "I'll catch up with you later."

"Terrific," McCade said dryly. "Be sure to bring your body."

"If you insist," Walker countered, and vanished into the crowd as the men surged forward and down the ramp.

As McCade emerged, he was almost blinded by the hot white glare from the powerful floodlights mounted on each crawler. Gradually his eyes began to adjust, and before long he could make out the other crawlers a short distance away, and the men which surrounded them.

A few hundred yards to the north, there was a low hill with an ominous-looking hole in its side. McCade didn't need a road map to know where they were going. The hole practically screamed, "I'm dangerous, don't come in here." So naturally that's where they'd have to go.

The land surrounding the hill faded off into soft darkness, interrupted here and there by rocky spires of denser black. After a brief moment of confusion, the guards herded the men into a single line, and then watched impassively as they shuffled by a large open box. "That's the tool line," Spigot said, appearing at his elbow. "Go ahead and I'll meet you at the other end."

McCade followed the little man's suggestion. The line moved quickly, and a few minutes later a bored-looking guard handed him a tool, before ordering him to move along. McCade examined it as he left the other end of the line. It was a durasteel rod, about two inches thick, and four feet long. One end was pointed for use as a pry bar, and the other was flattened out and bent at a right angle, kind of like a pickax. It had seen hard use and showed it. Which made sense, because you had to shift a lot of rock, and then break through the solidified goo the male worms used for a sealer, before you could get at the eggs. Or at least that's what he'd heard. Not something you'd want to do with your bare hands. He tried swinging the tool around. Not a bad weapon in a pinch, which explained why they were collected at the end of each shift. Torb didn't want the prisoners digging their way out of the dome's underground prison, or taking a swing at the guards.

"All right, meat, this ain't no damned picnic. Get you butts down there and find some eggs. Torb's offering five extra meal paks per egg, so keep your eyes open." The voice belonged to the same female guard who had been on the crawler. She wore her hair in a short crewcut, and her face was thin and bony. "If you don't," she cautioned, "you're all going on short rations. We're behind quota."

Her speech was met with mixed jeers and grumbling. One voice said, "Yeah? So what else is new?" Another said, "If you're so hot for worm eggs, then get your skinny ass down there and find 'em yourself." But in spite of their brave talk, no one wanted to charge the guard's riot gun, so slowly but surely they shuffled their way toward the dark mouth of the cave.

The path was quite worn, suggesting that they'd been coming here for quite some time. McCade wondered how long it took to exhaust a particular area. Or did the worms lay eggs so fast it didn't make any difference? But if that were true the eggs would be easier to find. Well, it made little difference to him. He was looking for something else, and making damn little progress. He'd spotted a couple of possibilities, but deep down in his gut he knew they weren't Alexander. No, so far his only lead was Walker.

The man was strange, but apparently quite real, and seemed to know all about McCade's mission. How and why? McCade swiveled his head right and left, but Walker was nowhere to be seen. He'd promised to catch up. How would he manage that down in the tunnels? But that thought, and all others vanished as they entered the dark opening in the hillside.

It was cold inside and McCade shivered. A slight breeze blew from somewhere up ahead, hinting at other openings, and bringing with it the smell of things long dead. McCade was one of the few who still hadn't turned on his headlamp. Now he did so, adding still another bobbing blob of light to the hundreds which already splashed the tunnel walls. Some of the men were grimly silent, others engaged in forced banter. "Sure hope we don't walk right up a worm's rear end," someone said. "Hell, you are a worm's rear end," another voice replied. "Nah, I've seen a worm's rear end, and it's better-lookin' than Frank is," a different voice said. There was general laughter which quickly died away as they entered a dimly lit open area. Countless tunnels branched off from all sides. The cavern apparently served the worms as a hub, much as the large subterranean vault under Torb's dome once had. Tilting his head back, McCade's light was quickly lost in the darkness above.

"All right, meat, listen up. I'm only gonna give it to you once." McCade recognized Whitey's voice right away. By standing on a small rock, he could see over the men in front of him, and sure enough there was Whitey, seated at some sort of makeshift console, peering into a portable terminal. The wash of light from the VDT gave Whitey's skin a sickly green appearance. The neanderthal, plus a mean-looking black man in worn leathers, stood to either side of him, their riot guns resting in the crook of their arms. "All right. Mendez, tunnel four. Riker, tunnel two. Mugabe, tunnel twenty..."

As Whitey read off their names and tunnel assignments,

the men reluctantly trudged off, presumably heading for their particular tunnels. McCade had no idea how they knew which tunnel was which. "McCade, tunnel thirty-four."

"Just follow me, Sam." It was Spigot. He had a water container in each hand but no tool. McCade followed, as Spigot wound his way around piles of fallen rock and pools of water, to the far side of the cavern. As they approached the dark mouth of a tunnel, McCade saw there was a small sign over the entrance, and sure enough, it read "34."

"They're numbered one through one hundred and forty-six, starting back where the entrance meets the cavern, and moving from left to right," Spigot explained.

He stepped into the tunnel, and motioned for McCade to follow. As McCade stepped inside, the walls seemed to close in on him, and suddenly he could feel the tons of rock pressing down on him. The passageway was barely six feet tall, and in places he had to stoop to pass. He knew it shouldn't bother him, after all he'd spent months at a time in some very small ships, but that was different somehow. Outside there had been the vast emptiness of space, not ton after ton of solid rock, and while that shouldn't make a difference, it did. Taking a deep breath, he forced the fear into the back of his mind, and followed Spigot's bobbing light.

Suddenly he slipped and almost fell down. Tilting his head forward to throw some light on the tunnel's floor he saw some sort of glistening substance. "Hey, Spigot, what's this stuff?" he asked, pointing down.

Spigot turned to see what McCade was referring to. "Worm slime," he answered matter-of-factly. "Some say they use it to lubricate their way through the tunnels." He smiled a toothless smile. "Others say it's how they shit. Personally I figure it don't make much difference."

McCade nodded at Spigot's obvious wisdom, and they moved farther into the stygian blackness. Every now and then, Spigot would stop to explain a fine point of egg

hunting, or tunnel survival. Once he pointed out a small
hollowed-out space just off the tunnel, and declared that a
prisoner named Hagiwara had found two prime eggs in it.
Scooping up what looked like crumbled rock, he held it out
for McCade's inspection. It had a slightly reddish hue.
"That's what you look for, Sam. It's what their sealer looks
like when it's all dried out. As you can see it's a different
color than most of this rock."

And about ten minutes later, Spigot stopped again, to
point out the side tunnel in which Samms had died.
McCade shuddered as Spigot described Samms' death,
how the worm had taken him feet first, and how he'd
screamed forever.

"But," Spigot added cheerfully, "don't let it worry you,
Sam. It actually improves your odds some. I can't remember the last time we lost two in a row in the same
tunnel. Anyway, this is where I leave you. Gotta make my
rounds. It's all virgin territory from here out. Keep an eye
out for color changes in the rock and watch for worms.
There's a buzzer built into your headlamp. When you hear
it, head back." And with that the little man was gone.

The next four hours were very strange. McCade had
decided to approach the situation systematically. For the
first four hours he would examine the right wall, and then
he'd turn around, and spend the next four hours on the left
wall. That should put him back at his starting point with
only an hour or so left to kill. As he moved cautiously
down the tunnel, there was an eerie silence, broken only by
the sound of his own footsteps and the occasional dripping
of water. Every now and then, he came to intersections
where other worm tunnels crossed his, or passageways had
been carved out of solid rock by a thousand years of running water. He ignored them. One tunnel was plenty, without adding the additional hazards of more. More than once
he slipped in the worm slime, and almost fell. Twice, he
spotted reddish places in the tunnel wall, and attacked them

with his tool. But all he found was solid rock. Apparently there was some reddish rock around. Finally, after what seemed like an eternity of darkness, the four hours were up. He had just turned around, and started back up the tunnel, when he heard someone call his name and saw a distant light. It bobbed closer and closer, until it was only feet away, casting long shadows down across Walker's face. He smiled.

"We've got to stop meeting like this."

McCade laughed in spite of himself. Then he said, "I suppose you used some more of whatever it is you do to find me."

Walker grinned and shook his head. "Nope. It seemed a lot simpler just to peek in Whitey's holo tank. There you were, checking out tunnel number thirty four, just like an old pro. Whitey was very impressed."

Of course. McCade wondered why he hadn't thought of it earlier. They'd be able to track all the prisoners via the beacons built into their headlamps. That way if someone decided to take a nap, or tried to take off, they'd know about it. Although there'd be damn little chance of that, since anyone who tried to escape would run out of oxygen a few hours later.

Walker looked around, selected a likely looking boulder, and sat down. He reached into an inner pocket and pulled something out. He handed it to McCade as he said, "I understand you like these things, so here's a little present."

As McCade accepted it he saw it was a cigar. "It may be a bit stale," Walker said apologetically. "I don't smoke. My predecessor did though, and left it behind."

McCade thanked him, and eyed the other man thoughtfully as he puffed the cigar into life and took a seat opposite Walker. "Your predecessor?"

"Yes," Walker answered. "We keep a one-man station on Worm. That's how we found out about the prince."

McCade felt his pulse quicken as he blew out a thin stream of gray smoke. Maybe he was about to get somewhere. "No offense, but it would really help if you could start at the beginning. First of all, who's *we?*"

Walker looked surprised. "You mean you don't know? I'm sorry, I guess I just assumed you did. I'm a Walker of The Way. That's why they call me Walker. Have you ever heard of us?"

McCade shook his head.

"Well, that's not too surprising," Walker said. "We avoid publicity. Simply stated we're a loosely knit group of sentients who follow The Way."

"It's a religion then," McCade suggested.

"No, not in the conventional sense," Walker replied. "For example, The Way isn't written down anywhere, it's discovered through the process of living and therefore accessible to all. We have no rites, no layers of priesthood to separate us from the truth, and we don't attempt to proselytize. In fact, we don't interfere with those around us unless asked, and even then there are severe limits on what we can do. That's why Torb and his guards tolerate me. Besides, I suspect he thinks I'm a useful figure, sort of a priest, or father confessor figure for the men. Frankly, I've encouraged them to view me that way . . . even though our organization doesn't have priests."

McCade shrugged. "Sounds good to me . . . although I've got enough problems in the here and now, without worrying about the hereafter. You said you maintain a station on Worm? Whatever for? Especially if you're not trying to convert the prisoners."

Walker smiled. "There was a need. I told you earlier that others have abilities far beyond my own. Well, some of them can read what they call the flux, which is simply the ebb and flow of cause and effect. I won't attempt to describe how they do it, because I don't understand it myself, but basically it amounts to a heightened form of meditation. Somehow they momentarily step out of their bodies and can see the complex patterns and relationships which flow out of all that we do. By studying these patterns they can predict trends and probabilities as to what may come. And sometimes, not often, but sometimes, we can use that knowledge for the greater good."

McCade tapped the ash off his cigar, and resisted the temptation to ask how they knew what the "greater good" was. Historically mankind had used religion, and the concept of "the greater good," to perform unspeakable acts of cruelty and barbarism on each other, usually because their leaders got their own personal "good" all mixed up with everyone else's.

Unaware of McCade's skepticism, Walker continued to speak. "Many years ago, one such read the flux, and discovered that Worm would eventually become a significant place in human events. So a call went out for volunteers to sit on Worm and wait. Each had the same orders. 'Watch, wait, help to whatever extent you can, but do nothing to change the status quo.'" Walker smiled. "That last order was necessary, for slavery offends all of us, and the temptation to interfere had been very strong. But to do so would change the flux, and that might erase our chance to accomplish an even greater good, so we have obeyed. And it's good that we did, because during my predecessor's stay the prince arrived, and suddenly we understood. Eventually the emperor would die, and if Alexander was allowed to die on Worm, his sister would inherit the throne. And given her beliefs, Claudia might start a war which could swallow all sentient life in this part of the universe."

There was silence for a moment, and then McCade cleared his throat. "How did your predecessor know Alexander's true identity? He didn't announce it, did he?"

Walker laughed. "No, he didn't. He arrived calling

himself Idono H. Farigo, like 'I don't know how far I go.' Get it?"

"Yeah, I've got it," McCade acknowledged dryly. "The prince is a thousand laughs. Then I suppose he did his 'I'm just one of the guys routine.'"

Walker shrugged philosophically. "Alexander was determined to live through the experience without recourse to either his father's power or position. But his actions quickly separated him from the rest—just as yours did—and my predecessor gradually learned the truth."

"Well," McCade said, watching his cigar smoke curl up through the light of Walker's lamp, "if it's any comfort, Naval Intelligence agrees with the conclusions of your flux readers. But since Naval Intelligence is usually wrong, that doesn't mean much. Nonetheless, just to be on the safe side, we might as well grab the prince and get out of here."

Walker only smiled.

McCade said, "Uh-oh, I've got a feeling I'm not going to like this."

Walker looked at him sympathetically. "The prince has been gone for some time I'm afraid."

McCade groaned. "Then why are you still here?"

"That's simple," Walker responded earnestly. "I've been waiting for you."

"Come on," McCade insisted. "I'll give you people credit for predicting something important would happen here on Worm, your presence seems to prove it, but there's no way you could've known I was coming."

Walker smiled patiently. "Not *you* personally. I was waiting for someone *like* you. No offense, but if it wasn't you it would've been someone else. Just as the flux predicted Alexander's coming, it also foretold your arrival. That's how I know the Emperor is dead. Only his death would force those who oppose Claudia to find out if the prince is still alive, and if he is, to place him on the throne.

You were picked for the mission, and the trail led you here."

The way Walker put it, everything sounded so simple, and lacking any other way to explain the man's presence and knowledge, McCade was forced to believe him. At least until a better explanation came along.

"So where is he?" McCade asked.

"On a planet called the Wind World," Walker replied. "My organization has a monastery there. Alexander spent a great deal of time talking with my predecessor and, after a good deal of soul searching, asked permission to go there and study. His request was approved."

McCade dropped his cigar into some worm slime where it hissed and went out. "Aren't you leaving something out? Like how Alexander managed to get off this pus ball?"

Walker grinned. "That was quite simple actually. One day Alexander went into the tunnels and was eaten by a worm. He's a bit of a ham, you know, and his screams sounded quite realistic. Afterward they found only his headlamp and one boot. Very touching, and very convincing, since no one willingly parts with their headlamp."

"And then you got him off-planet," McCade finished. "Very slick. And that brings us to the present. Are you willing to give me some help as well?"

Walker's light bobbed up and down. "That's why I'm here. Now that his father's dead, it's imperative that you reach Alexander and convince him to accept the throne."

McCade frowned. "Why me? He obviously respects you and your organization. Why not convince him yourselves?"

Walker shrugged and spread his hands. "We cannot interfere without risking negative changes in the flux. Besides, our role is to facilitate, not control. And while his father lived, there was no reason to force the issue. Now we can only hope that when you tell him of his father's death, he will see the need to assume the throne, and do so

of his own free will. But the decision is his. We will not try
to force him."

"Terrific," McCade responded sourly. "Thanks a lot.
Well, let's get on with it. Have you got a radio?"

"A good one," Walker replied, "though I have to be
careful how often I use it. Torb's under the impression that
I rely on his."

"Good," McCade said. "I've got some friends and a
ship just off-planet. At least I hope I do. If you'll call them
they'll come and pick me up. First, however, we'll have to
stage my death like you did Alexander's."

Walker agreed, producing a stylus and a small notebook
into which he wrote the frequency and code words which
would allow him to contact Rico and Phil on *Pegasus*.

"Just let me know a time and where to meet," McCade
added.

"No problem," Walker said, getting to his feet. "I'll try
to set it up for tomorrow or the next day. Meanwhile you'd
better start working your way back, before Whitey decides
you're taking a nap."

McCade stood, and the two men shook hands. "See you
soon," Walker promised, and hurried up the tunnel.
McCade watched until his bobbing light disappeared
around a gradual curve.

With almost half the shift still left to go, McCade took
his time working his way back up the tunnel, swearing
when he lost his footing on the slippery floor, and watching
the wall for color changes. But he felt good knowing that
Alexander was still alive, and apparently living like a
monk on some backward planet. It was just his style. Gam-
bler, slave, and now a reclusive mystic. The guy never
quit.

If he hadn't been thinking about Alexander, McCade
might have noticed a liquid grinding noise, or felt a slight
vibration in the surrounding rock, but he didn't. Therefore

it scared the hell out of him when solid rock parted with a loud crack, and the right side of the tunnel caved in. As the hole appeared, it was filled with an obscene bulge of glistening gray flesh, and McCade felt a lead weight drop into the pit of his stomach.

Thirteen

MORE AND MORE rock continued to fall, and McCade knew if he didn't move soon, he'd be trapped. Fortunately this section of the tunnel was larger than most, so the initial cave-in had failed to completely block it. He eyed the narrowing gap between the top of the rockfall and the ceiling. If he was fast enough, he just might make it. Forcing himself to ignore the loop of slimy gray flesh which now protruded out into the tunnel, he backed off a few feet, and then ran full tilt toward the pile of rocks. A series of quick leaps carried him to the top, and a shallow dive took him through the small opening. He fell head over heels down the other side, hitting and bouncing off a variety of rocks, before finally coming to rest at the bottom. With a roar of falling rock, the rest of the ceiling caved in, and the small opening disappeared.

His right knee hurt like hell, and he didn't feel like getting up, but the large rocks which continued to roll down and crash around him suggested that he should. Besides, at any moment the worm might decide to join him. Forcing himself to his feet, he limped up the tunnel, trying to put as much distance between himself and the worm as possible. After about fifty feet or so, he was suddenly short of breath, and noticed that his oxygen hose had pulled loosed from his nostril plug. As he stopped to fix it, he glanced back over his shoulder, half expecting to see the worm in hot pursuit. It wasn't. Maybe the rockfall had slowed it down, if so, good. Apparently the blasted thing had been busy creating another tunnel parallel to his own, when the thin rock wall separating the two tunnels had collapsed, causing the roof to cave-in as well.

By the time he emerged from tunnel thirty-four, McCade's right knee felt better, and his limp was almost gone. Making his way between the large rocks which littered the floor of the cavern, McCade caught occasional glimpses of the guards gathered around the makeshift console. When he got there, they would probably chew him out, and send him into another tunnel. After all, there were more than two hours left in the shift. But what the hell, maybe he could talk Whitey into giving him a break. It was worth a try. Either way, he'd soon be off Worm, and having a good meal aboard his own ship. Assuming of course that Phil and Rico had left anything edible in the galley. In the meantime he would do his best to take it easy, and avoid worms.

McCade put on his best hangdog expression as he approached the guards, and prepared to tell them a somewhat exaggerated version of his encounter with the worm. But much to McCade's surprise, all three ignored him in favor of Whitey's VDT. They glanced his way, but continued to talk excitedly among themselves, even allowing him to walk up and peek over their shoulders. Apparently his position as unofficial enforcer granted him a certain amount of privilege.

"Looks like the little creep's luck finally ran out," the

black man said cheerfully. "I'll bet you ten Imperials he doesn't last another ten minutes."

The neanderthal grunted his agreement.

McCade saw that the object of their discussion was a flashing green dot in tunnel seventeen. Whitey was tracing its progress with an electronic arrow. Strangely enough the dot seemed to be moving down tunnel away from the safety of the cavern.

"You're on, sucker," Whitey sneered, without taking his eyes off the screen. "Ten Imperials it is. Spigot's got a lot of tunnel savvy so I say he's good for twenty minutes easy. See . . . I figure the worm's right here"—Whitey pointed the red arrow at a spot just behind the green dot—"and Spigot's trying for this side passage down here." He pointed to a small tunnel which branched off from the larger one. "In fact, he might even loop in behind the worm and get clean away. How 'bout a side bet?"

But the black man didn't reply, because McCade chose that particular moment to crush his skull with a large rock. As the riot gun fell from the guard's lifeless fingers, McCade caught it and brought it to bear on the neanderthal. It pays to take out the worst of the opposition first. The big man wasn't too bright, but his reactions were just fine, and as his partner fell the neanderthal was already spinning in McCade's direction. But he was too late. His huge torso jerked three times, and fell over backward as McCade squeezed the trigger, and felt the heavy weapon buck in his hands. The sound was still echoing off the cavern walls as Whitey clawed for his sidearm with one hand, and tried to stop the slugs with the other. It didn't work. The automatic shotgun roared twice, taking his hand off at the wrist, and erasing his face. His body toppled sideways out of his chair and crashed to the ground.

"If it's any comfort, Whitey, you look better this way," McCade said as he rolled the corpse over and undid the gunbelt which circled its waist. McCade was strapping

Whitey's gun on, when three other prisoners ran up.

"Shit, boss, you don't mess around," a short blocky man called Fesker said. "God, look at that, he took all three of 'em."

"I'm glad you men showed up," McCade said. "I could use a little help. Are you with me?"

"You bet we are, boss," Fesker said, picking up a riot gun. "Right, Mendez? Right, Hawkins?"

"Count me in," Mendez agreed calmly, kneeling to strip off the neanderthal's gunbelt.

Hawkins just nodded solemnly, and ran his hand lovingly along the length of the second riot gun. He had even features, bright blue eyes and long brown hair, which hung down his back in two braids.

"All right," McCade said. "Now listen carefully . . . and do this exactly the way I tell you to. As the men come out of the tunnels, hold them right here. Whatever you do, don't let them leave the cavern. Otherwise the guards on the crawlers will know something's fishy, and mow you down before you even get close. The time to take them is at the end of the shift, when they expect us to come out."

"Right, boss," Fesker agreed enthusiastically. "It'll be just the way you said."

"Good," McCade replied. "How about radio? Do you know if Whitey had some way to communicate with the crawlers?"

Fesker shook his head. "Naw, the rock's too thick."

"Excellent," McCade replied. "At least there's one problem we don't have to worry about. Now, Hawkins, give me a hand with one of these bodies. Spigot's in a tight spot, but there's a chance we can pull him out." McCade bent over, struggled to get a hold on Whitey's body, and only barely managed to pick it up. It was damned heavy. Doing his best to ignore the nature of his burden, McCade headed for tunnel seventeen.

Hawkins slung the riot gun across his back, eyeing first

the black man, and then the massive form of the neander-thal. He quickly chose the black man. With one smooth motion, he lifted the corpse, and threw it over his right shoulder. Then, carefully picking his way through the rocks, Hawkins hurried to catch up.

As he entered the tunnel, McCade had only the vaguest of plans. But if Spigot was as elusive as Whitey gave him credit for, it might even work. Even so, speed was of the esssence. It wasn't easy to jog with a dead body in his arms, so McCade was forced to stop, and sling it over one shoulder as Hawkins had. Having done so, he made much better time.

Finally he saw it, a narrow slitlike crevice in the rock, cut by running water rather than worms. The opening was a tight fit, but he forced his way through it, with Hawkins right behind him. They couldn't run in the narrow passage-way, but they still made fairly good time, splashing through the shallow water until suddenly a rock wall barred their way. At the base of it there was a small hole through which the water gushed into the open space beyond. They could make it, but they'd have to lay down in the water to do so, and there was no guarantee as to what they'd find on the other side.

McCade dumped Whitey's body into the water. "You first," he said, pushing the guard's body down, and into the hole. It was quickly sucked out of sight. McCade motioned to Hawkins. "Your friend's next."

Hawkins grinned, and followed McCade's example.

As soon as the other body had disappeared, McCade gave Hawkins what he hoped was a confident smile as he lay down in the water, and shot through the hole feet first. First he felt bitter cold as the water hit his skin, and then pure terror, as the current grabbed him and pulled him through the opening. Suddenly he was falling, wondering if this was how he would die, and then he hit, plunging deep under the surface of the water. Kicking upward, he wondered why everything was black, and then realized his eyes were closed. He opened them to crystal-clear water, his headlamp shining up toward the surface, bubbles dancing in and out of the light. Then he was through the surface, splashing water against a rock wall, and gulping down air. He cursed himself for never wondering if the light was waterproof, and gave thanks that it was.

He heard a tremendous splash behind him, jerked around, almost laughing when he realized it was just Hawkins, shooting through the opening and into the pool. Turning his head McCade's light fell across a steeply shelving beach. He gave a kick and stroked toward it, almost screaming when he hit something soft, and Whitey's faceless corpse popped up in front of him. Forcing himself to push it in front of him, he heard Hawkins surface, coughing up water.

"Over here!" McCade shouted, and splashed the water to attract the other man's attention.

Hawkins coughed in reply, and began swimming toward the beach.

McCade felt his feet touch bottom, scooped up Whitey's body, and stumbled up and out of the water. Suddenly he froze. What the hell was that? Some sort of a noise. Then he heard it again and saw a flash of light over to his right.

"Take that, you big turd. I hope you choke on me and die." It was Spigot!

"He's somewhere to the right!" McCade yelled, lunging toward the flashing light. After a few steps, he came to a place where the wall opened to the main tunnel, and there was Spigot, one leg twisted awkwardly under his body, his headlamp swinging wildly this way and that, as he threw both rocks and insults at the worm.

The worm was by far the ugliest thing McCade had ever seen and, considering its size, moved with surprising speed. It made a sort of sloshing sound as it surged forward, its circular pink maw opening to reveal thousands of black teeth. As it moved, it belched out waves of rotten acidic breath. McCade felt the hair on the back of his neck stand on end. A primitive part of him started to gibber and scream deep in the back of his mind. He pushed it down and pretended not to hear it. Twenty-five more feet and the worm would have Spigot.

Hawkins appeared at his side, riot gun at the ready, reminding McCade of the task at hand. Apparently the other guard's body was still somewhere in the pool. "Well, I guess it's up to you, Whitey," he said to the corpse. Turning to Hawkins he said, "Grab Spigot, and get him out of there!"

Seconds later, Hawkins was dragging a surprised Spigot back away from the oncoming worm. Meanwhile, McCade forced himself to move toward the undulating monster. When he was about ten feet away, he dumped Whitey's corpse unceremoniously on the ground, and quickly backed up. As he did so, McCade drew Whitey's handgun, and Hawkins pumped a round into the chamber of his riot gun. For the first time since they'd met Hawkins spoke, *"Bon Appétit,* you sonovabitch." Spigot cackled gleefully from his position on the ground.

Then all three watched in horrified fascination as the Worm reached Whitey's body, delicately sucked the corpse into its mouth, and began to chew. The sound of Whitey's bones being ground into a fine paste sent chills up McCade's spine. but at least they'd bought some time, now all he had to do was find a way to use it.

"So far so good," McCade observed, turning to the others. "Now if there's only some way to get past the damned thing."

"This is no time to kid around, Sam," Spigot said. "The minute that thing's done with Whitey, it'll come for us. Let's leave the same way you came in."

"I'd like to, Spigot, but I'm afraid that's out." McCade

quickly described the passageway, the fall into the pool, and their subsequent arrival.

Much to McCade's surprise, Spigot laughed. "That's a new one on me, Sam. No wonder you're wet. I assumed you came through the side passage, that hits the main tunnel about twenty yards behind us. That's where I was headed when I slipped in the slime and broke my leg."

McCade looked at Hawkins, and they both laughed. "All right, Spigot," McCade said. "Let's get out of here." Carrying Spigot between them, McCade and Hawkins made their way down the tunnel. They went about twenty yards, and sure enough, there was the passageway, right where Spigot said it would be. It took a good twenty minutes of hard work to carry the little man through the passageway and out of the tunnel. As they emerged, McCade wasn't ready for the crowd of men, or their applause. The shift was about to end, and true to his word, Fesker had held all the men inside the cavern. He and Mendez were standing at the front of the crowd, having appointed themselves as McCade's assistants.

Turning to the crowd Fesker yelled, "There he is, men, he just snatched Spigot from a worm, and now he's gonna kick Torb's ass, are you with him?"

As the crowd roared their approval, Spigot grinned, and waved, as though they were cheering him. Suddenly McCade realized that things had gotten out of hand. What started as an effort to help a friend had somehow turned into a full-scale revolt. The men expected him to lead them against Torb, and having killed three guards, McCade realized he didn't have much choice.

As the crowd calmed down, two men took Spigot aside, and applied some rough and ready first aid. There wasn't much time, so McCade jumped up on a rock and motioned for silence. "Thank you, men. Now listen carefully, because if we don't do this right, the guards are going to cut us up into very small pieces." For the next few minutes

McCade outlined his plan, assigned responsibilities, and answered questions. Then it was time to move.

McCade nodded. "All right then . . . let's do it." There was a sense of subdued excitement, as the men walked out of the cavern, and into the early dawn light. They were different somehow, backs straight, heads erect, they no longer moved like slaves. McCade worried that the distant guards would notice the difference. If they did, the whole thing could turn into a terrible slaughter. They had to get close enough to take over the crawlers. Once they accomplished that, they'd have powerful weapons, plus a way to crack the dome itself. The chances were good that Torb would receive some sort of warning, and unless they had the means to break in, he could lock them outside the dome until they simply ran out of oxygen.

But his fears were groundless, because as they approached the crawlers, the guards regarded them with the same bored disdain they always did. McCade, Fesker, Hawkins, and Mendez were each leading a contingent of men toward one of the four crawlers. They had the only weapons, so it would be up to them to neutralize the guards, and McCade knew that even with surprise on their side, it wouldn't be easy. The guards were tough, and many were professional killers.

As the men lined up to throw their tools in an open box, McCade was watching both of his guards. The driver was sitting on the bow of the crawler, completely oblivious to his surroundings, reading a skin mag. The other guard was the same woman they'd had on the way out, and one glance told McCade she was suspicious. Her features were locked into a rigid frown, and her glittering eyes scanned the crowd, searching for something to confirm the feeling in her gut. She knew something was wrong . . . she just couldn't figure out what it was. Then McCade saw her eyes widen as she realized that Whitey and the other two guards were nowhere in sight. Her lips moved, and her hand dived for her sidearm, but the only sound was the roar of McCade's gun. The heavy slug hit her in the left thigh, and she went down hard, the gun spinning from her hand to land in the dirt. The driver was fast. He was up and scrambling toward the weapon turret so quickly that McCade fired three times before a slug finally caught him and threw him off the far side of the crawler.

McCade pointed at three of the nearest men. "You . . . you . . . and you. Get the men aboard and secure this rig. Find somebody who knows how to run it. And not some bozo either . . . our lives are going to depend on him in a few minutes. And get that guard some first aid. Watch her though, she's down, but she isn't out. Got it?" They nodded and scrambled off to obey his orders.

Suddenly Fesker appeared at his side. "Trouble, boss. We got two of em, but the guards on the fourth killed Mendez, and managed to button it up."

As if to punctuate Fesker's words, there was the whine of a starter, followed by a stuttering roar as the last machine in line started up, and then jerked into motion. "Hit the dirt!" McCade shouted, and promptly followed his own advice.

Incandescent pulses of blue light flashed and rippled toward them, slagging everything they touched, as the crawler gradually built up speed and rumbled away. Men ran screaming in every direction as the turret-mounted energy cannon cut them down in swathes. But suddenly two of the captured machines began to return fire, scoring at least one clean hit, before the escaping crawler disappeared around a spire of rock. "Damn," Fesker said as he got to his feet. "Sorry, boss."

McCade did likewise and shrugged. "Couldn't be helped. We were lucky it wasn't worse. Well, let's see to the wounded, and get organized. There's no reason to give Torb any more time than we have to."

An hour later they'd done what they could for the

wounded, passed out what weapons there were, and assigned the most experienced drivers and gunners to the
three remaining crawlers. As they neared the dome,
McCade was worried. They had an hour, two at the most,
before they ran out of oxygen. Torb knew that, and therefore knew exactly how long he had to hold out to win the
battle. An advantage to say the least.

McCade ran a critical eye over the outside of the dome
and didn't like what he saw. First, the base of the dome
was made out of durasteel reinforced permacrete; second,
the bubble was constructed of forty ply armaplast; and
third, the damned thing had four weapons emplacements,
one for each point of the compass. Bad—but not hopeless.
By the look of them, the multibarreled energy weapons
were intended for anti-aircraft use, and not for defense
against a ground attack. Since he had Worm to himself,
Torb had assumed that an attack would come from space.
McCade grinned as he remembered what they'd taught him
at the Academy. The first rule of warfare is, don't assume
anything. Spread out the way they were, McCade figured
he could neutralize two of the gun emplacements by attacking just one side of the dome. While that would leave
only two emplacements to deal with, they would be able to
support each other, and place his forces in a cross fire.

The only other thing going for him was Torb's sloppy
housekeeping. The junkyard of rusting metal surrounding
the dome would provide his crawlers with some cover. Lacking heavy weapons, or specialized explosives, he figured the
main door was his best bet. It should be the weakest point in
the dome's structure. For a moment he considered calling for
Torb's surrender, but quickly rejected the idea as a waste of
time. Torb had both time and oxygen to burn. He'd never
surrender in a situation like that.

McCade picked up the mic and keyed it open. He
smiled as he imagined Torb listening inside the dome. "All
right, men, let's do it by the numbers. Remember the sig-

nals we agreed on, remember your individual missions, and remember what an asshole Torb is. All right, let's go!"

As his crawlers jerked into sudden motion, McCade grabbed the twin grips of his energy cannon, and waited for the range to close. His job was to engage the left weapons emplacement. Meanwhile the second crawler would attack the door, and the third would tackle the right weapons emplacement. His head hit the side of the turret, as his driver made a hard right, and then a left, starting the evasive maneuvers they'd agreed upon. Ignoring the pain McCade concentrated on his target. Meanwhile the range was closing . . . closing . . . closing. At the precise moment when McCade squeezed his triggers, pulses of blue light also stuttered out from the weapons emplacements, trying to lock onto the swerving crawlers and destroy them.

As far as McCade could tell, both emplacements were firing independently of each other. Good. Tied together under computer control, Torb's weapons would be even more lethal.

Meanwhile, the third crawler, with Hawkins in command, had taken refuge behind a pile of rusty plating, and was doing battle with the right emplacement, while Fesker led crawler two against the doors. The metal was already glowing cherry-red under the determined assault of his energy weapon, but his machine was terribly exposed, and would soon draw fire from both emplacements. McCade doubled his efforts to hit the left emplacement, swearing when it suddenly ignored him, and went for Fesker. Seconds later the other emplacement did likewise. Torb was finally exercising some fire control.

As he glanced from one emplacement to the other, something kept bothering McCade, but he couldn't figure out what. Then he had it. Torb's forces couldn't depress their weapons any farther than they already were! Because they were intended for anti-aircraft use, their mounts limited how far down the barrels could be depressed. So, if Fesker moved in even closer, they wouldn't be able to hit him.

McCade keyed his mic on, and brought it up to his lips, just as Fesker's crawler took a combined hit. Flames poured out of the engine compartment as the driver spun the big machine around and ran for the shelter of a junked fuel tank. McCade and Hawkins provided covering fire as men poured out of damaged machine and ran for cover. Most had escaped by the time the crawler blew up a few seconds later.

Then, much to McCade's surprise, both weapons emplacements fell suddenly silent, and Torb's voice crackled over his radio. "Sam Lane, you out there?"

McCade keyed his mic open. "I'm here, Torb, what's for lunch? We thought we'd join you."

"You can't win, Lane," Torb said reasonably, "you're running out of oxygen . . . and there's no way you're gonna break into the dome to get more. Give it up. I promise you won't be punished. We'll just chalk it up to experience . . . and then go back to the way things were."

McCade squinted against the glare, and smiled grimly. "Screw you, Torb."

There was a moment of silence, and there was fury in Torb's voice when he answered. "Then you're dead, Lane. Good-bye."

Suddenly both emplacements opened up with renewed fury, and McCade wondered if Torb was right . . . maybe they were dead.

Inside the dome's com center, Walker conscientiously powered the equipment down, and returned all major systems to standby. Things were going fairly well. He had managed to reach McCade's friends aboard *Pegasus*, and they were on the way, ETA, about six hours. He had also programmed and activated one of the three message torps his organization kept in parking orbit around Worm. Within minutes it would break out of orbit, accelerate away from Worm, and go hyper. Eventually it would emerge near the Wind World, and play back its coded message. Then his superiors would know the Emperor was dead, and that McCade was on the way. He sighed. He'd also done his best to send the message in another way, but had apparently failed, since there'd been no acknowledgment. It seemed as though he'd never get the hang of that stuff. But at least the torp would get through. Now there was only one problem left to solve.

Walker stood, and turned out the lights as he left the room. He knew that outside the dome the battle still raged, and unless McCade won, the prince wouldn't take the throne, and a terrible war could result. And it didn't take a genius to see that McCade was going to lose. He wondered if the flux readers had known it would end up like this, although it didn't matter much. He knew what to do, but it scared him. What if his brothers and sisters were wrong? What if there was no life after death? He shrugged. Then that's just the way it goes, he decided.

Torb's guards ignored Walker as he strolled across the center of the dome. Most of their attention was directed outside, and besides, everyone knows a Walker doesn't take sides. As Walker approached the dome's huge doors, he was praying in a tongue no longer heard on Terra, and hoping that his action would be in concert with the flux. He was only feet from the control box when a guard shouted, "Hey, you! Walker! Get away from those doors!"

The guard was fast, but Walker was just a little faster, diving for the box, touching the controls just as the bullets hit him. Even as the slugs tore him apart, Walker held the button down, smiling because he'd fooled the silly bastards, and was far, far away.

Fourteen

McCade gritted his teeth, and ordered his crawler forward. With Fesker's rig out of action, someone had to tackle the doors, even though it seemed hopeless.

McCade was thrown in one direction, and then another, as his driver, Freak, did his best to avoid the flashing blue beams that stuttered out from Torb's weapons. Hawkins tried to provide covering fire, but Torb's gunners ignored him, throwing everything they had at the crawler racing toward them.

Then their port engine took a direct hit, and McCade was half blinded by the flash, and almost deafened by the loud explosion. An energy beam sliced through the right track, and the crawler slewed left as Freak dumped power and thumbed the intercom. "OK, people, this is the end of the line. Please pay the driver as you disembark. All gratuities will be appreciated."

As men tumbled out of the crawler and ran for cover, McCade did his best to cover them, but here and there they jerked and fell, as a hail of lead and lethal energy tossed them about like so many rag dolls. He felt sick. Now they were well and truly screwed. The whole thing was a complete disaster. It was time to surrender and save as many lives as he could. He was reaching for his mic when the radio squawked into life, and Hawkins said, "Damn! Look at that, boss! They're opening the doors!"

McCade looked, and sure enough, the huge double doors were slowly sliding upward. He couldn't be sure, but it looked like there was some kind of a fight going on inside the dome. It didn't make sense, but what the hell, some chance was better than none. He keyed his mic and said, "Go, Hawkins! Get the hell in there and secure the dome!"

Hawkins didn't reply. He didn't have to. His crawler spewed gravel, and threw up a cloud of dust as it swept around a big pile of empty cargo pods and roared toward the dome. McCade swore under his breath as he saw the doors reverse direction and start downward. Whatever the problem was, Torb's men had it under control, but could they close the doors in time? Hawkins was close, closer, through! The doors closed behind him.

Once inside the dome Torb's guards didn't stand a chance. Hawkins had a field day, grinning as he cut down the running guards, using the crawler to grind them into paste.

Ten minutes later the battle was over, and ten hours later, McCade was ready to lift off Worm. The dome had been secured, Torb and his guards were safely locked into their own underground prison, and the dead had been buried.

One grave stood above all the rest. It was located on top of the little hill where McCade had been tortured, and where the man with the cool green eyes had invaded his dreams. Walker was dead, and McCade didn't know how to mark his grave, or say good-bye. So he gave up, figuring that if Walker was still around, then he knew how McCade felt, and if he wasn't, then it didn't matter.

Turning, he walked down the slope, and headed for *Pegasus*. Her slender shape was a black silhouette against the last rays of the setting sun. Off to the right the glow of cargo lights revealed a small crowd. Some of the men had come to say good-bye. As he headed their way, he thought how good it would feel to leave Worm's eternal heat for the cool darkness of space. He threw the shovel toward the nearest pile of junk and quickened his pace.

A cheer went up as he approached. As McCade tried to quiet the crowd, Phil's shaggy form materialized beside him. The big variant shook his head in disbelief. "It's obvious they don't know you the way we do," he growled.

McCade laughed. "Unlike you, these men appreciate my finer qualities."

"And what finer qualities might those be, ol' sport?" Rico asked, appearing on his other side. "I'll bet the list ain't very long."

But before McCade could answer the crowd grew silent. Fesker stepped forward with Spigot and Hawkins by his side. Clearing his throat importantly, Fesker said, "Well, boss, with you liftin' an all, me and the boys thought we oughta come and say good-bye."

"I'm glad you did," McCade replied solemnly. "I've never served with a finer group of slaves."

They all laughed, shouted friendly insults, and congratulated each other on their wit. Fesker waited until they'd quieted down, and then cleared his throat once more. "As you know, boss, we found Torb's stash of Fire Eggs, and we figure to share and share alike. Well, the way we see it, if it wasn't for you we'd still be slaves. So we all voted, and everyone agreed to give you this."

With that, Spigot hopped forward on a single crutch, and proudly handed McCade a small package.

As the men looked on expectantly, McCade carefully

unwrapped the package to reveal a glorious Fire Egg. The very last rays of the sun hit the egg, exploding within to create a ruby red blaze of fire, shot through with iridescent sparks of blue and green. It was the most beautiful thing he'd ever seen.

Rico gave a low whistle. "Now that's some play pretty."

McCade looked up from the fiery egg to the waiting crowd. "Thanks, men, this means a lot. I won't forget you."

They laughed and joked, but as they waved and turned to go, he could see that they were pleased.

Spigot remained after the rest had gone. He grinned his toothless grin. "Thanks, Sam." He glanced at *Pegasus* and back, clearly curious, but too polite to ask. "It's been good knowing you."

"And you too, Spigot," McCade replied. "What's your real name anyway?"

Spigot blushed, looked over his shoulder to make sure the others couldn't hear, and then spoke in a secretive whisper. "You promise not to tell anyone?"

McCade nodded his agreement.

"Alfonso Esteverra Maxwell-Smith."

"It's a good name," McCade said solemnly. Spigot grinned his thanks, they shook hands, and the little man hopped off to catch up with the rest of the group. Occasionally one or two paused to look back and wave.

McCade waved back, and then, with Rico and Phil at his side, he turned and walked toward *Pegasus*.

"So what're they gonna do now?" Rico inquired.

McCade grinned. "Well, about half of them plan to stay awhile, and teach Torb and his guards how to find Fire Eggs."

Phil made a deep rumbling noise which was actually laughter. "And the rest?"

McCade shrugged. "They're happy with the Fire Eggs they've got, and plan to take over the next supply ship

Joyo sends out. There should be one in a couple of weeks."
The thought reminded him of Candy. Fesker had promised
to watch out for her, and make sure she didn't get hurt.

A few minutes later, the lock had cycled closed behind
them, and McCade was taking one last look at the Fire
Egg, before locking the ship's safe. The jewel's internal
fire lit up the inside of the armored durasteel box. It was
probably worth more than the ship itself. For one brief
moment, he considered quitting, hanging it up. After all,
why keep going, keep risking it all, when he had enough
for the rest of his days right here in front of him? As
quickly as the thought came, it disappeared, pushed aside
by Sara's trusting eyes, and Walker's bullet-ridden body.

Turning to Rico, McCade said, "Let's take a look at
those coordinates Walker fed you."

Rico's large fingers flew over the keyboard with surprising delicacy, and while most of the computer continued
its pre-flight check, a small subprocessor turned its attention to this new request. A second later the words "Wind
World" appeared on the master screen, followed by a long
list of numbers. McCade grinned. There it was, the end of
the search. The numbers were coordinates for the Wind
World, and the Wind World was where they'd find the
prince.

"There they are," Rico said, pointing a stubby finger at
the screen. "Just like your friend sent 'em."

"Speaking o' your friends," Rico continued, "that's
Cy's quite a character."

McCade laughed. "Yeah, he's definitely one of a kind.
Obviously he made it or you wouldn't be here."

Rico nodded. "There we were playin' cards, killin' time,
'n' waitin' for you to get tired o' the bright lights and come
back, when suddenly the chime for the main lock goes off.
You shoulda seen Phil, he damn near had a heart attack; I
mean, who the hell could it be? None o' the detectors had gone
off. He didn't pack enough mass or velocity. So we

looked at the vid pickup for the main lock, and there's this metal ball floatin' there, and it comes over the ship-ta-ship freq and says, 'Hello, could I borrow a cup of DC?'"

"I almost had a heart attack, did I?" Phil said. "Well, you might ask Rico who spilled the full cup of coffee in his lap."

McCade laughed. "That sounds like Cy all right. How did he manage to reach *Pegasus?*"

"Said there wasn't anything to it," Rico replied. "Bein' a cyborg, all he needs is a little 0^2 for his brain, and he's got that in a tank, so vacuum don't bother him a bit. He just locked onto a departing yacht, waited till they were free of Joyo's Roid, and squirted himself in our direction. It took him a few days . . . but he made it."

McCade tried to imagine what that would be like, launching yourself on a one-way trip toward a target you couldn't see, days passing as your precious reserve of power slowly dwindled away, knowing if you didn't find the ship you'd never make it back. It would take an incredible amount of guts.

McCade looked around. "So where's Cy?"

Rico shrugged. "We offered to bring him along, but he said he had unfinished business on Joyo's Roid, something about beating the odds. So as we headed this way, we dropped him off real close to the Roid. Last we saw him he was lockin' onta an incoming yacht. Crazy little beggar."

McCade shook his head sadly. Like most inveterate gamblers Cy just couldn't quit. Well, maybe one day he'd win really big. McCade hoped so.

His thoughts were interrupted as the computer announced the ship was ready to lift and started a countdown. All three men checked to make sure their harnesses were secure, and then someone dumped a couple of anvils onto McCade's chest, and *Pegasus* roared toward the sky, riding a lance of orange-red flame.

They hadn't even cleared Worm's thin atmosphere when

every proximity alarm on the ship started hooting, buzzing, or flashing. Someone was waiting for them in space, and when it comes to unexpected visitors, it's always best to assume the worst. Pinned to his chair by the ship's acceleration, McCade armed all weapons systems verbally, and struggled to see through blurred vision.

As *Pegasus* broke free of Worm's gravity the ship's computer quickly scanned the immediate area, evaluated the available data, and gave itself permission to use emergency voice simulation. "Prepare to surrender or abandon ship. Estimated time to total annihilation is one minute 43.2 seconds. Enemy forces include one major warship, cruiser or better, two lesser vessels, and a full wing of Interceptors. All ships provide a 99.9 percent match to Imperial design. Probability for successful engagement, none. Probability for successful escape, none. The autobar and showers will be closed until further notice. This ship's manufacturer will not be held responsible for damage incurred during contra-indicated combat."

"You'd better get that thing fixed, Sam, or I swear I'm gonna rip out its mother board, and dance on it," Phil growled as he unsnapped his harness, and half floated, half climbed up and into the top weapons turret. If they decided to fight, the computer would control the ship's main armament, since no mere human could track and hit multiple targets traveling at thousands of miles per hour. Not unless they got very close. That's when the ship's secondary armament could make the difference.

"Damn," Rico said in amazement as he scanned all the blips on their detector screens. "Where the hell did *they* come from? We weren't followed from Joyo's Roid, and they weren't here when we went dirtside."

Rico's questions went unanswered. Then the com set buzzed, and McCade flicked it on. The screen faded up from black to reveal a stern-looking naval officer. Her black hair was heavily streaked with gray, her eyebrows met just above her hooked nose, and her mouth was a hard straight line. "I'm Captain Edith Queet, commanding officer of the Imperial Cruiser *Neptune*. Cut your drives and prepare to be boarded."

McCade tapped a few keys, and *Pegasus* went into a series of stomach-wrenching evasive maneuvers, only barely escaping the massive tractor beams which lashed out from *Neptune*. In fact one came so close to lock-on that it rattled McCade's teeth.

Doing his best to assume a nonchalant expression, McCade switched the com set to send. "Captain, I'm afraid you're mistaken regarding your current tactical situation. It is you, not I, who should cut your drives and prepare for boarding. Otherwise I shall be forced to destroy your entire fleet."

Rico made a choking noise, and Phil shook his head in pained amusement.

Suddenly Queet's face disappeared to be replaced by Claudia's. There was no mistaking her blond hair, cold blue eyes, and bad temper. "Cut the crap, McCade, or we'll turn your pathetic little ship into so much free metal."

"My, but we're a bit testy lately," McCade replied, his eyes narrowing. "It must be a rough day for the royal retinue. As for blasting my ship . . . go right ahead. But keep in mind that your brother might be aboard, and then again, he might not. That's why you haven't blasted us already, isn't it? You don't mind killing him, but what if he's still out there somewhere? What if I'm going after him right now?"

"Cut your drives, McCade, or I swear I'll blast you, and sift the pieces for my beloved brother."

McCade's eyes flicked to his readouts and back to the screen. Just a little more time. *Pegasus* needed more velocity before she could go hyper. "Right . . . just give me a minute here . . . one of your tractor beams came damn close and I'm having control problems. How the hell did you find us anyway?"

To his surprise she took the bait. "When you started barging around Joyo's Roid, Joyo tried to check you out with his operatives on Earth, and one of them works for me. I sent Major Tellor to check it out; he ran a check on Joyo's computer, found the glitch where you accessed it, and the rest was easy. Knowing my brother's pathetic sense of humor, it didn't take long to see through his Idono H. Farigo nonsense."

Suddenly a computer-coordinated net of tractor beams flashed out from Claudia's fleet, just as McCade's fingers danced over the control board. She'd been stalling too, and had almost succeeded, but the tractor beams fell slightly short. *Pegasus* leapt outward, still steadily picking up speed.

"Damn you, McCade! I'll triple whatever they're paying you!"

"Thanks, your imperial wonderfulness, but no thanks. I'll see you around." And with that, McCade's stomach lurched, and he felt a brief moment of disorientation. *Pegasus* had entered hyperspace. Outside, the stars suddenly disappeared. Inside the ship's screens showed computer simulations of how the stars should look, would look, if the *Pegasus* wasn't traveling faster than the speed of light.

McCade lit a cigar, and leaned back, slowly allowing his muscles to relax. They were safe for the moment. Without the coordinates for their destination, Claudia couldn't follow, and by the time she did, he'd have the prince and heading for Terra.

"Is the bar open?" he demanded.

"Affirmative," the computer replied. Was it McCade's imagination, or was there a grudging tone to the machine's reply?

McCade shrugged off his harness and headed for the tiny lounge. Phil and Rico were right behind. "It would appear our troubles are over, gentlemen. The last one into the lounge cooks dinner!"

As she watched *Pegasus* disappear off her screens into hyperspace, Claudia swore and clenched her fists. "Damn that man. When I catch him he'll die by inches. Captain Queet, I want a report on that message torp, and I want it now."

Captain Queet nodded, and spoke softly into her headset. Around her the bridge crew literally sat at attention, eyes locked on their screens and multicolored indicator lights. By remaining perfectly still, and performing flawlessly, each hoped to avoid being singled out for one of Claudia's caustic remarks.

Lady Linnea stood toward the rear of the cavernous bridge, doing her best to maintain an expression of aristocratic superiority, while inwardly giving thanks that McCade had escaped. Had Alexander been with him? There was no way to tell, but she knew that if Claudia caught him, he'd soon be dead. Over the last month she'd become more and more obsessed with taking the throne, and now Linnea was convinced she'd stop at nothing to get it. She shivered, praying that wherever Alexander was, he'd never fall into his sister's hands.

Linnea's thoughts were interrupted as Captain Queet looked up, and smiled. "Crypto's very close, Your Highness. They're having trouble with the message, but they've got the coordinates."

"Excellent!" Claudia snapped, eyes gleaming. "Tell them I'm coming down." She spun on her heel, and marched off the bridge. Linnea reluctantly followed. Lately Claudia insisted she stay nearby. The more dictatorial Claudia became, the more she seemed to need Linnea's reassurance, and the harder it was to give.

When they entered the corridor, Major Tellor, plus a full squad of marines, snapped to attention. As Claudia and

Linnea passed, they fell in behind, their heavy boots hitting the deck in perfect cadence. Claudia rarely went anywhere without her bodyguard anymore. Maybe her own treachery led her to expect it from others. The thought made a hollow space in the pit of Linnea's stomach. Could she know?

When Claudia and her party entered the crypto lab, Lieutenant Chang barely glanced up from his work. Anyone else would have been dressed down, or even disciplined for such a breach of etiquette, but not Chang. At twenty-five, he was already a legendary genius and eccentric. A long series of frustrated instructors and commanding officers had finally given up, realizing that in order to exploit his brilliance, they'd have to put up with his personality. It was a high price for a military organization to pay, but Chang was worth it, because when it came to cryptology he was the very best. His long lank hair hung down into the inner workings of the long slender torpedo while smoke, from a non-reg dope stick, curled up and around his head. Long slender fingers made a final adjustment, and then he straightened up, wiping his hands on an already filthy uniform. Chang's almond-shaped eyes regarded Claudia with the same friendly enthusiasm he offered the lowliest ratings. "Hi, Princess, step right over here and I'll print out what we've got so far."

Claudia struggled mightily, and just barely managed to ignore Chang's familiarity.

At the cryptologist's touch, a printer began to whir, and while it spit out plastic fax, Chang provided a cheerful stream of conversation. "She's a beaut, isn't she?" he asked, indicating the torpedo. Its long black hull rested on four supports. Claudia knew it consisted of a drive, hyperdrive, and mega-memory. A minicomputer provided guidance and control. It was the mega-memory that held whatever secrets had been entrusted to it. At the moment, a maze of multicolored wires led from the mega-memory's circuitry to some specialized crypto equipment, which in turn was linked to the ship's main computer. Blithely ignoring Claudia's pained expression, Chang continued his monologue.

"I guess she gave our Interceptor jockeys a real run for their money. She was just about to go hyper when they threw some light tractors on her. I figure somebody's got something real important to say, because unlike our converted jobs, this baby was really designed to carry the mail. Someday we'll figure out how to punch com messages through hyperspace and these suckers will become so much scrap. Don't get me wrong though, you can't get anything better than a torp´ from Techno. I mean that sucker's built. It took me two hours to defeat the electro-mechanical traps, and another three to get around all the stuff hidden in the programming. Still," he added happily, "I showed those Techno types a thing or two."

The printer stopped whirring, and Chang ripped off the fax. Proudly he handed it to Claudia. She found herself looking at the words "Wind World," and a long string of numbers. "There you go, Princess, that's where the torp was headed, and although we haven't broken their message code yet, you'll notice they didn't try to encode proper names. For example, 'McCade,' and 'Farigo,' appear more than once. Does that help?"

Claudia's face broke into a rare smile. "It certainly does, Lieutenant, no, make that Lieutenant Commander, Chang. You've been a very big help indeed! Please feed those coordinates to the bridge, and tell Captain Queet I want to reach the Wind World in record time."

Claudia watched Chang as he called the bridge, and neither saw Lady Linnea as she slipped away on an errand of her own.

Fifteen

McCADE HAD NEVER liked hyperspace shifts in general. The whole concept of leaving normal space for some other reality, which only a few mathematicians understood, bothered him. But to do it without nav beacons seemed especially stupid. Oh, he'd done it often enough, one didn't have much choice out along the frontier, but he didn't like it. He preferred the situation in toward the Empire, where nav beacons marked all the major trade routes, and were taken for granted. Once each sixty seconds the beacons automatically shunted from normal, to hyperspace, then back. Meanwhile each nav beacon broadcast its own distinctive signal, thereby marking a proven entry and exit point. It was a very useful system. Unfortunately this was the rim, and one helluva a long way from any trade route, so they weren't going to run into any nav beacons. Of course as long as you had good coordinates you didn't really need a beacon. And they had the coordinates provided by Walker. "Which means we're in good shape," the optimistic McCade told himself.

"Sure," the pessimistic McCade answered, "but Walker was under a lot of pressure when he sent Rico those coordinates. What if he made a mistake? What if he transposed two digits for example? You might come out of hyperspace right in the middle of a sun . . . and that could be a tad uncomfortable. So why not just forget the whole thing and go home?"

The discussion was suddenly rendered academic, as the computer cut the ship's hyperdrive, and slipped *Pegasus* into normal space. There was a brief moment of nausea, followed by subtle changes in all the viewscreens as they switched from simulated to real space.

Rico gave a low whistle. "Well, ol' sport, your friend certainly liked 'em tight."

McCade nodded his agreement. They'd come out of hyperspace so close to the planet they were damned near in orbit. Walker liked them close indeed. Most pilots considered it prudent to leave a little more leeway, even if it meant a day's travel in normal space. It might be slower, but it was a lot safer.

McCade tapped some keys, and the ship's computer obeyed, taking *Pegasus* down into a high orbit. He wanted to look things over before trying to put the ship down. There was nothing in the ship's data bank on a planet called Wind World, and Walker had mentioned something about high winds.

"Well, Rico, let's see if anybody's home," McCade said. "Try all the standard freqs."

Rico ran through the most commonly used frequencies as McCade studied the fleecy ball below. It wasn't hard to see why they called it the Wind World. Here and there the clouds were shaped into huge whorls, and as he watched, he could actually see them move, driven no doubt by some

very strong winds. It didn't take a degree in meteorology to
see landing could be very dangerous indeed.

"Here we go, Sam, I've got somebody," Rico said. He
flipped a switch, allowing a cultured male voice to come
over the control room's speakers. Cultured or not, it was
clearly synthetic.

"Greetings, gentle beings. I am a weather and commu-
nications satellite known as FG65, in geosynchronous orbit
above a settlement known as Deadeye, which also happens
to be this planet's only spaceport. At this particular moment surface weather conditions are such that radio com-
munications with Deadeye are somewhat intermittent.
Perhaps I could be of help."

"This is the ship *Pegasus*," McCade replied, "request-
ing permission to land, and instructions on how to do so."

"Permission granted," the satellite responded gravely. "I
have scanned your ship for illegal weapons and technology,
and have found none. Providing that you agree to obey the
laws and customs of our planet, you are welcome."

"We agree," McCade said solemnly.

"Excellent. Now, if you will put your computer on
line," the satellite continued, "I will send it Deadeye's position, some basics on the planet's atmosphere, ecology,
laws, and so forth, plus the relevant meteorological information regarding current conditions."

McCade tapped a quick sequence of keys, and said,
"Our computer's on line."

Three seconds later, the satellite was back. "Please re-
view the information I've provided, and prepare to land in
approximately one half standard hour, on my command.
Current conditions suggest a brief period of calm at that
time. Until then, remember, 'Those who ride the wind
must accept where it goes.'" Then there was a click, followed by static.

McCade looked at Rico with a lifted eyebrow, and the
other man shrugged his massive shoulders. "I've seen

everything now, ol' sport, includin' a philosophical satellite."

For the next half hour they studied the information the
satellite had sent them. It quickly became clear that the
winds which whipped across the surface of the planet
below were not all that random. In fact most were quite
predictable. Which explained why the spaceport was located at the very center of a large, circular, semipermanent
storm. Although the storm occasionally shifted a little from
north to south, and from east to west, it didn't go far. In
fact, according to the information supplied by FG65, it
stayed right where it was most of the time. Once in a while
it would vanish for a time, but it always returned to take up
the same position.

The com set buzzed, and satellite FG65 said, "Please
initiate your descent. Based on past weather patterns, a
brief period of relative calm should prevail in all layers of
the atmosphere above Deadeye during the next hour or so."

"Understood," McCade replied. And while one didn't
usually thank computers, in FG65's case, it seemed quite
natural to say "thank you."

McCade assumed control from the ship's computer as
Pegasus entered the planet's atmosphere. Tricky atmospheric landings were one of the few things human pilots
usually did better than computers. Lots of research had
been done trying to figure out why, since logic seemed to
suggest it should work the other way around, but no one
had come up with any really believable answers. The best
they could do was suggest that sentients were capable of
something called kinesthetic intuition, which meant human
pilots could "feel" subtle things computers couldn't, and
could then "guess" what to do about them.

The ship shuddered as the wind hit and shoved it sideways. McCade corrected, and then swore when the wind
suddenly fell off, forcing him to compensate.

"If this is 'relative calm,' then I'm a Tobarian Zerk

monkey," Rico said, frowning at his instruments.

"Now that you mention it, I do see a certain family resemblance," Phil growled.

McCade grinned, but quickly lost track of their friendly insults as he fought his way down through layer after layer of disturbed air. Finally, after a braking orbit which seemed years long, they came in on final approach. Below, the storm which surrounded Deadeye raged on as it had for more than a thousand years. Ahead, clouds swirled around a vertical tube of calm air which marked the eye of the storm. All he had to do was stop *Pegasus* in midair and drop her straight down that tube. "Nothing to it," he told himself. "Child's play for a pilot of my experience." But as the critical moment approached, sweat trickled down his spine, and the tic in his left cheek locked into permanent spasm. Then it was too late to worry. He killed power, kicked the nose up, felt her drop, goosed the drives to slow their descent. Now all he could do was sit back and hope for the best.

And much to his surprise he got it. *Pegasus* dropped as smoothly as a lift tube in an expensive hotel, giving him a chance to grab a quick look at the planet's surface. Where the rest of the surface was hidden by wind-driven sand and dust, the area directly below was clear. The first thing he noticed was the relative sameness of the land. Yes, he could see distant mountains poking their peaks above the roiling storms, but directly below the land was flat, ridged here and there where the eternal hand of the wind had carved topsoil away from solid rock, but otherwise smooth and featureless. He saw nothing resembling vegetation, and quickly checked the computer to confirm a breathable atmosphere. Sure enough, the atmosphere was within a couple of points of Earth normal, so there was some bio-mass somewhere even if he couldn't see it at the moment.

His thoughts were interrupted by the buzzing of a prox-imity alarm as the ground rose to meet them. He turned his attention back to the controls, and a few minutes later felt a gentle thump as the ship settled onto its landing jacks.

He was still congratulating himself when the com set buzzed. This voice was real, somewhat nasal, and belonged to a fat woman. Her hair had been braided and then piled on top of her head. She had laughing eyes, a button nose, and at least four chins. Due to where the viewscreen cut her off, McCade couldn't see below the level of her chest, but if her enormous bosom was any indication, she was very, very large. "Hey, good lookin', unless you plan to stay here the rest of your life, you'd better move that toy. The winds'll shift soon, and when they do, that little thing's goin' bye-bye. So follow the red drone, and then come on down to Momma's Saloon for a drink." She winked a tiny eye, and then disappeared.

McCade had dropped into some pretty casual spaceports in his time, but this was the first time he'd run into a combination air traffic controller-saloon keeper. He checked the main viewscreen, and found a large red sphere had indeed appeared, and was waiting for them to move. The words "follow me" flashed on and off across the front of it, and as a small gust of wind hit, the drone bobbed slightly.

McCade fired his repellors, lifted the ship off the ground, and danced her toward the red ball. The drone drifted left and he followed. As *Pegasus* moved, her repellors cut shallow trails through the dirt, throwing up rooster tails of dust, which were quickly blown away by the light breeze.

There wasn't much to look at, and what there was didn't qualify as works of art. To the right, a heavily reinforced, all-purpose antenna housing pointed a dark finger toward the sky, looking like some sort of primitive obelisk. And to the left, a pylon shaped like a vertical airplane wing soared upward, ending in a sleek housing, and a slowly turning propeller. When the wind was blowing full force, the aerodynamically shaped pylon would rotate to meet it, and the propeller would turn at incredible speeds. Wind power made practical. So, while the surrounding countryside looked a bit bleak, at least the locals had plenty of cheap nonpolluting power.

And things did look bleak. The sky, the ground, and the rocks were all done in different shades of gray. As a result, the red ball seemed even brighter than it was. It stopped, and McCade did likewise, noticing that the ground below had given way to a huge durasteel plate. Now the words "follow me" disappeared, and were replaced by "cut repellors." McCade obeyed, dropping *Pegasus* gently onto the scarred metal surface.

Moments later he felt a slight jerk, and the metal plate, ship and all, began to sink underground. It didn't surprise him, since the arrangement was quite similar to the underground hangars on Alice, which also served to get ships down and out of the weather.

The rock walls which slid upward around them were as smooth and uniform as duracrete. Suddenly the walls vanished, giving way to a large, brightly lit open space, rectangular in shape, and quite uniform in construction. This was no work of nature but a well-executed creation of man.

The red ball had dropped with them, and now its "follow me" sign reappeared. McCade fired his repellors again, lifting *Pegasus* only inches off the deck, and followed the sphere into a rather generous berth. Once in place, he killed the drives, and delegated control to the ship's computer. It began a post-flight diagnostic check on all systems. When McCade looked up he found the red ball had disappeared.

"Well, gentlemen," McCade said, releasing his harness, "the lady said we should have a drink, and I think it would be rude to ignore her invitation."

"Hear, hear," Phil said. "Never let it be said that we were rude."

"I wouldn't think o' such a thing," Rico agreed solemnly, heading for the lock.

A few minutes later, McCade and Phil waited as Rico set all the ship's security systems. It never hurt to be careful.

McCade noticed there were only three other ships in sight, although the hangar could have easily handled three times that number. One was a beat-up lifeboat, with a FOR SALE sign painted across its port side in sloppy lettering, the second was a fairly well-maintained freighter, probably on a supply run, and the third was a wreck, a twisted pile of junk only vaguely resembling a ship. Although there was no one in sight, the scaffolding which surrounded the wreck suggested an optimist at work, someone who thought it could be put back together. He'd seen a few spaceports even more deserted, but not many.

Rico sealed the ship's lock and then joined them. Together they followed a series of signs which simply read, "Momma's," through a series of clean, but deserted passageways. A short time later they descended a steep flight of stairs, and went through a narrow doorway. Over it hung a sign which spelled out "Momma's" in pink neon letters.

They found themselves in a large open room. In the tradition of bars everywhere it was dimly lit and filled with smoke. A huge mirror dominated the far wall making the room seem bigger than it really was. Below it was a massive bar of polished black rock. Huge columns of the same stuff reached up at regular intervals to support a vaulted ceiling. The columns and the high ceiling combined to give the bar an aura of dignity more appropriate to the lobby of a grand hotel than a spaceport saloon on a remote frontier planet. It was also well furnished and quite clean. A most unusual rim world bar indeed.

As he approached the bar, McCade felt the other customers watching him. Not too surprising, since the newcomers were probably the most interesting event of the day, or maybe the week. Nonetheless he sensed that while most were simply curious, others had deeper, darker thoughts. He sighed. Some things never changed.

As they bellied up to the bar McCade found himself face-to-face with the combination air traffic controller-saloon keeper. "Well, look what the wind blew in. Welcome to Momma's, and if ya ain't guessed yet, I'm Momma." Her eyes twinkled, and her chins rippled when she spoke. "Your berth is costin' you two hunnert credits a day, my rooms are clean, the food's good, my booze ain't been watered down, and if you shoot anybody in here, you pay for damages and clean up the mess. Now what'll it be for you, gentlemen?"

"Let's start with some o' that booze which ain't been watered down," Rico said pragmatically, "and then maybe some o' that food you mentioned."

"An excellent choice," Phil rumbled. "Make that two."

McCade nodded in response to Momma's inquiring look, and as she waddled off to fill their order he used the big mirror behind the bar to check out the rest of her clientele. Off to his right there were three women and a man all seated together. From their matching uniforms, he figured them for the freighter crew, and the oldest of the three women as the captain. A short distance away, an older man and a boy still in his teens sat locked in earnest conversation, their worn gear somehow reminding him of the wreck he'd seen in the hangar. Beyond them sat two men and a woman, all dressed in gray one-piece suits of a style he'd never seen before, and all watching him while pretending not to. As their eyes brushed his, he nodded gravely, as if already acquainted. And in a way he was. He'd met their kind a thousand times before, in a thousand other bars. The users and the takers. Every planet had its share, and the Wind World was apparently no exception. They avoided his gaze as they stood, threw something metallic on the table, and ambled toward the door. He noticed all three wore blasters.

"Cute, aren't they," Phil said, his eyes on the mirror.

"Probably on their way to church," Rico observed, picking up the large tankard Momma had just placed before him, and taking a noisy sip.

"Not unless it's worth robbing," McCade said dryly, pulling out a cigar and puffing it into life.

And then an interesting thing happened. A tall black woman stepped into the bar and stopped as the three hardcases blocked her way. She wore a seamless, black one-piece suit and two blasters, one low on her right thigh, the other in a shoulder holster under her left arm. Except for a round island of kinky black hair on the very top of her skull, her head was shaved, and she was very beautiful. Her eyes flashed when she spoke. "Either get out of my way . . . or make your move." Her fingers hung just above the butt of her blaster.

The three hardcases just stood there, fingers twitching, trying to decide. They'd seen her in action, and knew that even with the odds on their side, the outcome was still in doubt. Even if they won it would be a close thing.

As the seconds ticked slowly by, McCade blew smoke at the mirror, and allowed his left hand to drift down toward his handgun. Finally, when the moment was stretched thin, one of the men said, "This isn't over, Mara."

"Thanks for the warning," she replied calmly. "I'll watch my back." Then she walked straight toward them, showing no surprise when they parted to let her through.

She seemed to take the bar in with one sweeping glance, her eyes stopping on McCade as she headed for the bar. McCade turned in time to see the hardcases leave the bar, and to accept her out-thrust hand.

She had a strong grip and a low melodious voice. "Welcome to Wind World. I'm Mara, the Walkers of The Way sent me to meet you." She looked from one to another. "Which one of you is Sam McCade?"

"I am," McCade replied, "and I'd like you to meet my friends, Rico and Phil." As Rico and Phil said their hellos, McCade had already taken a liking to her, and knew his friends had too. Rico insisted on giving her his seat, while Phil kissed her hand, something most men couldn't do gracefully, but which worked somehow when the big variant did it.

Then a brief battle was fought to see who would buy her a drink, with Rico emerging the winner, and Mara laughing at the competition. "Really, gentlemen, this will never do. I'm supposed to guide you to Chimehome, not sit around while you buy me drinks."

"Chimehome?" McCade asked.

Mara threw her drink back and nodded. "Chimehome's the name of the Walker monastery. Say, where's my old friend Pollard? Isn't he with you?"

At first McCade didn't understand, then he realized that "Pollard" must be Walker's real name. For a moment he said nothing, stubbing out his cigar, and stalling for time. Finally he looked up into deep brown eyes.

"I'm sorry, Mara, but Pollard's dead. Right after he programmed that message torp and sent it your way he was killed. He saved my life, along with quite a few others."

He saw his words hit Mara like physical blows. She looked down at the surface of the bar and closed her eyes. It didn't take a genius to see that Mara and Pollard had been more than just friends. They sat that way for a couple of minutes, Mara silent and withdrawn, the three men awkward and embarrassed. Then she looked up and smiled, twin tracks marking the path of the tears which had trickled down her cheeks. "This round is on me."

As if by magic, Momma appeared with a new round of drinks, and then waddled away to serve other customers. Mara raised her glass. "To one helluva man."

"To one helluva man," the others echoed, and drained their glasses.

"Tell me about Pollard," Mara asked softly.

So McCade told her: How they'd met, the plan they'd agreed on, and how her friend had died. To his surprise she showed no further signs of grief as he spoke. She laughed when he described how Pollard invaded his hallucinations, nodded while he explained their plan, and winced when he told her about the door. But she didn't cry, and remembering his own farewell at Pollard's grave, McCade knew that at least for the moment, she too had found a way to deal with his death.

When he'd finished both were silent for a moment. Hoping to take her mind off Pollard, and genuinely curious, McCade cleared his throat. "Now it's your turn. Tell me all about a beautiful lady who packs two blasters . . . and doesn't step aside for anyone."

Mara laughed. "You make me sound so dangerous! There isn't much to tell. I was born on an ag planet called Weller's World. Ever heard of it?"

McCade nodded. "I've been there."

"You're one of the few," Mara replied with a grin. "Anyway, my mother died while I was still quite young, and my father raised me. He's the one who taught me how to fight. 'When it's you or them, honey,' he used to say, 'make damn sure it's them.'"

"Words to live by," McCade agreed solemnly, sipping his drink.

"Ain't it the truth," Mara said, her face softening. "He never told me everything, but I suspect he was a soldier of fortune . . . or maybe something worse before settling on Weller's World. I know this for a fact, during my childhood he never worked a single day on planet, yet we lived quite well. Once each year he always went off-planet saying, 'I've got some business to take care of, honey . . . I'll be back in a few weeks.' And sure enough, a few weeks later he'd be back, wearing a big smile and loaded down with presents."

Mara frowned. "I didn't think anything of it, back then, but now I believe those trips were somehow connected with money, and whatever he did to get it. Anyway the years passed, and as my father grew older, he became increasingly interested in religion. He was never willing to admit it, but I suspect the prospect of death scared him, and like many others, he hoped to find some guarantee of continued existence. Yes, please."

Mara paused while Momma freshened her drink, and then picked up where she'd left off. "During his research, Father came across occasional mention of the Walkers and their philosophy. For some reason it fascinated him. The funny thing was he didn't know that much about them or 'The Way,' but nonetheless he became certain they were right. Somewhere he learned of the monastery here on Wind World, and decided to come." Mara smiled as she remembered. "Frankly I opposed it, but his mind was made up and he was determined to go, with or without me."

Mara looked up into McCade's eyes. "By this time Father was quite elderly. I couldn't let him go alone. So we sold our place on Weller's World, and hopped a series of freighters, eventually landing here. During the trip, Father's health deteriorated, and by the time we arrived was quite bad. At his insistence we finished the trip to Chimehome, and he died a month later. His last words to me were, 'Take care, honey, I'll be around.' And you know what?"

McCade shook his head.

"Every now and then I think he is . . . although maybe it's just my memories of him. Anyway, after Father's death, the Walkers invited me to stay and I accepted. I've learned a lot . . . and used some of the things Father taught me to help out." Her right hand strayed to the butt of a blaster. "Meeting you is a good example."

McCade smiled. "We can sure use the help."

Mara looked thoughtful for a moment. "And that brings us back to the present. Something you said is bothering me. Something about Pollard launching a message torp. What message did he send?"

McCade lifted one eyebrow in surprise. "Beats me. I just assumed it was his way of letting you know about us. You mean the torp never arrived?"

Mara smiled and shook her head.

"Then how did you know we were coming?"

She laughed. "How did Pollard get inside your head?"

McCade looked her right in the eye, and knew she wasn't kidding. "I don't believe it.'

"The facts speak for themselves," she replied lightly. "We haven't received a torp, but I knew your name, your mission, and approximate time of arrival. All were given to me before I left Chimehome." She chuckled. "It sure sounds like Pollard. Like you, he always had trouble believing in anything beyond the physical, and therefore doubted his own abilities. It would be just like him to use a message torp as a backup."

It all seemed pretty strange to McCade, but as Mara pointed out, the facts seemed to support her contention that Pollard had used nonphysical means to send his superiors a message. If so, what had happened to the torp? They weren't infallible, but they were fairly reliable, and it seemed strange that it hadn't shown up. He felt a cold hand grab his stomach. What if Claudia had managed to intercept the damned thing? It would be just like the miserable bitch. He picked up his glass and finished off his drink. As he turned toward the others, he wiped his mouth with the back of his hand and plastered a grin on his face. "Well, here's to a quick and successful journey."

Sixteen

THE NUAGS FILLED the dimly lit staging area with their bad-tempered grunting and the stench of their excrement. Tons of flesh pushed and shoved, eager to reach the succulent roller bushes just dumped into their pen. The smaller animals, males mostly, were quickly pushed toward the rear while the dominant cows took their rightful positions in the front. Like pink snakes their long, greedy feeding tentacles slithered out from under leathery gray armor, to snatch up prickly round balls of vegetation and pull them back toward hungry mouths. It wasn't a pretty sight. The sounds that went with it weren't all that great either, McCade decided, as the nearest cow put away another roller bush, slurping and gurgling with happiness. In addition to their other unpleasant traits, Mara informed him Nuags were also lazy, stubborn, and not very bright. In other words they'd make outstanding admirals, McCade thought.

"So why keep them around?" he asked.

"Because," she answered, "they are also big, strong, and perfectly happy to spend the night in the middle of a storm which would kill us. All of which makes them perfect for hauling you around."

"Couldn't we use a nice cozy crawler instead?" McCade asked wistfully, imagining one equipped with a small, but serviceable bar, and some comfortable bunks.

"Because," Mara replied patiently, "our storms tend to pick up crawlers, and toss them around like feathers, something which rarely happens to Nuags. Follow me and you'll see why."

So he followed her down to the staging area where the Nuag convoys were loaded and unloaded. It was a huge man-made cave which served as both a barn and warehouse. At the moment the place was packed with milling Nuags. Mara was forced to shout over her noisy subjects.

"Look at how they're shaped!" Mara shouted. McCade looked, and saw that most Nuags were about thirty feet high, and forty feet long. Their smoothly rounded gray armor made them look like huge beetles. Only beetles have heads and Nuags don't. In fact, with the exception of some narrow breathing vents, their exterior coverings were completely smooth. "The wind just flows over and around them," Mara yelled. "They can travel during even the worst storms."

McCade nodded his understanding, and followed as she waded into their midst, kicking, pushing, and swearing. Much to McCade's surprise, the Nuags did what Mara told them, albeit reluctantly, as if respecting anyone as mean and crotchety as they were. As she shoved her way through the crowd, McCade did his best to avoid their prodigious droppings, making a face at her when she turned and laughed.

"They may be ugly, Sam, but once you've tried getting somewhere without them, they start looking a lot better. Besides," she shouted, adopting a professional air, "each

one is a masterpiece of evolutionary engineering. Take
those breathing vents for example." She pointed toward the
nearest Nuag. "Each one is protected by a flap which
closes automatically when the wind hits it. Meanwhile the
ones on the opposite slope of the mantle remain open, allowing the Nuag to breathe. Neat, huh?"

"Incredible," McCade agreed, ducking as one of the
miserable beasts relieved itself of sufficient gas to power a
small city.

Mara laughed. "It's a good thing you weren't smoking a
cigar. Now, take a look at this." She hammered her fist on
the side of the nearest animal. Its armor started to flex, and
then curled slowly upward, until it was about four feet off
the ground. "After you," she said politely, delivering a formal bow.

"You're too kind," McCade replied dryly, ducking
under the edge of the raised armor. She followed, the
Nuag's protective covering dropping into place behind her.

To McCade's surprise, he found the interior to be well
lit, and rather spacious. The light originated from some
chem strips fastened to the animal's belly with some sort of
adhesive. But even more interesting was the large gondola
suspended below the Nuag's midsection by a massive harness. The gondola was made of light plastic boasting both
windows and a door. Taking a peek inside McCade saw
comfortable seats, an array of darkened viewscreens, and
even a tiny galley. He groaned.

"Don't tell me, let me guess. We get to travel in this
thing."

Mara shook her head in pretended amazement. "Amazing. It'll be tough putting anything over on you."

McCade decided to ignore her sarcasm. "How the hell
do these things see anyway? I didn't notice anything resembling eyes out there."

Mara nodded. "Right, there weren't any. Follow me."

McCade followed her toward the front of the animal. He

noticed it had no head to speak of, just a rounded area above its chest, which was mostly mouth. At the moment two feeding tentacles were busily stuffing a gray roller bush into the large pink maw. Mara pointed, and McCade saw there was a single eye located just below the Nuag's mouth, right in the middle of its massive chest. The eye was red in color, and seemed to regard McCade with considerable hostility. "Their eyes are located down here," Mara said, "safe from windblown dust and sand."

McCade looked up from the Nuag's baleful red eye, and into her pretty brown ones. "Kind of a limited point of view, isn't it?"

She shook her head. "Not really. First you must realize that because of the frequent storms, the surface visibility is often zero. And second, it happens that Nuags have no natural predators other than man. And, since they navigate using some sort of biological direction finder we haven't figured out yet, all they have to see is the next few feet of trail."

"Very impressive," McCade said politely, eyeing the gondola dubiously. "How far did you say it was to this Chimehome place?

"I didn't," Mara replied, grinning. "But you'll be pleased to know that it's only a hundred miles or so."

Six hours later, McCade tried to ignore the swaying motion of the gondola, and convince himself that a hundred miles was no big deal. Uncomfortable though it was, he consoled himself with the thought that if the viewscreens meant anything, it was much worse outside. Before departing Deadeye, Mara had placed heavy-duty vid pickups on the outer surface of the Nuag's armor. During the early part of the trip the pickups had provided a somewhat monotonous view of windswept plains. Now even that would be welcome. For the last hour or so all he'd seen was a brown mist of windblown dirt and sand.

Even though he couldn't see it, McCade knew Rico and

Phil's Nuag was close behind, with still another animal
bringing up the rear. In fact, he could have called them on
the radio had he wished to. Although the storms made
long-distance communication difficult, short-range stuff
worked just fine. Nonetheless he resisted the temptation.
They were probably sacked out. That was the weird part of
traveling by Nuag. You didn't have anything to do.

Apparently early settlers had wasted a great deal of time
and energy trying to train the Nuags like horses or other
domesticated riding animals. Eventually, however, they
noticed that each herd had its own migratory paths, and
that animals from a particular herd refused to walk any
paths except their own. They also observed that Nuag
herds were fairly well distributed across the surface of the
planet. So, knowing when they were beat, the colonists
quit trying to train the Nuags to go everywhere, and took
advantage of the places they went on their own. Research
stations and mines were placed along secondary paths,
while major settlements were generally located where a
number of primary walks came together.

Deadeye was a good example. Approximately one third
of all ancestoral routes passed through Deadeye. This was
due to the plentiful supply of roller bushes pushed there by
the circulating winds. It seemed all the Nuag walks had
evolved from the eternal search for food. Like the Nuags
themselves, their food also roamed around, searching for
windblown nutrients. And because the major weather patterns were quite repetitive, the windblown food tended to
end up in certain places, at certain times of the year. So,
while the colonists hadn't managed to train the Nuags, they
had found ways to use them.

McCade had to admit that the system seemed to work.
For hours their Nuags had trudged along without any sort
of guidance. Still, he thought Mara's attitude a bit too re-
laxed, and was determined to keep a careful eye on the
viewscreens. So he scanned them one after another, fight-

ing the hypnotizing movement of the brown mist, completely unaware when he drifted off to sleep.

He awoke with a guilty jerk. The horrible swaying motion had stopped, Mara was no longer asleep beside him, and the door to the gondola was wide open. Glancing at the viewscreens he saw that either the storm had stopped, or they had moved out of it, and into an area of momentary calm.

He climbed down from the gondola, and thumped his fist against the inside of the Nuag's armor, just as he'd seen Mara do. The beast uttered a grunt of protest at this unreasonable demand, but grudgingly lifted its armor, allowing McCade to duck under and out.

Outside, a chill breeze tried to penetrate the stiff fabric of his seamless one-piece windsuit, failed, and whistled past, searching for easier victims. The sky was a dark gray color, and McCade imagined that somewhere above the clouds, the sun was nearing the horizon. About fifteen or twenty other Nuags dotted the area. Most were motionless, resting or asleep, almost covered by windblown sand. But others were awake, and pulling restlessly against whatever held them in place, eager to socialize with the newcomers. McCade looked around but there was no one in sight.

Hearing a noise, he walked around the nearest animal to see Mara feeding the third, with Rico and Phil looking on. The Nuag was grunting contentedly, as Mara pushed a roller bush under its mantle with the help of a short pole.

"So, sleeping beauty awakens," Phil said cheerfully. "It's about time." McCade noticed that due to his thick fur, Phil had seen fit to dispense with a windsuit, and wore only his traditional kilt.

"Hello to you too," McCade replied good-naturedly. "Where are we anyway? And why?"

Mara wrestled the pole away from a playful feeding tentacle, and gave McCade a smile. "We're at Thirty Mile Inn, which is where we're staying tonight."

McCade lifted one eyebrow as he pretended to scan the horizon. "I don't want to seem ungrateful, but at first glance the accommodations seem somewhat spartan."

In response, Mara reached into the cargo pocket on her right thigh, and pulled out a small black box. It had only two buttons and a short antenna. She thumbed the top button, and McCade heard a crunching sound to his right, as a thin crust of dirt and rock parted, making way for a metal shaft. It rose from the ground with a whine of hidden hydraulics. The shaft was about six feet square, had one large door, a lot of smaller hatches, and a pointed top. A number of cables led out of the smaller hatches to disappear under the sand. As it ground to a halt, a sign lit up above the door, WELCOME TO THE THI TY MILE INN.

"Don't tell me, let me guess," McCade said. "The Nuags always stop here for the night . . . so this is where they built the inn."

"Like I said before," Mara grinned. "There's no fooling you. Now, if you gentlemen would give me a hand, I'd sure appreciate it."

She led them over to the metal shaft and opened three small hatches. Behind each door was a power lead. Pulling one out, she handed it to Rico. "If you'd be so kind, sir. You'll find a connector mounted on the rear of your gondola. Just plug it in and flick the mode switch to charge. That way your gondola will have a full charge by morning . . . plus your Nuag will still be here. They tend to drift a bit if you don't tether them, and I don't know about you, but I don't need a mile hike first thing in the morning."

"Yes, ma'am," Rico replied cheerfully. He trudged off toward his Nuag, dragging the power lead behind him. McCade did likewise, quickly discovering that after a few feet the cable got damn heavy.

Meanwhile Mara and Phil headed for the third beast, which though equipped with a cargo gondola, still required power for various passive systems. The big variant used only his thumb and two fingers to haul the heavy cable. It was hard to tell if Mara was impressed or simply amused.

A few minutes later they all met in front of the metal shaft. Mara palmed the lock and the door whined open. A gentle blast of warm air hit them, bringing with it the faint smell of cooking, and the less pleasant odors of stale smoke and beer.

It was crowded inside the small elevator but their journey was soon over. Apparently the inn was just deep enough to keep it out of the wind. After all, McCade thought to himself, why dig any deeper than necessary?

As they got off the elevator, it became quickly apparent that the management of the Thirty Mile Inn never did anything they didn't have to. Where Momma's place was squeakily clean, and therefore the exception to rim world bars, this one was all too typical. The metal grating under McCade's boots just barely managed to keep him up out of the muck below. The walls of the corridor were bare earth, and what little light there was came from some tired chem strips dangling from the ceiling.

"How quaint," Phil growled. "Sam always takes us to the nicest places."

"Yeah," Rico agreed, "I wonder what time the string quartet performs."

Just then the corridor opened into a large open room and McCade knew they were in trouble. As they entered, the normal buzz of conversation suddenly stopped, leaving an unnatural silence broken only by the steady drip of a leaking faucet. Tension drifted with the floating smoke to fill the room and dim the light.

Nine heavily armed people stood with their backs to the bar. None of them looked too friendly. Especially the three hardcases Mara had faced down back in Deadeye. They stood at the very center of the semicircle. One of them, a weasel-faced man with short black hair, wore a shit-eating grin. When he spoke there was a general scraping of chairs as noncombatants scrambled to get out of the way. "Well, bitch, say whatever prayers the Walkers taught you, cause you're about to die."

McCade couldn't believe it. The idiot was a talker. One of the stupid-scared ones that always have to explain how tough they are before they beat up some old geek, and take his drinking money. After a while they get in the habit, and eventually they wind up talking when they should be shooting. Weasel face died getting his next sentence ready. Mara's blaster bolt drilled a neat hole through his chest, hit the full tankard of beer behind him, and turned it to steam. Suddenly all hell broke loose.

Rico and Phil had already spread out right and left. Phil went into full augmentation ripping off the first burst from his machine pistol before McCade had even pulled his slug gun. Two men were still falling, their bodies riddled with Phil's bullets, when McCade's gun leaped into his hand and roared four times. His first shot kicked a leg out from under the woman in the middle, the other three punched black holes through the guy on her right, slowly climbing until the last one erased his face.

Out of the corner of his eye, McCade saw Mara stagger and spin as she took a hit, and saw Rico nail the man who'd shot her. Then death plucked at McCade's sleeve as someone opened up with a flechette gun. Picking them out of the crowd, Phil roared with rage, and leaped across the intervening space to bang two heads together, dropping the limp bodies like so much dead meat. Limp fingers released the flechette gun and it clattered to the floor.

That's when the man on Phil's right brought out a ten-inch blade and prepared to ram it into the variant's back. McCade fired twice and the man toppled backward, landing in a pile on his own guts.

For a long moment there was silence in the bar, interrupted only by the groaning of a wounded man, and the whimpering of a female bystander. Then, as though coming out of a trance, the room gradually came back to life. Rico and Phil gave Mara some first aid, simultaneously chewing her out for scaring them half to death. Phil breathed a sigh of relief when he found the slug had only creased her side.

Meanwhile McCade methodically searched the room. Others eyes met his, but saw only death, and slipped away to look at something else. Satisfied that the immediate danger was past, McCade felt the adrenaline start to ebb away, and cursed the twitching in his cheek.

Thirty minutes later the bodies had been hauled away and the worst of the gore had been mopped up. At Mara's insistence they took seats at a circular table, and waited while a nervous old man placed drinks in front of them.

McCade watched Mara as he slowly rotated a cigar over his lighter. "Maybe you'd better tell us what this is all about."

She shook her head regretfully. "I'm really sorry you got caught in the middle of it. I didn't think they'd make a move this soon. The three in the center were Wind Riders; the rest were just local muscle, waiting for the next caravan out, and eager to make an easy credit."

"Who are these Wind Riders?" McCade asked.

"Basically they're bandits. The name stems from the powered hang gliders they use to attack settlers."

"Wait a minute," McCade interjected with a wave of his cigar, "I thought atmospheric flight was supposed to be impossible here."

"Dangerous and inefficient, yes," Mara replied, "but not impossible. Although long-distance point-to-point flight is so difficult, it's just about impossible. However, that still leaves localized flight outside the storm zones, or on the edge of them, and that's what the Wind Riders specialize in. They use ultra-light aircraft to make aerial attacks on Nuag caravans or settlements. They take great pride in their skill, and rightfully so, because they're very good at it."

McCade sighed. Great. Now in addition to Claudia,

they had a bunch of flying bandits to contend with. He tapped his cigar in the general direction of the floor, and said, "OK, the Wind Riders are in the robbery business, but why are they so fond of you in particular?"

Mara shrugged, and then winced slightly as the motion pulled on her wound. "It's not me so much as it is the Walkers. As a group we oppose the Wind Riders, and encourage the settlers to do likewise. So, when I'm not running supply convoys in from Deadeye, I spend a lot of time helping the locals fortify their homes, and organize commandos."

Phil nodded proudly. "That would piss 'em off all right. No wonder they tried to take you out." Then he turned to McCade with an expression which seemed to say, "So there. You were wrong. The woman's a saint."

"Excuse me, noble ones . . ." The shaky voice belonged to the old man who had served them earlier. He'd watched the fight from the safety of a dark corner, and now he was scared, positive that the people sitting at this table must be even worse than the Wind Riders. His rheumy eyes darted this way and that, like frightened animals trying to escape a trap. "Is one of you noble gentlemen named Sam McCade?"

"Yup," Rico answered, waving his drink in McCade's general direction. "Sam's the ugly one."

Terrified that McCade might resent Rico's joke and take it out on him, the old man began to shake. "I . . . have a message for you . . . you, sir. It . . . It just came in from Deadeye. They picked it up from a ship . . . ship in orbit."

"Once in a while Deadeye can use high-speed transmission to squirt something through during a moment of calm," Mara explained. "They never know exactly when that moment will come, so they record the message, and if it's important enough, broadcast it for days at a time." She turned to the old man. "Take it easy, old one, we won't hurt you. What was the message?"

Relief washed over the old man's face as he fumbled a

piece of fax out of his pocket, and read it in a quavering voice. "'An open message to the citizens of Wind World, from Her Royal Highness, Princess Claudia, Empress pro tem of the human empire. Greetings. It is my unpleasant duty to inform you that a fugitive from Imperial justice has taken shelter among you. Do not believe his lies. Aid him at your peril. He is guilty of murder, treason, and flight from Imperial justice. His name is Sam McCade. I will pay fifty thousand credits for his body—dead or alive—no questions asked.'"

Seventeen

THE WIND FIRED the tiny grains of sand across the plain, like miniature bullets. They stung McCade's cheeks and hands and splattered against his goggles. Sand was everywhere. It had worked its way past the seals of his windsuit, sifted through his underclothes, and was gradually filling his boots. For hours he'd labored in a windblown hell, where everything was gray-brown, and nothing came easily.

Standing only three feet tall, the wall represented hours of back-breaking work, and didn't deserve the title "fort." But a fort it would have to be when the Wind Riders attacked, as Mara assured them they would. At Mara's insistence they had left the questionable hospitality of Thirty Mile Inn, and resumed their journey. Before long the Wind Riders would hear of Claudia's offer and come after them. The opportunity to get Mara, plus the bounty for McCade, would make it irresistible.

Meanwhile, the fugitives decided to make as much

progress as possible. It wasn't easy to convince the Nuags to move at night, and they didn't move fast, but every mile would put them that much closer to their goal and safety. So they left the inn hoping to reach the protection of the next way station before dawn.

They hadn't even come close. A storm came up slowing the Nuags to a crawl. All through the long hours of the night, the Nuags struggled against the wind. Even with their streamlined bodies and phenomenal strength, the big animals were unable to do more than about two miles an hour.

Finally, with dawn only hours away, Mara ordered a halt, pointing out that when the storm cleared, they'd be sitting ducks. And due to the Nuags' predictability, the bandits would know exactly where to find them. They'd simply cruise along the appropriate Nuag path from Deadeye to Chimehome, and bingo, there they'd be, easy targets.

Soon the air would become warmer, creating thermals, and helping the Wind Riders into the air. Shortly thereafter the bandits would locate their prey.

Suddenly Phil appeared at McCade's side, touching his arm, and pointing to the right. Turning, he saw Mara as a black silhouette against the gray dawn. Beneath her feet was the rounded shape of a Nuag. Most of the sound was whipped away by the wind, so McCade heard only a dull thump as she fired Rico's heavy slug gun. The animal's legs collapsed and the poor beast slumped to the ground. It was the last. In spite of his distaste for the animals, McCade couldn't help but feel sorry for them, and for Mara. Tears had streamed down her face as she killed the first two. The Wind Riders would have killed them anyway, and by positioning them evenly around the perimeter of their makeshift fort, she'd at least put their bodies to good use.

The bandits made it a practice to kill Nuags first. Doing

so prevented any possibility of escape, immobilized their loot, and demoralized their opponents all in one easy step. Besides, they couldn't carry the animals on their ultra-light aircraft, and even if they could, the Nuags refused to deviate from their ancestral paths, and were therefore useless to the bandits.

McCade slumped down in the shelter of the stone wall. By connecting the three Nuags it created a large triangle. Its main purpose was to provide cover for anyone moving between the three strongpoints, and for use in the case of a ground attack. According to Mara, the Wind Riders often ran short on fuel, forcing them to land and attack on foot.

Reaching inside his windsuit, McCade found a cigar, and used the protection of the rock wall to light it. Moments later Mara and Phil joined him.

"You might as well grab some shut-eye, Sam. They won't be coming until the storm's over, so jump in the nearest gondola and get some rest. There's enough juice left in the storage cells to keep it warm for a while. Rico volunteered to take the first watch."

"How 'bout you two?"

Mara smiled while Phil tried to look innocent. "We're going to talk for a while . . . and then we'll get some sleep too."

McCade nodded and got to his feet. More power to them. Grab a little happiness when you can. Maybe Mara was reacting to Pollard's death . . . and maybe not. Either way it was none of his business.

A few minutes later he'd managed to pry up a section of Nuag shell and was stretched out in a nice warm gondola under several tons of dead Nuag. It seemed sleeping under dead bodies was getting to be a habit. Sara wouldn't approve. As he drifted off to sleep, he held a picture of her in his mind, and wondered if he'd ever see her again.

He tried to lose himself in total darkness, but found he couldn't. A jumbled montage of thoughts and pictures floated by. A strange face kept inserting itself between them. This had happened once before, but he couldn't remember why, or when. It was a woman's face, pleasant, but somehow concerned. She felt good. Like peace and warmth and comfort. He liked her. She was talking, but he couldn't make out what she was saying.

"I can't hear you," he shouted, his words echoing endlessly back.

She frowned. Her lips moved once more, and this time there was sound, but it was slow and distorted, like a tape playing at half speed.

"Faster," he shouted. "I can't understand you!"

"How's this?" she asked, her voice soft and melodic.

"Much better," McCade sighed, feeling the tension flow away.

"Good," she replied. "By the way, I know the answer to your question."

"I'm glad," McCade said happily. "What was the question?"

"You wondered if you'd ever see her again," the woman replied patiently.

"I did? Oh, yes, I did." McCade thought of Sara and suddenly a lump of fear filled his gut. What if the answer was no?

"Shall I tell you what I see in the flux?" the woman asked.

"Thanks, but no thanks," McCade replied. "I couldn't stand it if the answer was no."

"Very wise," the woman said, nodding her agreement. "Now there is something you must remember when you awake."

"Something I must remember," McCade agreed stupidly.

"Yes," she said. "There will be a fight."

"A fight," McCade agreed.

"Do not kill the blue one."

"No," McCade said, "I won't kill the blue one. . . . What blue one?"

But she was gone, leaving only darkness in her place. "What blue one?" McCade demanded, feeling silly when he realized he was sitting upright inside the gondola talking to himself.

Having people messing around with your dreams can be a bit unnerving, and having dealt with Walker, scratch that, Pollard, he felt sure that someone new had just gone for a stroll through his head. He shrugged and glanced at his wrist term. It was time to relieve Rico. He opened the door to the gondola and crawled out into the morning light.

Jubal stepped out of the shabby dome and finished zipping up his bulky flight suit. It seemed to get tighter every time he put it on. He wasn't tall, and he'd always been beefy, only now some of the beef was turning to lard. "Still," he assured himself, "there's plenty of muscle under the fat, and my reactions are still good."

He closed the final zipper and sniffed the morning breeze. It smelled like easy pickings. Thanks to Princess Claudia, there was a rich prize out there, just waiting to be claimed. Having the Emperor's daughter drop in out of nowhere was a bit weird, but the timing couldn't have been better. The strategy meeting the night before had almost turned into a disaster. He'd barely gaveled the meeting to order when word arrived from Thirty Mile Inn that the bitch Mara had not only escaped, she'd completely wiped out the team he'd sent to kill her as well. Damned embarrassing, and potentially dangerous, when there were scumbags like Yako around just waiting for a sign of weakness. Oh, how that scrawny little runt would like to take over leadership of the Wind Riders! And he might too—if there were any more disasters like the Thirty Mile Inn episode. Stupid buggers.

As Jubal strolled between the low domes, skirting the

junk and piles of garbage, a big smile creased his puffy, unshaven face. Children scurried to get out of his way, their parents shouted greetings, and he lifted a noble hand in reply. "Maybe we aren't rich," he told himself, "but we're a damned sight better off than most of the dirt-scratching settlers." Yes, all things considered, the Wind Riders had prospered under his leadership. Under his predecessor, ol' one-eyed Pete, they'd been living in caves. He grinned wolfishly. It was too bad the way ol' Pete just disappeared like that. He wouldn't let the same thing happen to him.

As Jubal approached the flight line, Yako was already sitting in the seat of his tiny aircraft, running a pre-flight check. Where Jubal was beefy, Yako was wire-thin, having both a body and a personality like a ferret. As Jubal approached, Yako watched him out of the corner of his eye, while pretending to check out the twin energy weapons mounted on either side of the cockpit.

"Good morning, Yako," Jubal said cheerfully as he passed. "Should be a good day for you youngsters to gain some experience."

Yako knew the older man was needling him, and it made him mad, but he managed to swallow his pride and smile. "Good morning, Jubal. I hope you're right."

The other man waved nonchalantly and continued on his way.

Good luck on getting your fat ass off the ground, Yako thought after him.

Two-faced bastard, Jubal thought to himself as he nodded to his ground crew and heaved himself into the seat. There was a provision for a rear seat, but at the moment the space was occupied by a reserve fuel tank. Like all their aircraft, Jubal's was little more than an alloy frame partially covered with thin duraplast. The cockpit was completely open. Above it, the wing itself was surprisingly long, and mounted a tiny engine. The engine was used primarily for gaining altitude and for flying against the prevailing wind. When possible the engine was shut off, and the plane was flown like a glider, explaining its considerable wingspan, and the lightweight construction.

Unlike many of the Wind Riders Jubal found no joy in gliding. Given the choice he would have used his engine constantly. Unfortunately that wasn't possible. Since the Wind World didn't have any oil reserves, all petrochemicals had to be imported, and that made gasoline a very valuable commodity indeed. Outside of expensive antigrav technology, gasoline engines were the only thing light enough to do the job.

Having completed his perfunctory pre-flight check, Jubal used a thick finger to stab the starter button, and smiled his satisfaction as the engine stuttered into life. Just one of the many benefits of leadership. His plane always got the best maintenance. Glancing to the left and right, he saw all five members of his wing were ready. They were older men like him, veterans of many raids, and getting a bit long of tooth. Nonetheless he preferred them to the greenies in Yako's wing. At least you knew what they'd do when the poop hit the fan. They weren't in any particular formation. He didn't go in for all that precision crap like Yako and his flying fruitcakes. "Get your ass in the air and the job done." That was Jubal's motto.

Yako watched Jubal's wing stagger into the air with open contempt. The whole bunch of them should be in a museum somewhere. They'd simply been at it too long. Gone were the days of easy pickings. Thanks to the Walkers the settlers had started to fight back. Hell, they'd started using surface to air missiles for God's sake! When was Jubal going to wake up and see that the old ways weren't good enough anymore? When the wind stops blowing, that's when.

Glancing right and left, Yako saw his own wing was ready to go. There were three ultra lights to either side, each perfectly aligned with his own, each awaiting his command. His pilots were young, eager, and impatient to make their mark. Yako chinned over to his wing frequency. "All right, let's show the old farts how to do it right."

All seven pilots revved their tiny engines, the sounds merging into a single high-pitched scream. "Hold . . . hold . . . get ready . . . now!" As each pilot released their brakes, the tiny planes surged forward, springing into the air a few feet later.

Suddenly Jubal's cheerful voice crackled over Yako's headset. "Tally ho! Last one there's a Nuag's rear end!"

Sure, now that you've got a five-minute head start, Yako thought to himself, putting his plane into a climbing turn. The old clown was obviously in a good mood. And why not? The miserable bastard was about to wiggle out of the trap he'd put himself in. Assuming things went well, they'd punch Mara's ticket, and pick up a nice little bonus from Princess Claudia in the bargain. A success like that could keep Jubal in the driver's seat for some time to come. It was a depressing thought.

The distant planes sounded like angry insects. Even standing on top of a dead Nuag, McCade still couldn't see them yet. Nonetheless, he checked the energy rifle Mara had given him. The power pak registered a full charge, plus he had a pak in reserve. Wind Worlders favored energy weapons because they were equally effective in all kinds of weather. Heavy winds can play hell with a projectile but they don't affect an energy beam in the least. Phil and Rico had energy rifles too and were dug in near the other Nuags. Between the three of them they hoped to catch the Wind Riders in a cross fire.

Mara however was their secret weapon. In spite of Phil's repeated objections she had insisted on hiding in a pit about five hundred yards out from their makeshift fort. They'd used a roller bush to disguise the opening, and tied some more down as well, since they were usually found in groups. Nonetheless it was a dangerous place to be. Once they located her, the bandits could easily cut her off. On the other hand they wouldn't expect her to be outside the fort, and the combination of surprise, plus her mini-launcher might just do the trick. "Well, it oughta scare the hell out of them anyway," McCade told himself.

Jubal grinned. There they were, just waiting for him to come along and scoop 'em up. How considerate! He pushed the stick forward, putting the plane into a long shallow dive. Up ahead he saw three dots which quickly grew into Nuags. They were spaced out to form the three points of a triangle. At first he thought they'd been hobbled that way. Then he realized they were dead. And someone had built a low wall between them too. Smart. But it wouldn't do any good. Flipping a switch on his instrument panel he activated both energy weapons. There was no point in getting tricky. Just strafe the area until everything was dead. Simple and effective. He grinned. Given the chance, Yako would no doubt waste a lot of time creating some fancy strategy to accomplish the same thing. Silly bastard. Now the ground was rushing up fast. Jubal released the safety and pushed the red button mounted on the top of his stick. Twin beams of lethal energy lanced down to cut parallel black lines across the ground below.

The little plane came in much faster than McCade had expected. Instead of shooting back, he found himself diving for the ground, hoping he wouldn't get his ass shot off. The energy beams sizzled as they cut a deep trench through the Nuag's corpse. McCade spit sand and swore. At this rate their fort wasn't going to last very long.

One after another the planes screamed over, their energy beams crisscrossing the compound, quickly reducing the Nuags to large lumps of charred meat. Try as they might, the three men found they could do little more than snap off an occasional shot. The little planes were just too fast and maneuverable.

Yako kicked his right rudder pedal and banked left. By now both wings had made two or three passes apiece, and as far as he could see, all they'd done was cook a few Nuags, and waste a lot of gas. At this rate they'd soon be forced to land and fight on foot, something which not only reduced their advantage, but seemed somehow demeaning. Pilots should fly, not slog around on the ground. As usual Jubal was using brute force instead of brains. Of course you can't use what you don't have. Down below he saw the occasional wink of an energy weapon, but thus far their fire had been completely ineffectual. He'd counted three defenders so far. Yako frowned. Shouldn't there be four? According to the messenger, two men and some sort of an alien had been with Mara at Thirty Mile Inn. So where was number four?

Mara peeked out from under the roller bush to see the planes buzzing and diving over the fort like motorized birds of prey. It was time to make her move. She'd forced herself to wait until the bandits were completely occupied with the fort. Ignoring the pain in her side, she eased the launcher up, until it was just barely sticking out from under the prickly vegetation. Peering into the tiny sight the planes suddenly grew larger. She noticed half were red and the other half bright blue. Each had a number painted on its wing. A blue plane with the number one inscribed on its wings was circling the compound, apparently looking the situation over. "Good, number one. You can be the first to die." She squeezed the trigger, and there was a whoosh of displaced air as the heat-seeking missile went on its way.

McCade looked up at the blue plane with the number one painted on its wings. The "blue one"! The one he shouldn't kill! And he hadn't told the others. They'd maintained radio silence for fear the Wind Riders would monitor their frequency, but McCade felt sure this was important, so he touched his throat mike. "The blue plane with the number one—whatever you do—don't shoot it down!"

"What?" Mara demanded. "Why? Not that it matters because I just . . ."

She never finished her sentence because at that moment the missile hit and exploded. Hot shrapnel flew in every direction, and by chance, a chunk of hot metal hit another plane's fuel tank and blew it out of the air as well.

Chunks of wreckage crashed all around the fort sending up a cloud of billowing black smoke. Mara was still reloading when the blue plane with the number one painted on its wings dove out of the smoke and came her way. She hadn't hit it after all! Not that she could see why it made a difference. One of the other blue planes must have swung in front of it and been hit instead. Oh, well, better late than never, she'd nail him now. The plane quickly filled her sight, and her finger was resting on the trigger, when McCade said, "Don't fire, Mara! Let him go!"

She dived for the bottom of her hole and swore when an energy beam sliced along one side of her hole splattering her with globs of melted sand. Suddenly her side began to hurt even more. Reaching down, Mara found her wound had opened up. She fumbled out a self-sealing battle dressing and slapped it on. "Damn you, McCade, you'd better have one helluva good reason for this!"

"I do," McCade replied, "at least I think I do. I'll explain it later, when you're in a better mood. In the meantime perhaps you'd oblige us by cooking a few more of these bastards. Just leave number one alone."

Twisting herself around in the small hole, Mara managed to gain her feet once more. Picking up the launcher she aimed it toward the wheeling planes and picked out another blue target. "All right, I'll try." She saw movement out of the corner of her eye. The bastard in the "blue one" had located her, and was coming in for the kill. She forced him out of her mind as she picked a target.

Yako was shaking with rage. Two planes! Two pilots! He'd kill her for that. He could see her clearly. Her damned launcher was aimed toward the other planes. Why not him? Surely she must see him coming. Well, never mind. All he had to do was hold it steady and then fire. There was a puff of vapor and he knew another missile was on its way. He knew he shouldn't look, but found he couldn't resist. Damn! The miserable bitch had done it again! Another blue plane exploded into a thousand pieces. Why didn't she aim at one of Jubal's planes? Suddenly he realized he'd already passed over Mara's hiding place, and there, right in front of him, flying like he didn't have a care in the world, was Jubal. Something deep inside Yako suddenly snapped. A wave of anger and resentment flooded through him. When he squeezed the trigger he did it without conscious thought. The twin beams of blue energy cut Jubal's plane in half. Both pieces spun into the ground with tremendous force and burst into flames. For a moment there was silence, as they worked to absorb what they'd just seen, and then there was chaos, as everyone tried to talk at once.

"Did you see that? Yako just killed the boss! Let's nail the bastard."

"Try it and you're dead meat," a blue pilot replied.

"Oh, yeah?"

And suddenly the sky was full of dueling planes. McCade looked on with amazement as the ultra lights wheeled, soared, and dived in a clumsy parody of air combat. In spite of the way the blue plane had blown the red plane out of the air, the dueling pilots didn't seem to be doing much damage to each other, although they were putting on a spectacular show. Even though McCade didn't have the slightest idea why the two groups were fighting, he felt sure it had something to do with the woman in his dream, and what she'd told him. And he knew it was going to save their lives. As the Sky Riders fought each other, they moved farther and farther away, until finally disappearing toward the west.

Mara walked in, and one by one the exhausted defenders emerged from their hiding places to sit slumped in the shelter of a half-burned Nuag. McCade told them about the dream, and though Mara had seen the Walkers do even stranger things, she was still amazed, and said, "Then help is probably on the way."

They all nodded, just happy to be alive, too tired to worry about the future.

Eighteen

McCade rubbed a bleary, bloodshot eye, and looked again. It was still there. Maybe he wasn't hallucinating after all. Maybe there really was a big yellow sail coming his way. He'd been watching it for some time now. It had gradually grown from a drifting dot to a large splash of color. The sail was triangular in shape like those used on any planet with enough water to float a boat. But according to Mara's maps they weren't near any water, so the sail must belong to something else. The sail suddenly flip-flopped. Whatever it was had just tacked, and was now headed directly at him. The Wind Riders again? Coming to finish them off? Or some of Mara's friends—coming to the rescue. Which? There was no way to tell.

They had discussed the possibility of hiking to the next way station but Mara had objected. She felt they were better off staying where they were. In her opinion McCade's dream proved that the Walkers knew where they were, and knew they needed help. Something about the way she said it made McCade wonder if she wasn't just a bit jealous. After all, she was a Walker herself, but for some reason he'd had the dream. Anyway they'd agreed to wait for a while and see if some help came along. Now somebody was coming . . . and the question was who.

He pulled back the corner of the emergency tarp and touched Mara's shoulder. Rico woke in midsnore, and jumped to his feet, while the other two were still untangling themselves. "What's up, sport?"

McCade nodded toward the plain. "We've got company."

"Bandits?"

McCade shrugged. "Maybe . . . maybe not. Let's see what Mara thinks."

Mara had overheard, and wasted no time scrambling up onto the Nuag. She gave a whoop of excitement, turned, and slid to the ground. "I told you they'd help us! They sent a wind wagon. Grab your stuff and let's go. We'll have to jump it on the run. Once they stop it takes 'em forever to get going again."

Each grabbed their weapon and a pack prepared earlier, slipping their arms through the straps as they followed Mara out onto the plain. In spite of her wound, Mara was way ahead of them. Phil had given her some kind of a painkiller and apparently it was working.

The sail was closer now, and McCade saw it was supported by a metal mast, which jutted upward from a low boxy platform. Since the wind wagon was coming straight at them it was hard to see much more, but it was certainly fast, bearing down on them at twenty or thirty miles an hour.

Phil frowned. "Aren't they going to slow down?"

Mara laughed. "'They' are an 'it,' and the answer is 'not much.' Come on!" And with that she started running again.

There was little the others could do but follow. As he

broke into a run McCade decided he'd finally lost his mind. What a silly way to die. Run over by a landlocked sailboat on some rim world! Claudia would love it. She wouldn't even pay a bounty on him. That at least would have cost her something. It was close now, so close he could see the welds holding it together, and hear the big sail slapping against a stay. Just as he decided his only chance lay in falling flat and letting it roll over him, he heard a klaxon go off, and the machine began to turn. It was starting to tack!

"Now!" Mara yelled, leaping for the short ladder which was welded to the hull. Three quick steps and she was over the top, turning to shout encouragement at the others. Phil went into partial augmentation. He took three giant strides and jumped. Huge paws caught the top edge of the hull, while powerful muscles pulled him up, and over. Rico, meanwhile, had managed to jump onto the lowest step of the ladder. He hung on with one hand, stretching the other out towards McCade.

"Come on, ol' sport, you can make it."

But McCade knew Rico was wrong. He was running as fast as he could, and he still wasn't going to make it. Bit by bit the distance between him and Rico's outstretched hand grew larger. Then he heard a crack of sound, and the sail started to flap as it lost the wind. Out of the corner of his eye he saw the heavy boom swinging toward him. He jumped, wrapped his arms around the boom as it passed overhead, and swore as it picked up speed. He'd have to drop off when it passed over the hull, otherwise it would throw him off when it crossed over the far side and was jerked to a halt. Everything was a blur, so he closed his eyes, let go, and hoped for the best.

He landed on his pack. It broke his fall but knocked the wind out of him. The part of his mind not occupied with obtaining more oxygen suddenly realized that he'd lost his energy rifle. That wasn't exactly good news, but it was better than lying in the dirt, watching the wind wagon race away. He opened his eyes to find himself looking up at Rico. The wind tugged at Rico's hair and ruffled his beard. He wore a big grin. "Always showin' off. Maybe if you'd cut back on them cigars you could run a bit faster."

Still unable to speak due to a lack of oxygen, McCade offered the other man an ancient gesture. Rico laughed and helped him up.

The wind wagon had come about, and was making good time back across the plain. Now that he was on his feet McCade saw the hull was a large metal triangle. The sides were low but strong. The mast was made of metal, and was located about halfway down the wagon's length. A quick glance over the side confirmed his original impression that it was equipped with three wheels. Two were located on either side of the stern, and one in the bow, which was used for steering. The hull was about fifty feet across at its widest point, and seventy or eighty feet long. A network of wire stays supported the mast, while a host of lines snaked down through pulleys and power winches, to disappear into a sealed metal box. Since there was no crew in sight, and nowhere for them to hide, McCade assumed the metal box housed some sort of a computer, which controlled the ship via sensors and servo motors. The whole thing was scarred and pitted from countless collisions with windborne debris. Almost every square foot of sail showed signs of repair. The whole thing worked nonetheless.

"Well, what do you think?" Mara asked, gesturing toward the rest of the machine. McCade's reply was forestalled when a sudden gust of wind hit the sail, causing the left rear wheel to leave the ground, and throwing them off their feet. A few seconds later the computer made a minute correction and the wheel thumped back down.

McCade looked at Mara, and they both laughed until Mara grabbed her side, and said, "Enough . . . it hurts when I laugh."

As they helped each other up McCade said, "It's a bit treacherous, but it sure beats walking."

"Or watching Nuags rot in the sun," Mara agreed, brushing herself off. "Apparently this was the best the Walkers could come up with on short notice."

"I won't even ask how they knew we needed it," McCade said, looking around. "What are these rigs normally used for anyway?"

"Ore carriers," she replied, gesturing toward the bow. "And," she continued, "once you've built a wind wagon it's cheap to run. As you can see, they don't need any crew, and the computer's solar powered. Besides catching the wind, the sail also acts as a solar collector and, even with all our clouds, puts out more power than the computer can use."

"So why the Nuags then?" McCade asked, leaning back to look at the huge sail. "Why not use these babies instead?"

Mara smiled. "They're great out on the plains, but completely worthless in the hills and mountains. Which by the way is where we're headed." She pointed toward the distant horizon.

By squinting his eyes, McCade could just barely make out a dark smear above the plains, and beyond that a vague darkness that might have been mountains.

Hours passed, interrupted only by the hooting of the klaxon each time they tacked, and a somewhat spartan meal of emergency rations. Like the others, McCade passed the time by taking short naps, and then getting up to see how much progress they'd made since the last time he'd looked. Finally he stood to find that what had once been a dark smear had now resolved into low rolling foothills, and the darkness beyond them had indeed turned into mountains, which though rounded off by a million years of wind and rain, still reached up to hide their peaks in low-lying clouds. Now the sun was low in the sky, throwing softly rounded shadows out beyond the foothills, making even the Wind World's harsh landscape seem pretty.

"Is that smoke?" It was Rico, pointing off to the right.

McCade looked out beyond the bow, and sure enough, smoke was pouring up from the edge of the plain. Now Mara joined them and eyed the column of smoke with obvious concern. "It's coming from Trailhead, a small settlement, which also happens to be our destination. I can't imagine what's burning. The whole place is made out of shaped earth, reinforced with rock."

McCade noticed the smoke went straight up for several hundred feet before strong winds whipped it away. He had a pretty good idea what could have caused the smoke, but he hoped he was wrong. He'd seen smoke like that before. A glance in Rico's direction told him the other man had similar thoughts. They'd know soon enough.

Twenty minutes later the wind wagon's klaxon sounded three short blasts. There was a whine of servo motors and the clacking of winches as the computer started to lower the sail. At the same time the boom began to rotate, winding the sail around itself, creating a neat cylinder of fabric. Meanwhile the wagon slowly coasted to a stop. There were three similar craft moored a short distance away, and beyond them McCade could see the outskirts of the settlement. Low rounded warehouses and the like mostly, the kind of buildings that go with light industry. Behind them smoke billowed up to fill the sky and the crackle of flames was clearly heard. Now McCade was almost certain this was no ordinary fire.

They climbed over the side and helped Mara snap the mooring lines to the large eyebolts sunk into the plain for that purpose. Otherwise the large vehicle could be blown away by a sudden storm. Once the wagon was secure they followed her toward town. The sun was dipping behind the horizon now, soon to disappear.

The flatness of the plain quickly gave way to a gentle

slope. Their path was wide and unpaved but rock hard
from constant use. Up ahead McCade could see the dim
shapes of the outlying domes and hear the shouts of those
fighting the fires. Smoke swirled everywhere, irritating his
eyes and making it hard to breathe. They came to a stop
when a middle-aged man with a blackened face and a grim
expression appeared out of the smoke. He nodded in
Mara's direction.

"Hello, Mara. So you're here. The Walkers sent word to
expect you." There was no welcome in his voice or his
eyes. They were angry and resentful. He turned to the
others. "My name's Nick. Welcome to Trailhead . . . or
what's left of it. I don't know what this is all about, but I
sure hope it's worth it." And with that he turned his back
on them and started back up the trail.

McCade looked at Mara and she shrugged. Silently they
followed Nick up the trail. It didn't take long to see why he
felt the way he did. For all practical purposes Trailhead
was a memory. Many of the low earthen domes had been
crushed. Others were surrounded by flames fed by some
sort of liquid that burned with intense heat. As they
reached the top of the low hill Nick stopped and pointed
wordlessly down into the center of the settlement below.
McCade looked and found his worst fears had come true.

Sprawled across the small valley was the long broken
shape of an Imperial Intruder. There was no mistaking the
ship's lethal ugliness. Intruders were specifically designed
for landings under combat conditions, but the Wind World
had turned this one into a pile of useless scrap. The fires
which burned around it, and reflected off its polished surface, made it look like a vision from hell. Muffled explosions could be heard as internal fires found and set off
stored explosives. Rivers of flame were born deep inside
the ship to flow out and between the domes. Here and there
figures darted through the flames, searching for survivors,
salvaging what they could.

Mara turned away from the destruction and placed a hand on Nick's shoulder. "I'm sorry, Nick. I know that doesn't help, but please believe me, it's more important than you can imagine." She hesitated for a moment as if considering her options, and then spoke in a low, urgent voice, quickly outlining what was happening and why.

When she'd finished, much of the anger had disappeared from Nick's eyes, leaving only sadness behind. He nodded. "Yes, I'll do what I can. You'll have to catch those bastards before they can reach Chimehome."

"Catch them?" McCade and Mara asked together.

"Yes," Nick replied, anger flooding his features once more. "Right after the ship crashed, a hatch opened and an armed crawler rolled out. An officer, Major Tell, Tellor—something like that—asked me for directions to Chimehome, and like an idiot I told him. Then they took off. Didn't even try to help their own . . . much less ours."

The three men looked at each other. Major Tellor! Here. It certainly sounded like him. All three remembered the enjoyment in his eyes as he'd left them to die in the coliseum. Their situation had just gone from bad to worse.

"All right," McCade said grimly. "They've got a head start . . . and we've got to stop them before they reach Chimehome. Is there anything around here which can match that crawler for speed?"

Nick thought for a moment, and then shook his head. "No, we've got a few tractors for pushing ore around, but nothing to match that military job."

Mara shook her head. "Even if there was, we'd be crazy to race them, that crawler won't make it even halfway to Chimehome."

Nick nodded his agreement.

Seeing the doubt in McCade's eyes Mara said, "The planet will stop them. That's why we don't use crawlers ourselves. This world turns unprotected machinery into junk faster than you can bring it in. All we have to do is grab a couple of Nuags and plod along. They'll be waiting for us."

McCade had his doubts, but Mara seemed certain, and from what Nick said there wasn't much choice. Of greater concern was what lay ahead. Assuming Mara was correct, something nasty would eventually happen to the Imperial crawler, and as a result, they would run into Major Tellor and an undetermined number of marines. And knowing Tellor, his troops wouldn't be sitting around reading poetry to each other. They'd either be hiking toward Chimehome on foot, a less than pleasant experience on the Wind World, or, more likely, laying in ambush, hoping to acquire some new transportation. Like a couple of Nuags for example. With us thrown in as a bonus, McCade thought to himself. It wasn't a very pleasant thought.

Nineteen

AT SOME TIME during his long career Tellor had probably been more uncomfortable than he was right now, but he couldn't remember when. For almost half a day he'd been waiting. It was the sound that bothered him most: a low rumble, which rose and fell endlessly. Try as he might he couldn't get rid of it. He'd tried ignoring it, accepting it, and humming over it. Nothing worked.

Gritting his teeth, he stared at the point where the path disappeared around the bend, and willed some sort of transportation to appear. Anything. Anything that would get him up the path to Chimehome. Sweeping his powerful glasses across the land his eyes confirmed what his mind already knew. Had known even in orbit. Out here it was a long way between bars.

The space jockeys had provided a fairly decent aerial survey map showing all the major roads, settlements, and ground features for the area. The cloud cover had obscured a few areas, Chimehome among them, but all things considered it was a good map. One glance told him: One, this was wide open country with very little vegetation or other natural obstacles, in other words, tank country, and two, for some stupid reason all the roads meandered from place to place. Solution, ignore 'em. The quickest way from point to point is always a straight line. So Tellor laid his plans accordingly, but instead of a nice neat landing, the damn winds had smeared the Intruder all over the landscape.

Luckily, about ten percent of his insertion team survived the crash, as did one of his five armored vehicles. Not good, but not bad all things considered. The idea of aborting his mission never even occurred to him. Duty first.

They had made pretty good time at first, slowed by the wind, but still burning up the miles. As the only surviving driver, Blenko had the con. He was a homely man, with raw asymmetrical features, stooped shoulders, and tiny little white hands. As he drove they darted here and there, uncertain and afraid.

The road was not a road in the conventional sense. No intelligence had planned and then paved it. It went where Nuags had gone for thousands of years.

Seeing no reason to follow the road's meandering course, Tellor ordered Blenko to ignore it. So the crawler cut across great loops of road doing in minutes what it took Nuags hours to do. It looked like they'd reach the settlement in time for lunch the next day. And then, just when things were going so well, it all came apart. They were rolling across the floor of a valley, heading toward the far slope, when disaster struck.

Looking left, Blenko saw a brown wall of wind-borne sand scudding toward them, and shrugged. No big deal he told himself, just another dust storm. Since leaving the ship they'd rolled through three or four small ones without a hitch, and no wonder, it takes a lot to stop an armored crawler. Blenko's flat brown eyes flicked over the gauges.

All four intake filters looked good, both engines, okay, all systems go. Satisfied there was nothing to fear, Blenko slumped back, returning his attention to a well-worn fantasy concerning Sergeant Okada.

At first Tellor agreed with Blenko's superficial assessment of the storm, but as he watched it race toward them, he began to wonder, and wonder turned to doubt, and then doubt to certainty. Punching the port screens up to full mag he felt the bottom drop out of his stomach. Sol! That thing was carrying more than just sand! It was picking up boulders and tossing them around like feathers! Other shapes were dimly visible within the brown mist too, including something which looked a lot like one of those big animals the local colonists used, and other stuff as well. Now the brown wall was only a mile away and moving with incredible speed. They'd never outrun it, and if the storm hit them broadside, those rocks would pound the crawler into pieces.

"Turn into the storm, Blenko! Turn left, damnit!"

Tellor could still see the vacant look in Blenko's eyes as the marine slowly turned his attention from a vision of Okada's naked buttocks to his commanding officer's urgent voice. Finally Tellor's words seemed to register, and Blenko's tiny white hands fluttered from one control to the next, slowly turning the crawler into the storm. Had he reacted faster they might have made it.

Thunderclaps of sound came at them as the storm beat the crawler like a gong, pushing it higher and higher, finally flipping it over altogether, and exposing its vulnerable underside to the full fury of the storm. Within seconds the rock bombardment had destroyed the crawler's drivetrain, ripped off a track, and holed the main fuel tank. Ten minutes later the storm was gone, leaving three dead marines, a wrecked crawler, and a furious Major in its wake. Once he realized the storm was over Tellor grabbed Blenko from behind, with every intention of killing him. Unfortunately his hands encountered no resistance. The driver was already dead.

Salvaging what they could from the wreckage, the marines trudged to the nearest loop of road, and dug in. Tellor sighed. So instead of rolling into Chimehome, he was lying on some very uncomfortable rocks, trying to shut out the sound of the blasted wind. Even if the interference suddenly disappeared, their remaining com set wasn't powerful enough to reach into space, so help was out of the question, and the storms made continuing on foot impossible. So, all he could do was wait, and hope some transportation would come along and fall into his trap.

And then, as if in answer to his prayers, something moved in the far distance. Whipping the binocam left, he stopped, hitting the autofocus button, and marveling at his good luck. He certainly deserved some, and there it was, one, no, two of those beetlelike animals. Where were their heads anyway? They'd been included in the pre-drop briefing, but he hadn't paid much attention. Nugs? No, Nuags. All he remembered was people rode under them, instead of on top, and that Nuags refused to deviate from their ancestral paths. Well, it didn't matter. A ride's a ride. Carefully chinning his mic on he whispered, "Objective in sight. Range, two thousand yards. Hold for my signal."

Eight double clicks echoed in Tellor's ear as each member of his team flicked their mic on and off twice. Good. Everyone was awake and paying attention.

The Nuags were closer now. Just a few more minutes and he'd spring the trap. His troops would slip out of their hiding places quickly surrounding the animals. They'd call for the passengers to surrender, and if they refused, go in after them. Either way they'd have to die. On a mission like this one it's a mistake to leave enemies or witnesses behind you. Those were the rules—good rules—rules which had protected him for many years. After all, what if by some twist of fate Claudia lost her bid for the throne?

His sponsor would be gone, along with her the legal protection he presently enjoyed.

Suddenly something hard and cold was jammed into Tellor's right ear. He knew what it was. A gun barrel. The damned wind had allowed someone to sneak up on him unheard.

"Move and you're dead." For a split second Tellor considered going for his blaster but didn't. The voice was as hard and as cold as the steel in his ear. He felt an expert hand remove his sidearm, combat knife, and the tiny backup needler strapped to his ankle. He still had a small knife concealed in his belt, but that wasn't going to accomplish much against someone with a gun. Best to wait and see how things went.

"OK, you can turn . . . slowly." A chill ran down Tellor's spine. There was something familiar about that voice. It couldn't be. Nobody could have luck that bad. As the gun barrel left his ear he slowly turned his head. Shit! It was Sam McCade.

McCade grinned. "Hello, Major, fancy meeting you here." He placed a finger over his lips. "Mums the word though. We wouldn't want to distract your team with our idle chatter."

McCade used his left hand to remove the binocam from Tellor's unresisting fingers. He used his left hand to sweep it across the hillside below, while his right hand kept the slug gun centered on the marine's spine. Tellor didn't even consider testing McCade's reflexes. Not after seeing tapes of the battle in the Imperial Coliseum.

McCade saw that the Nuags were almost in position. "All right, Major, in a moment I'm going to say 'now.' When I do, give your team the go ahead. Get fancy and you're dead. It's up to you. OK . . . ready . . . now."

Tellor chinned his mic switch, and said, "The objective is in position . . . go!"

And they went. Rising from the ground like ghosts they

swept down the hillside to surround the Nuags below. The moment they were in position, Sergeant Okada bellowed, "You're surrounded. In the name of the Emperor, throw down your weapons and come out!"

For a moment nothing happened. Then, just as Okada started to order the team in, the lead animal gave a snort of protest, and grudgingly lifted an armored skirt. An attractive black woman emerged. As she straightened up, Okada saw both her hip and shoulder holsters were empty. "Where's the rest?" Okada demanded.

The black woman smiled. "Behind you. Throw down your weapons and surrender."

But Okada was having none of that. She knew what her job was, and it didn't include dropping her weapon for some unarmed colonial. Her blast rifle was already spitting blue energy as she spun around. Her dying brain barely registered the flash of light that killed her before a wave of darkness snuffed her out. Two more marines fell to Rico's and Phil's markmanship, before the rest gave up, and threw down their weapons. As Rico and Phil made their way down from their hiding places at the top of the hill, Mara forced the marines to sit on their hands, while she gathered their weapons into a pile.

As McCade followed Tellor down the hill, he gave thanks the plan had worked. About a hundred things could have gone wrong but didn't. They'd been very lucky to spot the marines while they were too busy carving hiding places to notice.

After forcing the Nuags out of sight down the trail and sneaking up to the crest of the hill, they'd watched the marines for a while, counting the opposition, mapping their locations, and planning their counterambush. Unfortunately the Nuags wouldn't leave their ancestral path, so there was no way to circle around the ambush. After that, it was a matter of creeping into position, and hoping for the best.

As McCade and Tellor reached the bottom of the slope, Phil said, "Welcome, Major, if you'd just step over there." He pointed to the group of angry-looking marines.

Tellor did as he was told. Rico turned to McCade. 'What's the plan, sport, we can't take 'em with us."

McCade ran his eyes over the marines. They were a bedraggled bunch, but far from beaten, and even unarmed they were dangerous as hell. He hated to leave them behind, but Rico was right, they didn't have room for prisoners. If the positions were reversed, McCade knew what Tellor would do. But McCade had no stomach for cold-blooded murder. They'd have to leave the marines behind and hope for the best.

Tellor sneered, as if able to read his thoughts, and amused by his weakness. McCade ignored him as they made ready to depart. They left the marines their food and medical kits, nothing more.

Thirty minutes later they were on their way. Mara and Phil rode together, suspended under the first Nuag, while McCade and Rico followed along behind.

The marines were just a dwindling image on the rear screens. They stood in a clump apparently listening to Major Tellor. A little pep talk perhaps, or maybe a major ass chewing, with the Major doing the chewing.

Hours passed and it seemed as if their luck had taken a turn for the better. The wind died down, the clouds vanished, and the Nuags walked along under blue skies. Soon they were out of the foothills and working their way up into the mountains beyond.

Occasionally they took turns walking beside the Nuags, enjoying the fresh air and the exercise. There were lots of things to look at. Rocks shimmered and sparkled in the sun. Flowers shaped like dinner plates, which turned toward the sun and shook off layers of windblown dust to reveal their brilliant colors. Small animals scurried here and there, largely ignoring human and Nuag alike, intent on their various errands. Mara told them that while the clear weather wouldn't last long, it arrived with a certain regularity, and played an important part in the local ecology. Each period of clear weather functioned like a Terran spring, setting off a frenzy of feeding, mating, and other behaviors. As a result, many life forms had very short birth to death cycles, though some—the Nuags were a good example—had evolved adaptations allowing them to live to a ripe old age.

Once, McCade sighted a distant speck in the sky. It moved in wide lazy circles, riding the thermals upward. Thinking it a bird, he pointed, and asked Mara what kind it was. She took one glance and swore. "Wind Riders." She spat the words out one at a time. Moments later the speck disappeared into the distant haze. There was no way to tell if they'd been spotted, but the incident worked to dampen their spirits, and Mara urged the Nuags to move faster.

Night had come and gone, and all were walking in the early morning light when McCade heard the music. At first it seemed part of the gently rising wind. However, when the wind dropped off for a moment, and the music continued, he knew it was real. It had a strange haunting quality, quite unlike anything he'd heard before, yet familiar somehow. It managed to make him both happy and sad at the same time. Looking at the others McCade saw they heard it too. Their expressions reflected mixed emotions. Except for Mara. Her expression was different. She was happy— like someone greeting an old friend too long absent.

Now the wind reasserted itself, and as they walked the music became louder and louder, until the air seemed saturated with it, driving McCade's emotions up until he thought they could go no farther, and then releasing them to slide quickly downward, to start all over again.

A few minutes later they rounded a bend, and there, spread out below them, was Chimehome. The village was nestled in a small valley between twin mountain peaks.

The valley served to protect the small collection of white domes from storms, and also acted as an acoustic enclosure for the huge wind chimes, which gave the place its name.

A single glance told McCade the chimes were a work of nature. Eons ago a spire of volcanic rock had been upthrust from the planet's molten core. Millions of years came and went. By now the rock had cooled, and the winds had come to rule the planet, bringing their endless cycles of good and bad weather. With them came the countless snows which blanketed the surrounding peaks with white, melted during brief periods of sunny weather, to run gurgling and splashing down into the valley below. As it passed, the water pushed and tugged at the small spire of rock, as though considering the various uses to which it might be put. Then, as if decided, it went to work. With eternal patience, the water probed and pulled, carving soft material away from hard, smoothing here, and shaping there. As the water dug deeper the spire grew taller, until finally it stood like a sentinel, guarding the valley from harm. And then one day, long before Nuags evolved from small animals which burrowed in the earth, the water cut one last tendon of volcanic flesh, and a large plate of delicately balanced rock broke free. For a moment it hung there, twisting slightly back and forth as the wind played with its new toy. Then a sudden gust pushed it sideways to strike a hard surface and the first note rang out. At first the chimes had only that single note to play, but as the years passed, and the water continued its marvelous work, other notes were added, until finally an intricate maze of delicately balanced rock produced an endless symphony of sound.

As they followed the path down into the valley below, McCade was amazed at how quickly his mind accepted the music produced by the chimes. Somehow it flowed in and around him without dominating his emotions or interfering with his thoughts. As they drew closer to the whitewashed domes which nestled together on the valley floor, he realized the whole place felt right somehow, as if expressing some internal harmony. Was that an expression of the Walkers and their philosophy? Or a manifestation of the place itself? There was no way to know, but the name Chimehome certainly fit, and the village seemed the perfect place for a monastery.

They had almost reached the village when a small group of people started up the path to meet them. They wore a variety of clothing, ranging from the somber to the gay, but all were smiling, and the young man leading them looked familiar somehow. Then McCade had it. The biosculptors had roughened his features slightly, but he was still tall, handsome, and blond like his sister. There was laughter in his sparkling blue eyes. As they shook hands the blond man smiled. "You must be Sam McCade. My name's Alex. I understand you've been looking for me."

Twenty

McCADE WAS ALONE in the observatory. Outside, the storm still raged, though more slowly now, much of its energy expended during the night. The rising sun was a dusty glow in the distance, still barely visible through the curtain of windblown sand. Eventually the wind would die away, but until then they were prisoners of the storm.

McCade lit another in a long series of cigars, blowing the blue smoke upward, to gather toward the top of the transparent duraplast dome. It swirled there for a moment, until the nearest exhaust vent sucked it away to become part of the storm. The last day and a half had left him with mixed emotions. On the one hand there was the satisfaction of finding Prince Alexander, and on the other, there was the growing fear of losing him. The longer the storm kept them captive, the more time Claudia had to find them. And that would be very bad, not just for them personally, but for the Empire as a whole.

Reluctantly, and against his better judgment, McCade

had come to admire Prince Alexander, or Alex, as he preferred to be called. This was no spoiled princeling, insulated from the real world, and demanding respect he didn't deserve. No, there was a quality to the man. A questioning spirit, which had caused him to gamble his inheritance, plus a wealth of intelligence and courage which had seen him through when he'd lost. Those qualities, combined with a self-deprecating wit, made the prince hard to resist. It was as if Alexander had inherited his father's pragmatisim, but invested it with a genuine concern for other people. They had talked for many hours, waiting for the storm to pass. Alexander had put him immediately at ease by saying, "I already know about my father's death, Sam, and have for weeks."

Seeing McCade's confusion, the prince smiled. "I know all this must seem very strange to you, Sam—Chimehome, the Walkers, and the rest. Believe me, I felt the same way at first, but it's all quite real, and very useful. My father's death is a good example. You've heard about what the Walkers call the flux? Good. Well, the concept fascinated me from the start. However, the elders were reluctant to provide me with instruction. They are rightfully wary of novices who care little about learning The Way, and seek instead special powers with which to elevate their own egos, or gain advantage over others. But I argued long and hard, worked to understand the principles which light The Way, and finally received their permission. I was taught to meditate, to work through a variety of exercises, and, most of all, to consider what good I might accomplish if I succeeded. For as the elders pointed out, such abilities are nothing but tools, worthless unless applied to some purpose.

"So one day, there I was, working my way through a series of exercises, and not making much progress, when suddenly I was somewhere else, standing in a matrix of multicolored energy. It pulsed and flowed all around me, and somehow in its movement I saw shapes and patterns, people and events, all moving and interacting in accordance with their own free will, and the immutable laws of the universe. Millions and billions of variables forming to create endless combinations of cause and effect. It was incredible, Sam."

As Alexander spoke, his eyes glowed, and his whole face seemed to light up. "For one splendid moment it all made sense. Each life seemingly isolated, but part of the whole, just as each drop forms part of the ocean. At first I couldn't understand what I saw, overwhelmed by the sheer size and complexity of it all, but eventually I began to focus on smaller areas, and things began to have meaning. Here and there I saw patterns emerge, saw energies gather, build, and then release themselves to create what we know as reality. It was then that I saw my father's death, knew it had already taken place, and understood the forces it had set in motion."

For the first time since they'd met, McCade saw Alexander's face darken, as if a cloud had just passed between him and the sun. "Up ahead, I saw a branching, a division of energies which I somehow knew represented two possible futures, each equally possible based on past events, each dependent on the free will of certain individuals. In one case Claudia took the throne, and the tendril of energy which symbolized her rule led off into what seemed like a final darkness. The other path was mine. It was weaker, less likely, but led to a future which seemed to swirl and shift with many possibilities, some good, some bad. And then it was over, and I've never managed to duplicate the experience since." Here Alexander laughed. "So beware, Sam, even if I take the throne, the Empire's problems aren't over."

McCade half smiled, and flicked some cigar ash toward a nearby receptacle. "I'm glad you said that, Alex. Otherwise it would be tempting to shoot you here and now. One Claudia's enough."

For a moment the prince frowned, as if thinking McCade's comment through, and then he laughed uproariously, almost falling out of his chair. "And you would too! By God, if we get out of here alive, remind me to surround myself with people like you. In fact, how would you like a job? I could use you on my staff."

McCade smiled. "Thanks, but no thanks, Alex. I don't think I'd fit in around the palace."

"Well, at least consider it," the other man replied seriously as he leaned back in his chair. "Anyway, after my experience with the flux, I approached the elders, and they confirmed what I'd seen. At first I was angry—why hadn't they told me? Then as I began to calm down I was glad they hadn't. My experience with the flux was something special, something I'll never forget, and all the more valuable because I'd experienced it firsthand. So I spent a couple of days thinking about it, and although I still wasn't thrilled with the idea, it seemed as if I should return and, God willing, take the throne. In fact, I was preparing to leave when word came through that you were on your way. All things considered, it seemed wise to wait for some help. I understand Claudia is trying to find and kill me." He shrugged sadly. "It pains me that she would do that, but doesn't especially surprise me. Looking back I realize she's got a lot of her grandfather in her. Whatever it takes to get the job done. Well, anyway, now you've heard my story, so let's hear yours."

So McCade recounted the adventures leading up to his arrival at Chimehome. Every now and then Alex interrupted with a question. The first concerned Swanson-Pierce. "This Rear Admiral who engaged your services, what was his name again?" As McCade answered he realized he was probably doing Swanson-Pierce an enormous favor. Damn! Walt was bad enough as a rear admiral; if he made full admiral he'd be completely insufferable. Chances were, Alex was putting together a mental list of those deserving a reward after he took the throne.

Having explained who Walt was, and how they happened to know each other, McCade continued his story. It went smoothly until he reached the meeting with Lady Linnea. Then the prince stopped him again, his expression was one of eagerness mixed with suspicion. "How did she look?"

McCade repressed a smile as his mind conjured up an image of Lady Linnea in the nude. "Very beautiful. As a matter of fact she sent you a message."

Alexander became suddenly impatient and annoyed, providing McCade with a glimpse of his royal upbringing. Alex might be a regular guy in some respects, but deep down he was still a prince. "Well, man, out with it. What did she say?"

"She said I should tell you she loves you, and that the Empire needs you."

For a moment Alexander's face softened, and McCade was reminded of the holo showing the two of them in the garden. There seemed little doubt that he loved her, yet his face hardened as he asked, "But what of her friendship with my sister?"

McCade shrugged. The conversation was becoming distinctly uncomfortable. "I'd say she's on your side. Apparently she's forced to maintain the appearance of friendship with your sister."

Alexander nodded thoughtfully as if the whole thing made perfect sense. "Yes, otherwise my sister might destroy Linnea's father . . ." For a moment he seemed lost in thought, then he motioned for McCade to continue.

As McCade did so, he felt that more and more of plain old Alex was dropping away, gradually revealing something that looked a lot like an Emperor. A nice Emperor

. . . but an Emperor nonetheless. Well, it made sense. After all, he'd been born and raised to the job.

From that point on, the prince restricted himself to an occasional chuckle, or a spontaneous "well done," making no other comment until McCade reached Pollard's death. As McCade described how the Walker had died letting them into the dome, a great sadness came over Alexander's face, and he looked down toward the floor. They were both silent for a moment, and when Alexander finally looked up, tears were running down his cheeks. He made no effort to wipe them away. "I lost a good friend, Sam, but my tears are for myself, not Pollard. He's where no one can hurt him."

McCade had never been able to decide about the question of life after death, but he nodded his agreement anyway, hoping it was true. They drank a series of toasts to Pollard, and by the time McCade finished his story, they were both slightly drunk. "To you, Sam McCade," Alex said, forming each word carefully, and holding his glass up high, "to one helluva bounty hunter. No, let me rephrase that, to the best damn bounty hunter in the Empire! Nobody else could've done it."

"Thank you," McCade replied, trying not to slop any of his drink on his lap. "And here's to you, the only Emperor stupid enough to give it up, and smart enough to get it back!"

Alex roared with laughter, and the two of them proceeded to drink and tell lies, until McCade began falling asleep. Tactfully suggesting they both needed some sleep, Alexander had gone to bed, allowing McCade to do the same.

Now, nine hours later, McCade felt slightly hung over, and wished the storm would abate, allowing them to head for Deadeye and *Pegasus*. Fortunately they wouldn't have to spend days riding under a Nuag. Instead, they would use some large gliders which belonged to the Walkers, and could be launched from high in the mountains. Weather and thermals allowing, the gliders could make it to Deadeye in just a few hours. Later they would be torn down, and brought back to Chimehome by Nuag caravan. It was a lot of work, and therefore something the Walkers seldom did, but this was an emergency, and they had gladly offered McCade and Alex use of the system.

Of course, once they made it to Deadeye, there was still the matter of getting safely off-planet, and finding a way to slip through Claudia's blockade undetected. McCade stubbed out his cigar and stared out into the storm. They had a long way to go.

Twenty miles to the north, the storm continued to blow, but more gently now, as it gradually lost its strength. Yako completed his inspection of the ultra lights, located the flashing blue beacon marking his survival shelter, and struggled toward it through a brown mist of windblown dirt and sand. Other identical shelters surrounded his, each housing two members of his wing, and each having its own colored beacon. It wasn't a pleasant place to camp, but it was close to Chimehome, and when the storm died down, that might become important. Getting down onto his hands and knees, he wriggled his way through the low entrance into the relative comfort of the interior.

"Welcome home," Major Tellor said with only a trace of sarcasm. He was sitting with his back against a pile of equipment, an open meal pak steaming beside him. The light suspended from the roof reflected off his recently shaven head, and cast deep pools of shadow beneath his eyes. "Everything all right?"

"Good enough," Yako grunted as he found a place to sit. "The storm's dying. In four or five hours we'll be able to fly."

"And so will they. That's when they'll try the gliders." Tellor made it more a statement than a question.

Yako shrugged. They'd been over this many times and the marine never seemed to listen. What the hell did he want? A gold-plated guarantee? "There's no way to be sure, Major. If they're in a hurry, the gliders are the fastest way to reach Deadeye. On the other hand, the Walkers rarely use them, partly because of us, and partly because of all the work involved in carting them back. So this McCade guy might opt for ground travel instead."

"In which case he'll run right into my team . . . and this time he won't be so lucky," Tellor said thoughtfully. "My people have orders to blast anything that comes down that path."

"Right," Yako said reassuringly, remembering the weapons he'd sold to the marines at incredibly inflated prices. "No matter what they do, you've got 'em."

"Why gliders anyway?" Tellor asked.

"Beats me," Yako replied. "Someone told me it's part of their harmony with the planet thing, but you'd have to ask them." Asshole, Yako added silently.

Tellor nodded, and proceeded to eat his food, chewing each bite with military precision. He was staring off into space, as though he could see right through the wall of the shelter, all the way back to Terra.

Happy to end the conversation, Yako fumbled around inside an open duffle bag until he found a meal pak. Damn. Pseudo meat again. Yako ripped off the tab and waited for the contents to warm up. He didn't like Tellor much and was doing his best to hide the fact. First because the Major had promised him enough credits to last the Wind Riders for a long, long time, and second, because the marine scared the hell out of him. After all, it sounded like half the Imperial fleet was in orbit around the Wind World. Something like that could be real bad for business. But it wasn't. In fact he'd had a lot of good luck lately. Take Jubal's untimely demise for example. Sure, he'd lost some good people in the brawl with Jubal's wing, but he'd also wound up in command, something which had seemed hopeless just a few days before. Then, just to put the icing on the cake, one of his scouts had stumbled across Tellor and his marines. The scout had been looking for Mara and McCade; after all, Jubal or no Jubal, they had a score to settle with those bastards. So here comes a pack of marines willing to pay him for doing exactly what he wanted to do anyway! What could be better? Yako chuckled deep inside. In spite of Tellor's efforts to gloss it over, you didn't have to be a military genius to see that he'd been ambushed, stripped of all his weapons, and left to make his way on foot. If Tellor failed to find McCade and kill him, Claudia would have his ass. Yako found the prospect quite appealing.

"What's so funny?"

Yako looked up, startled. He wasn't sure that he'd laughed out loud. Tellor's eyes were narrowed, as if he somehow knew the laughter was directed at him. "Nothing special, Major," Yako replied. "Just a joke someone told me earlier today."

Tellor nodded, but continued to watch Yako suspiciously, until the little man grew so uncomfortable he decided to take a nap. Anything was better than Tellor's unwavering gaze. A few minutes later Yako was asleep, dreaming about a monster who wouldn't stop staring at him, and a man named McCade who was supposed to die but wouldn't.

McCade watched the preparations with a jaundiced eye. He'd flown gliders before, but usually they were towed into the air behind an aircar, not launched off the side of a seven-hundred-foot cliff. In front of him two skeletal-looking ramps swooped down the steep hillside to end at the edge of the abyss. People were climbing all over the durasteel structures making sure that recent storms hadn't damaged them. Meanwhile a white glider sat poised at the top of each ramp. They were pretty craft, made out of lightweight duraplast, and gracefully shaped. So much so that the energy weapons mounted under the long slender wings and behind the canopy looked foreign and out of place. McCade prayed they wouldn't need the weapons. Flying a glider after so many years without practice was bad enough, but having people shoot at you while you did it, well, that was just too much. However, it seemed like he didn't have much choice. It turned out the gliders were two-place craft, which meant they'd have to leave Mara behind, and do their own flying. And while Alexander had flown just about everything else, he'd missed gliders, and Phil's experience was limited to aircars. So McCade and Rico would have to get behind the controls and hope for the best. He looked up toward the sky. At least the weather was right. The wind had died down to a gentle breeze, and here and there, the sun peeked through the eternal overcast.

There was the shrill sound of a whistle, and turning toward the sound McCade saw the inspectors had scrambled down off the ramps, and were gathering around the gliders. Rico waved in his direction and shouted, "Come on, ol' sport, all aboard the Deadeye express!" With a jaunty wave Rico climbed into his glider, settling himself behind the controls.

Forcing a grin McCade climbed up the path leading to the launching platform. Off to one side he saw Phil give Mara one last bear hug, before lumbering over, and climbing in behind Rico. Earlier, while saying his good-byes, McCade had noticed Mara's eyes were red. Phil hadn't said anything, but apparently there'd been a parting of the ways, and not at his request. If so, McCade wasn't too surprised. In order for the relationship to succeed, one of them would have to make a very large sacrifice. While he hadn't complained, Phil's variant physiology made life on anything but an iceworld distinctly uncomfortable. And, in her own way, Mara was just as tied to her world. She had an almost mystical understanding of it. Besides, she clearly wished to continue her studies with the Walkers, and that would be impossible if she left.

As he climbed onto the platform Alex was there, shaking hands and exchanging hugs with various friends, turning mischievously as McCade arrived. "Oh, driver, do try to be more prompt in the future. Imperial affairs await, you know."

"A thousand pardons, Your Supreme Effluence," McCade replied, bowing deeply. "If you would be so kind as to lower your Imperial posterior into the cockpit, we can depart posthaste."

"It's so hard to find good help these days," Alex confided to an amused woman with long black hair. "One must put up with the most outrageous incompetence." With a grin and a wave, Alexander followed McCade into the cockpit, and helped slide the canopy closed over their heads.

McCade put on the pilot's helmet and chinned his mic. "Rico? Do you read me?"

"Loud and clear, Sam," Rico answered from the other glider, grinning from behind his plastic canopy.

McCade quickly scanned the simple instrument panel. With no engine to worry about, there weren't many instruments, and very little which could go wrong. Except getting our rear ends blown off, he thought to himself. However, due to the height of their launching platform the altimeter already showed 725 feet, and that made him feel better. At least they wouldn't have to go through a long vulnerable climb up from the ground.

"All set, Alex?"

"Ready when you are, Sam."

"OK, the last one to Deadeye buys the beer!" And with that McCade hit the lever marked release, and felt his stomach lurch, as the glider slid downward. The aircraft quickly picked up speed, moving faster and faster, until they shot off the end of the ramp and their wings cut into the air. Pulling the stick back, McCade started looking for more altitude. In spite of the seven hundred feet they already had, it wasn't nearly enough to reach Deadeye. Because a glider has no engine, it spends a great deal of its time falling. Glider pilots like to call this part gliding, but in reality it's nothing more than controlled falling, which accounts for the sport's relative lack of popularity, and also explains why gliders aren't used for serious transportation. "Except on this stupid planet," McCade said through gritted teeth as he felt the nose drop and the glider start downward.

Banking to the right, McCade tried to find some warmer air which would buoy them upward. Meanwhile the altimeter continued to unwind. Six hundred and fifty, then six hundred and twenty-five, and finally six hundred feet came and went, before he cut across a thermal and felt it lift his wings. Circling to stay with the warm air, the glider soared upward, first regaining the lost altitude, and then picking up even more, until the thermal disappeared, and McCade leveled out at eight hundred and seventy feet. A glance to the right confirmed that Rico was still with him. The other pilot gave him a cheerful thumbs-up, and McCade waved in return. Then he checked his course to make sure they were headed for Deadeye, and allowed himself a smile of satisfaction. They still had a long way to go, but it was a pretty good start.

Then Alex's voice came over the intercom. It was tense and concerned. "Looks like we've got company, Sam, behind us about eight o'clock high."

McCade craned his neck to see, and swore softly when his eyes confirmed Alexander's report. They were just black specks for the moment, gradually climbing, but there was no doubt as to who they were. The Wind Riders had found them.

Twenty-one

THE WIND RIDERS were steadily gaining on them. Each time McCade lost altitude, and was forced to circle searching for a thermal, the bandits got closer, their engines buzzing like a flight of angry bees. Then, just when the bandits got close enough to fire, the gliders had always managed to find an updraft warm air, allowing them to soar up and away. However the Wind Riders knew how to use the thermals too, and were in fact better at it than either McCade or Rico, and that had allowed them to slowly close the gap. It was just a matter of time before they caught up.

Nevertheless, McCade was determined to stretch that time out as long as he could. The chase was more than an hour old, and they had already covered more than half the distance between Chimehome and Deadeye. It was funny in a way. On any other planet a hundred miles would have seemed insignificant. A fifteen-minute ride in an aircar. But not here. Here one hundred miles was an eternity, a long passage requiring days of grueling travel in a Nuag caravan, or in the case of air travel, hours of fear, wondering if at any moment unpredictable gusts of wind might reach out and smash you into the ground.

There was a burst of static over McCade's headphones. "They're closin', Sam. Looks like a fight comin' up."

"I'm afraid so, Rico. But let's drag it out as long as we can. Since they've got powered aircraft they'll have the advantage. The most important thing is to reach *Pegasus* and lift. So don't let 'em sucker you into mixing it up. Dodge and duck, but keep your nose lined up on Deadeye."

"Roger," Rico replied.

Suddenly laughter cut through the light static. "You call that a plan?" Both the laughter and the voice belonged to the same man. Major Nolan Tellor. McCade felt the muscle in his left cheek begin to twitch. Somehow the miserable bastard had hooked up with the Wind Riders . . . and was still on their trail. He should have shot the sonovabitch when he had the chance.

"Why, Major, I see you've found some new recruits for the Imperial air force. A scruffy lot, I must say. Still, I suppose this beats lying around in the dirt waiting for a Nuag caravan to happen by, doesn't it?"

For a moment the Wind Riders filled the air with mixed laughter. None of them liked Tellor, and they all knew McCade and his friends had ambushed the officer and his team, stripping them of their weapons. So in spite of McCade's reference to them as being "scruffy," they still had a good laugh. Then Yako's voice cut in. "Shut up, you idiots. So far the joke's been on you. So save the laughs for later."

After that both sides maintained radio silence. McCade and Rico concentrated on eating up as much distance as possible, while the bandits held on, throttles full out, grimly watching as their fuel gauges steadily dropped toward empty.

Then everything seemed to happen at once. McCade spotted the heavy-duty antenna and pylon which marked Deadeye's location up ahead, and hit a pocket of cold air at the same moment. Even though he put the glider into a shallow dive, it seemed to fall like a rock, and he had to either find a thermal or put it down miles short of Deadeye. Recognizing the problem, Yako's pilots began to shout with excitement. By God, the quarry wouldn't escape this time!

As luck would have it, McCade and Rico found a thermal rather quickly, but were still fighting for altitude when the Wind Riders attacked. The first energy beam was just a hair off, but close enough to leave a black line across the top surface of McCade's port wing. "Try and keep their heads down, Alex!" McCade yelled over the intercom. "Make 'em keep their distance."

Alexander didn't answer. He was lining up his first target. By working two foot pedals he could swing his seat and the gun mount 360 degrees. Twin pistol grips were built into the arms of his chair, and by squeezing them he could fire one, or both, of his two energy weapons. As the ultra lights swarmed after them, he smiled a predatory smile. He didn't know it, but it was the same smile his grandfather, the first emperor, had smiled as he led his fleet into battle. And it expressed similar feelings. He'd found their weakness. Although the Wind Riders were excellent pilots, they didn't know a damned thing about air combat! With the single exception of their fight with Jubal, they'd always attacked ground targets prior to this, so instead of coming up under the gliders, and attacking their most vulnerable point, the bandits were coming in from above, exposing their own bellies. Though not a professional like his sister, Alexander had served in air reserves, and had a reputation as something of a jet jockey. Aerial gunnery had been one of his favorite exercises. So he waited until two of the blue machines were hanging just above him, spitting out lethal bursts of energy, and missing as McCade dodged back and forth. Having never practiced aerial combat before this, their markmanship was very poor. But Alexander's wasn't. He squeezed both grips, literally cutting one ultra light in two, and blowing the second out of the air.

As the wreckage of Alexander's kills went tumbling toward the ground, Phil took out a third, and suddenly Yako's force of eight aircraft was almost cut in half. Yako was stunned, scared, and secretly glad to be alive. He forced himself to think. What the hell was going on? We're better pilots than they are, so how come they're winning? Because they know some tricks we don't, he realized. What are we doing wrong?

"What are you idiots doing?" The voice came from Major Tellor in the backseat. "You call yourselves pilots? Go for their bellies for God's sake. My grandmother could outfly you."

Yako instinctively knew Tellor was right. They'd been attacking from above, right into those rear turrets. He banked right and dove, pulling back on his stick, and sliding up under the nearest glider.

Glancing left, McCade saw one trying to come in from below. The bastards were learning fast! Slamming the glider into a barrel roll he lost some precious altitude but did manage to come out below the attacking ultra light. Seeing the opportunity, Alex squeezed both pistol grips, and flamed Yako's starboard wing.

As the ultra light tipped, and went into a final spin, Yako closed his eyes, and wished he could listen to something besides Tellor's enraged swearing. What a miserable way to die.

McCade tried to look everywhere at once. As the burning ultra light smashed into the ground, he turned to see smoke streaming from a dark hole in the side of Rico's glider, and the brown smear of ground beyond. However, both men seemed to be okay, Rico giving a cheerful thumbs-up, and Phil waving an empty fire extinguisher. What's more, Rico had apparently scored another kill, because only three Wind Riders remained. And they seemed to suddenly think better of it, banking right, and circling down to search the ground for survivors. Looking forward, he saw Deadeye's antenna and pylon just ahead.

Both gliders made decent landings, were taken in tow by a couple of the now-familiar red drones, and were soon lowered into the underground hangar. As the elevator moved smoothly downward they climbed out of the gliders and brought their energy rifles with them. The underground hangar would make a perfect place for an ambush. So when the walls dropped away they were crouched behind the gliders ready for anything. Anything except total silence. No energy beams screamed around them. No Imperial marines rushed forward to kill them. Nothing happened at all. In fact, except for an old man and a teenaged boy working on the wrecked ship in one corner, the place was empty of all life.

As they stepped off the elevator, the boy eyed them with open curiosity but, after a whispered word from the old man, turned back to his work. McCade noticed that the freighter which had been there earlier had disappeared, and been replaced by a beat-up old tug, but the old lifeboat was still there, and still for sale.

Pegasus was just as they'd left her. McCade palmed the main lock, entered, and initiated a pre-flight check. The computer assured him no one had attempted to enter, or had disturbed the ship in any way. Nonetheless, he left via the main lock to perform a visual inspection of the entire ship. It always pays to be careful . . . especially when you've been away for a while. Just because the computer said no one had bothered the ship didn't make it necessarily true. What if Claudia's people had found a way to fool his sensors? Attached some sort of explosive device to the hull, for example? As he ran his eyes over the ship, McCade wondered why Claudia's forces hadn't tried to ambush them inside the hangar. Maybe Claudia had that much faith in Tellor. Or maybe she had something even worse up her sleeve. Time would tell.

Rico and Phil had gone off to pay Momma for their berth. When they returned both wore big smiles. McCade suspected they'd found time to put away a beer or two. "We're cleared for take-off, Sam," Rico said. "By the way, Momma says an Imperial Intruder put down here about two days back. Some second louie and half a section searched the place, warned her how evil ya are, and lifted. Kinda makes ya wonder, don't it?"

"It sure does," McCade answered grimly. "Why leave *Pegasus*? Why not take her? Or disable her? It doesn't make sense."

"Oh, but it does," Alex answered, joining them under a stubby wing. "I overheard the last part of that, and it's exactly what Claudia would do. She *wants* us to lift. Chasing us all over the planet isn't working, so she'll allow us to lift, and then grab us in space."

McCade reluctantly nodded his agreement. "Viewed that way it does make a twisted sort of sense. So what do we do? We can't sit here forever."

"True," Alexander agreed. "And time's running out. How long before she takes the throne by default?"

"Three standard months from your father's death," McCade said. "And there's about a week of that time left."

"Just enough to reach Terra if I start now," Alexander mused.

"So," Rico said, "we have ta lift . . ."

". . . but if we do she'll nail us," McCade finished.

Phil had remained silent so far. Now he cleared his throat with a deep growl. "True . . . but maybe we can at least give ourselves something to negotiate with."

The other three turned to look at him. "I'm all ears," McCade said.

"Well," Phil said thoughtfully, "seeing that lifeboat over there gave me an idea." He pointed to the decrepit-looking boat with the FOR SALE sign scrawled across its hull. "We could have used yours, but you left it on Joyo's Roid."

"I'll try to be more considerate next time," McCade said dryly.

Phil ignored McCade's comment. "We buy the lifeboat and load it aboard *Pegasus*. Then we have Alex here dump the full story of what's happened into the boat's vocorder, preset its course for Earth, and dump it the second we clear atmosphere. Maybe we find a way through Claudia's blockade, and maybe we don't, but even if she grabs us it's too late. No matter what she does the lifeboat's gonna show up in Earth orbit and spill the beans. Knowing that, she lets us go!"

McCade lit a cigar, took a deep drag, and blew a column of blue smoke toward the floor. There were a number of holes in Phil's plan. The largest and most obvious was that the lifeboat in question wasn't equipped with hyperdrive. A single glance told him that. So, by the time the boat arrived in Earth orbit and delivered its message, Claudia would have been dead for hundreds of years. Assuming the old tub didn't fall apart along the way. Not much of a threat. While Phil was an excellent biologist, he didn't know much about ships. Nonetheless, maybe there was another way to use the lifeboat to their advantage.

"With a couple of slight alterations, your idea might give us an edge, Phil. Now here's what I have in mind . . ." After McCade presented his idea, a lengthy technical discussion ensued, eventually ending with general agreement that while the plan might work, chances were it wouldn't.

"Nevertheless," Rico summarized, "Sam's had even

worse ideas than this one, and some of those worked, so why not give it a try?"

"Thanks for the overwhelming vote of confidence, Rico," McCade said.

The others laughed, and split up to handle their individual assignments. Rico and Alex took off to acquire the lifeboat, and program its vocorder, while McCade and Phil raided the supply lockers aboard *Pegasus*. A short time later they started the alterations to the lifeboat's tiny drive.

About four hours later the alterations were complete, the lifeboat had been loaded aboard *Pegasus*, and they were ready to lift. McCade fired his repellors, and carefully danced his ship out of her berth, and over to the elevator. There was the hum of hidden machinery as they rose toward the surface and emerged into the beginnings of a storm.

"It's a good thing we're liftin' now," Rico said from the copilot's position. "Another hour and this place'll be socked in but good."

McCade looked out at the swirling dust and nodded his agreement. Apparently the perpetual storm which usually surrounded Deadeye was about to reassert its authority. With a gentle touch on the controls he slid *Pegasus* off the elevator. "Stand by to lift. Five from now."

As he spoke, his eyes scanned the banks of indicators, and his hands moved over the controls with the surety born of long patience. Then with a final glance at the viewscreens, his right hand came to rest on the red knob located just over his head. "Hang on, gentlemen, here goes." And with that he gave the knob one turn to the right and pushed it in. The ship vibrated for a moment as her engines built thrust, and then she was gone, a momentary pinpoint of light high in the sky, glowing for a moment, and then gone.

As they cleared the atmosphere, McCade felt the weight come off his chest, and shook his head to clear his vision.

"OK, Rico, stand by to eject the boat. On five. One . . . two . . . three . . . four . . . five."

Rico touched a key on the panel in front of him, flipped up a hinged cover, and flicked the switch it protected. Halfway down the hull a hatch slid open and the lifeboat shot out. Seconds later its drive kicked in, and it swung off on a course which would eventually take it to Earth, about three or four hundred years hence.

Hitting the power, McCade accelerated away as fast as possible, but he didn't get far. Suddenly all sorts of proximity alarms went off. Lights flashed, buzzers buzzed, and klaxons hooted. And before he could do much more than swear under his breath, *Pegasus* was locked in a matrix of Imperial tractor beams. They had obviously tracked him from lift-off. Claudia didn't even bother to call them up and gloat. She just reeled them in.

Locked in the embrace of the tractor beams, there was no reason to remain at the controls so McCade and Rico released their harnesses, joining the other two in the ship's small lounge. Dropping into a chair, McCade lit a cigar, and watched the main screen. The Imperial Cruiser *Neptune* got larger and larger, until it blocked out the star field beyond it, and *Pegasus* was pulled through an enormous hatch and into a brightly lit launching bay. McCade saw Claudia had turned out an entire section of marines to welcome them. They wore full space armor.

"It appears my sister has sent an honor guard," Alex said dryly. "How considerate."

McCade laughed. "Your sister is quite generous with honor guards. We always get one, isn't that right, gentlemen?"

"Absolutely," Rico said, eyes twinkling.

"Every time," Phil growled.

The com set buzzed and lit up to reveal Captain Edith Queet. She looked very, very tired. "I will say this once, and once only. After the bay has been pressurized, open

your main hatch. Come out unarmed, with your hands behind your heads. Failure to obey my orders will result in
death." Then she was gone.

Time passed as *Pegasus* was maneuvered into a berth
next to a supply shuttle, the huge launching bay doors were
cycled closed, and a thin atmosphere was pumped in to
replace vacuum. "The Captain seems a bit testy," Alex observed, releasing his gunbelt and throwing it onto a chair.

"No offense," Phil growled, "but your sister does that to
people."

Alex grinned. "Ain't it the truth!"

McCade activated the main hatch, and they left the ship
as ordered, unarmed, and with hands behind their heads.
They were quickly surrounded by ominous-looking marines. The marines' features were hidden by reflective
visors and their actions were hard and jerky in the bulky
armor. McCade couldn't hear what they said via their suit
radios, so they seemed to move silently, in perfect harmony. It made them look even more menacing.

Working quickly and efficiently, the marines shackled
their hands behind them, using two sets of restraints on
Phil instead of one. Apparently someone remembered his
performance in the coliseum.

Then they were shoved and pushed into a single file,
herded through an inner airlock, and marched down a
gleaming corridor. After what seemed like miles of corridors, they were ordered to halt, and forced to wait outside
the ship's wardroom. Whether the wait was intended as a
psychological device, or simply meant Claudia wasn't
ready, McCade couldn't tell. Either way he was sure that
she had caused it. After about thirty minutes they were
finally ushered in.

The wardroom was large and spacious, boasting a long
bar against one bulkhead, with a mirror behind. Claudia
had staged the scene very carefully, using the bar and mirror as a backdrop. She sat in a chair on a raised platform,

which though not a throne gave that impression. She was dressed in a simple white gown. Her blond hair was draped over her left shoulder, her hard blue eyes sparkled with excitement, and her lips were curved upward in a smile of triumph. Her personal bodyguard stood in a semicircle behind her looking ominous in their reflective visors and black armor. However, what grabbed and held McCade's eyes were the two people standing to Claudia's right. Rear Admiral Walter Swanson-Pierce and Lady Linnea Forbes-Smith stood there with hands shackled, and under guard.

Alex surged forward only to be knocked down by a rifle butt. Claudia laughed, and said, "Welcome aboard, dear brother. I see you're still alive. Well, that's easily remedied."

Twenty-two

THINGS WERE NOT looking good. As a marine jerked Alex to his feet, McCade felt his spirits fall. Things were a lot worse than he'd expected. Deep down he'd hoped for a last-minute rescue by Swanson-Pierce, or maybe some secret assistance from Lady Linnea, and those possibilities were now eliminated. Both his rescuers needed rescuing themselves. Neither looked very good. Their clothes were soiled and ripped, and they swayed, as if barely able to stand. Swanson-Pierce kept trying to jerk his head up, but each time he tried it seemed to weigh too much, and it fell back to his chest.

As though reading McCade's mind, Claudia's eyes flicked over to the prisoners, and then back to him. "Well, we meet again, Citizen McCade." She nodded toward the two prisoners. "Pathetic, aren't they? Good examples of what happens to those who would betray me. You at least fight your battles directly. These," she said disdainfully, "cower in the shadows, too scared to come out and fight.

That one"—she pointed at Lady Linnea—"pretended to be my friend, while behind my back she sent secret messages to him." She indicated Swanson-Pierce.

The naval officer tried to bring his head up to respond, but failed once again.

Claudia laughed. "He actually tried to sneak aboard, from a supply ship, disguised as a Chief Petty Officer." She shook her head in amusement. "Who knows what kind of absurd plan he intended to carry out. As you can see we've been asking him a few questions, but so far he's proved quite stubborn. A credit to the Academy."

To McCade's amazement there was pride in her voice. Even as she tried to break Swanson-Pierce, she took pride in the fact that she couldn't, and credited the Naval Academy for his strength. She was even more bizarre than she'd been the first time they'd met. Still, he'd learned something valuable. She didn't know why Swanson-Pierce had tried to slip aboard. Good for you, Walt, McCade thought to himself. Now I wonder what you had up your sleeve, and if it's still operational.

"But wait!" Claudia said, her face lighting up with sudden understanding. "You graduated from the Academy too, didn't you, McCade? Of course! That explains why you've been so effective."

Alex and McCade exchanged glances. Claudia was obviously a few planets short of a full system. Somehow, in her mind, the Naval Academy had become elevated to the status of something very special, something with the power to confer unusual strength and power in its graduates.

Meanwhile Claudia continued to talk, apparently oblivious to their reaction. "Fortunately I'd been on to Linnea's treachery for months, and when she went sneaking off to meet Swanson-Pierce, I had her followed. It was as easy as that.

"Which brings us to you and my dear brother," Claudia said thoughtfully, fastening Alex with a hostile stare. "The

Academy wasn't good enough for you, was it?" Apparently she didn't expect an answer, because she kept right on talking. "We found the lifeboat, you know, and I must say, as ideas go it was just as inferior as you are. By the time it reached Terra and delivered your pathetic message, we would've all been dead. Not a very good idea, was it, McCade?"

McCade felt his heart begin to beat faster. They'd fallen for it! Part of it anyway. Now, if only the lifeboat was aboard *Neptune*. If they'd put it aboard some other ship, or simply blasted it, then this was the end of the road. But at least there was still hope. And with Swanson-Pierce and Linnea out of action it was their only hope. He slapped a confident grin on his face. "You can't win 'em all."

"How profound," Claudia observed dryly. "I'd forgotten what a brilliant conversationalist you are."

"Claudia, why don't you just cut the crap and get on with it," Alex said wearily. "You've got what you want, so do your worst, and let's get it over with."

"Why, Alex," Claudia said in mock surprise, "whatever do you mean? I wouldn't dream of hurting my own brother. In fact, I'm going to turn you loose." She paused for a moment to run her tongue over thin lips, enjoying her power over them, intentionally dragging out the suspense. "Yes, I'm going to turn you loose . . . in your own lifeboat."

She laughed as she saw their expressions. "Don't blame me, I got the idea from you. After I listened to your message on the lifeboat's vocorder, I thought, how dramatic! Hundreds of years after the fact, a message arrives from the long-lost prince, describing how his evil sister robbed him of the throne! The public would love it! The historians would go crazy! I'd be even more famous! In fact, the idea was so appealing, I almost let the boat go, message and all."

Claudia paused, assuming a look of pained regret. "But

then I realized how selfish that would be. Surely you would prefer to deliver your message in person! True, the trip would last hundreds of years, but I knew you wouldn't mind. A message is always so much more personal if you deliver it yourself!"

Alex shook his head sadly. "No wonder Father wanted me to assume the throne. You're sick."

Claudia's eyes flashed a brilliant blue, all color draining from her face. "Sick? You call me sick? Why you . . ."

Suddenly there was the muted thump of a distant explosion. The whole ship shook like a thing possessed, and since McCade was expecting it, even hoping for it, he was ready. As he fell he managed to take two marines with him. A distant part of his mind heard the emergency klaxons going off, knew the exploding lifeboat must have done a lot of damage to *Neptune*'s launching bay, and hoped it would keep the crew busy for a while. The lifeboat's drive had gone critical and blown up a full half hour later than he'd originally estimated. But, he thought as he hit the deck and managed to kick one of the marines in the head, sabotaging drives is not an exact science.

McCade looked up just in time to see Rico put his head down, run full tilt into a marine's stomach, and fall as a vicious blow from a rifle butt brought him down.

Phil had already gone into full augmentation, snapping his durasteel shackles as if they were made of cheap plastic, and charging Claudia's bodyguard all in one continuous blur of motion.

Already confused by the explosion, and safe inside their armor, the guards saw Phil coming but didn't take him seriously. After all, what could a shaggy-looking freak do to them? By the time they found out, it was way too late. Phil peeled their armor off like tin foil. Then he went to work with razor-sharp durasteel claws, slicing through flesh and bone, killing anything that moved. As the marines tried to fight back, they found themselves slipping and sliding in their own blood. And as they died, they couldn't believe what was happening. How could this be? What kind of creature can tear armor apart with its bare hands?

However, Phil didn't escape untouched. He was soon bleeding from a dozen wounds, adding his blood to that of the marines.

Claudia tried to run. As she launched herself toward the open hatch her face was frozen in a mask of terrified desperation. She had thought herself invulnerable, absolutely inviolate, and the ease with which Phil had decimated her bodyguard had shaken her to the core.

McCade swore. She was going to escape! Desperately he slammed the heel of his hand into the marine's nose, pushing the cartilage up into his brain, killing him instantly. Then he tried to get up, knowing he'd never make it in time. By now the only obstacle between Claudia and the hatch was the swaying figure of Swanson-Pierce. The explosion had knocked Lady Linnea to the floor, but by virtue of some miracle, or just his own stubborn pride, the naval officer still stood. With a tremendous effort of will, Swanson-Pierce managed to bring his sagging head up, and smiled at Claudia as he toppled forward into her path.

She tripped over the officer's body, skidded across the slick floor, and crashed into a console. Before she could recover, her brother had rolled over to lock powerful legs around her neck, squeezing until her eyes bulged and her face turned blue.

McCade yelled, "Alex!" but the other man was already releasing her.

"Freeze!" McCade's heart sank as Captain Queet stepped through the hatch, a blaster in each hand, and a squad of heavily armed navy ratings right behind her. Seconds later a doctor and a number of medics rushed in and began to tend the wounded.

Phil froze as ordered, but it didn't make much difference, because every marine in the room was either dead or wounded.

"On your feet!" Queet ordered. McCade struggled to comply, and then realized the naval officer wasn't even looking in his direction. Instead her blasters were pointed at Claudia.

Claudia's face registered disbelief as she stood with help from one of the medics. Her hands went up to touch her bruised throat as she croaked, "What's the meaning of this, Captain Queet? How dare you give me orders!"

"You!" Claudia pointed a trembling hand at a Chief Petty Officer who stood just behind Queet. "I order you to arrest Captain Queet for insubordination. Lock her in her quarters."

The Chief, a slender man named Lister, didn't move an inch. His blaster remained where it was, lined up on Claudia's chest. For a moment there was complete silence, and then Claudia seemed to slump inward, her eyes on the floor, her lips a hard thin line.

Queet turned to Alexander with a questioning look. "Sir?"

Alex nodded.

Turning to Lister, Queet said, "Lock her in her quarters, Chief. No one comes or goes without my permission."

The Petty Officer nodded, and motioned with his blaster. Claudia obeyed, stepping through the hatch without a word. As the last of Claudia's escort disappeared from sight, Queet turned, and snapped to attention. "Captain Edith Queet, commanding the Imperial Cruiser *Neptune*, at your service, sir."

Alex smiled. "At ease, Captain. Thank you."

She obeyed, already liking his style better than Claudia's. For months she'd been working with Swanson-Pierce, feeding him information, but hoping she would never have to come into direct conflict with Claudia. They'd agreed to move against her only if Alexander were found. But eventually it became clear that Claudia would do anything to take the throne. Then Claudia had discovered Swanson-Pierce and Lady Linnea, leaving only Captain Queet to make the final decision. Strangely enough, when Swanson-Pierce was no longer there to guide her, the same Academy training Claudia was so fixated on provided Queet with the answer. Ironically it was in the form of a maxim originating with Claudia's own grandfather, and drummed into every cadet: "An officer's ultimate duty is to the good of the Empire regardless of personal cost." Thinking about that made her feel better as she moved off to restore order to her ship. The damage was considerable, and that made her mad, but what could she do? Chewing out the Emperor didn't seem like a good career move. As she strode down the corridor Queet allowed herself a rare smile, much to the shock of a passing tech, who wondered if she'd smiled at him.

For a moment Alexander allowed his eyes to rove the wardroom. The price of victory had been very high indeed. It looked like a butcher's shop. Mangled bodies lay everywhere. Sadly enough the marines had died defending the Empire. His empire now. His marines. Knowing nothing of the issues involved, the marines had simply done their duty for Claudia, as they would for him. Of course, if it hadn't been for Phil, Rico, and McCade, those same marines would have happily sealed him into an old lifeboat and sent him off to die in space. He sighed. It didn't make much sense.

Over to one side, McCade and Rico were helping two medics load Phil on a stretcher. The big variant had collapsed. As always, full augmentation had left him drained, plus he'd lost a lot of blood. He'd probably sleep for about sixteen hours. Meanwhile, the rest of the wounded had been loaded onto auto stretchers, and the worst cases were already headed for sick bay. As they took Phil away, Rico went along to make sure his friend received good treatment, and McCade watched them go. He knew he should feel bad about the marines, but he didn't. He was just damned glad his friends were alive.

As the last of the stretchers were rolling out, Alex spotted Linnea. Her auto stretcher was gliding toward the hatch under the control of a rather plump young doctor. "Linnea!" He rushed to her side. Looking down, he felt heartsick. "My God, what have they done to you?"

Her beautiful face was pale and drawn. Her eyes fluttered open and she managed a weak smile. "Welcome home, Alex, we need you." Then her eyes closed again and her head fell to the side.

Alex looked up at the doctor, who smiled nervously, and shook his head. "She'll be just fine, sir." Under Claudia's orders the doctor had been present during Linnea's interrogation. Now it appeared her brother was suddenly in charge, and he was obviously concerned about Lady Linnea's health. What would she tell him? The doctor felt himself start to sweat.

Alex found he had to clear a lump from his throat before he could speak. "Good. Lady Linnea is to receive your personal attention. God help you if anything happens to her."

The doctor nodded, and started toward the door, jerking to a stop when Alex held up a restraining hand. Whirling around Alex said, "The naval officer who was with Lady Linnea, Swanson-Pierce, where is he?"

"Over here," McCade answered. "At the moment he's out of it, but I suspect he'll survive to make my life miserable."

"Him as well," Alexander admonished the doctor. "I want reports on their condition every four hours."

By now the doctor was quite pale. He nodded nervously, steering Linnea's auto stretcher himself, and urging the medic in control of Swanson-Pierce's stretcher to hurry up. He didn't understand what was going on and didn't want to. Safety lay in the direction of sick bay, and he unconsciously urged Linnea's stretcher to greater speed.

McCade was lighting a cigar when the Emperor walked over to join him. "Well, Alex, or should I say 'Your Highness'? The empire is yours. Wear it in good health."

The Emperor laughed. "It may be mine, but I don't think it's possible for you to say 'Your Highness' and mean it. So let's agree that you'll always call me Alex instead." And with that the Emperor held out his hand to the bounty hunter.

McCade stuck his cigar between his teeth and shook the Emperor's hand. "It's a deal, Alex."

The Emperor looked serious for a moment. "I'd say 'thanks,' but thanks isn't good enough, Sam."

"Then just make sure Swanson-Pierce comes through with my bounty," McCade answered with a grin. "He may be an Admiral, but he's still a bastard."

"The empire could use more bastards like him," the Emperor countered. "Which brings me back to my earlier offer. I could use you, Sam. I know you don't trust the Imperial government, so why not become part of it? I'll give you any job you want. That way you make sure we don't screw up."

McCade blew a stream of gray smoke toward the overhead. "Thanks, Alex, but I wouldn't fit in."

The Emperor shrugged. "All right, Sam, I respect your wishes. Nonetheless, I owe you one. Don't hesitate to call it in."

"I won't," McCade assured him. "Just out of curiosity, what will you do with Claudia?"

The Emperor smiled as his grandfather and father had before him. "Why, turn her loose, of course. All my opposition will flock to her, and then I'll be able to keep an eye on all of them at once."

McCade shook his head in amazement. "It's obvious you're the right man for the job."

"It's in the genes. Well, I'm heading down to sick bay. You coming?"

"In a few minutes. I'll catch up."

"See you there." And, with a cheerful wave, the Emperor was gone.

McCade stepped over to the bar and punched in a request for a Terran whiskey. While he waited, he took a deep drag on his cigar and then crushed it out. He knew, deep down, that in spite of everything, all they'd managed to do was buy a little time. Under Alexander's leadership, war with the Il Ronn would be delayed, but not prevented. The forces pushing both sides toward it were just too powerful.

With a gentle hum the autobar produced his drink. Turning his back to the rest of the room, he faced the mirror, and lifted his glass. The man he saw there looked older but not, he decided, that much wiser. Nonetheless he was alive. Thanks to some very good luck and some very good people. "To you, Cy, may you always win. To you, Spigot. And to you, Pollard, wherever you are. And, finally, to you, Sara, I'm coming home." And with that he drained the glass to the very last drop.

THE NEW SHARED WORLD ANTHOLOGY!

THE FLEET

EDITED BY DAVID DRAKE AND BILL FAWCETT

Featuring a who's who of science fiction, including
Poul Anderson, Piers Anthony, Gary Gygax, Anne McCaffrey,
Margaret Weis, and an unprecedented host of others, the Fleet is
military science fiction at its best. Join the Fleet as they take on
the Khalians—vicious carnivores who take no prisoners. Ever.

THE FLEET—*Pledged to protect us all,
they're mankind's last line of defense.*

AND BE SURE TO LOOK FOR THE NEXT ADVENTURE OF THE FLEET, COUNTERATTACK, AVAILABLE IN DECEMBER!

MORE SCIENCE FICTION ADVENTURE!

AWARD-WINNING
Science Fiction!

The following works are winners of the prestigious Nebula or Hugo Award for excellence in Science Fiction. A must for lovers of good science fiction everywhere!

☐ 0-441-77422-9	**SOLDIER ASK NOT,** Gordon R. Dickson	$3.95
☐ 0-441-47812-3	**THE LEFT HAND OF DARKNESS,** Ursula K. Le Guin	$3.95
☐ 0-441-16708-3	**THE DREAM MASTER,** Roger Zelazny	$2.95
☐ 0-441-56959-5	**NEUROMANCER,** William Gibson	$2.95
☐ 0-441-23777-0	**THE FINAL ENCYCLOPEDIA,** Gordon R. Dickson	$4.95
☐ 0-441-06797-2	**BLOOD MUSIC,** Greg Bear	$2.95
☐ 0-441-79034-8	**STRANGER IN A STRANGE LAND,** Robert A. Heinlein	$3.95

SCIENCE FICTION AT ITS BEST!

____ **THE CAT WHO WALKS THROUGH WALLS**
Robert A. Heinlein   0-425-09932-8 — $3.95

____ **TITAN**
John Varley   0-441-81304-6 — $3.95

____ **DUNE**
Frank Herbert   0-441-17266-0 — $4.50

____ **HERETICS OF DUNE**
Frank Herbert   0-425-08732-8 — $4.50

____ **GODS OF RIVERWORLD**
Philip José Farmer   0-425-09170-8 — $3.50

____ **THE MAN IN THE HIGH CASTLE**
Philip K. Dick   0-425-10143-6 — $2.95

____ **HELLICONIA SUMMER**
Brian W. Aldiss   0-425-08650-X — $3.95

____ **THE GREEN PEARL**
Jack Vance   0-441-30316-1 — $3.95

____ **DOLPHIN ISLAND**
Arthur C. Clarke   0-441-15220-1 — $2.95